Aunt Nellie B

by

Dixiane Hallaj

Other Works by Dixiane Hallaj

Born a Refugee
A Novel of One Palestinian Refugee Family

Refugee Without Refuge
A Novel of One Palestinian Refugee Family
(out of print)

It's Just Lola
(a novel)

The 5th Wish
(a children's picture book)

Caught by Culture and Conflict
A study of illiteracy among Palestinian refugee women

Find out more about my work and my interests:
http://www.dixianehallaj.com

Dedication

To my wonderful husband for 51 years of love and support.

This is a work of fiction and is not intended to represent any of the members of my fabulous family — especially my delightful daughters-in-law.

➤➤ ONE ◄◄

Melissa gasped for air and willed her legs to keep pumping. She saw the safety of a heavily trafficked street at the end of the alley. She wanted to scream for help, but her body needed the oxygen too badly. Footsteps pounded behind her…

The shrill ring of the telephone plucked me off the streets of Tangiers and back to the reality of my office. "Hello?"

"Hi, Mom, can I come over for tea?"

"Absolutely." My daughter-in-law almost never came for tea. I closed my computer, leaving my heroine in mid-stride, put the kettle on, and found some cookies.

It didn't take Susan long to come to the point. "David and I are worried about you."

That caught me off guard. "Worried?" What had brought this on? Had Sharon or Colleen been spreading vicious truths of me drinking wine and telling dirty jokes at the writers' conference? Did someone tattle about how fast I drove on the highway?

Susan took a deep breath. "Now that the kids are out of school, we decided to move farther south. We know how much you rely on us, and we'll make sure you're taken care of before we move."

In my head, a man in a trench coat and fedora, his face clouded by cigarette smoke, says, "Vinnie, take care of the old lady, and make it look like an accident." Susan kept talking, not leaving enough space between words for me to insert a reply.

"We've been looking into retirement homes in the area for you."

I inhaled bits of cookie and coughed violently. It was several seconds before I managed to squeak, "Retirement homes?" Eyes watering, I got up for a glass of water.

Her voice followed me into the kitchen. "Don't worry, it won't be right away. We haven't put the house on the market yet. We just wanted you to start thinking about it and get used to the idea."

My mouth opened and closed as I searched for words. Susan gulped her tea, looked at her watch and said she had to run. My anger kicked in before she was even out of the driveway. Steam still coming out of my ears, I watched the postman drive past the mailbox toward the house. He had a package that needed a signed receipt.

My anger evaporated when I read the return address: Robert Aldeman, Attorney at Law—Aunt Nellie's lawyer. With a sense of foreboding, I opened the package. There in my hand lay the dog-eared, yellowed notebooks of my childhood journal, along with a fat envelope that I knew held photographs and documents. I'd entrusted them to Aunt Nellie nearly a half-century ago, yet each one stood out sharp and clear in my mind. Blinded by tears, I sank into the nearest chair. Aunt Nellie was gone.

I didn't even have to close my eyes to see Aunt Nellie sitting across from me, her eyes as bright as the blazing red hair that framed the porcelain perfection of her smiling face. Her wind-chime laugh echoed in my mind, and I pictured her swinging her shapely leg as she flashed perfectly painted toenails surrounded by Italian leather. It wasn't the way I'd last seen her, but it was the way I'd always remember her. Aunt Nellie was everything my mother wasn't, and I owed her my life—literally. I dialed the phone, blinking away tears and wondering if I could still get into my black suit.

"Hello. This is Charli in Virginia. May I speak to Mr. Aldeman?"

"Charli?"

Condolences are always awkward, but what did one say to the son of your aunt's long-time lover? "Hello, Bob, I know this is hard for you. When's the service? I can probably get a flight out tonight."

"I'm so sorry, Charli. Didn't you read my letter?" I reached for the package with my free hand. Yes, there was a letter, but I hadn't seen it. Bob didn't wait for my answer. "The service was last week. I tried to call, but the number we have for you was disconnected, and we couldn't find you. I didn't even know the package existed until I read the will." The advantage of using a pen name is that readers only connect with the writer, not the real you; the disadvantage is that no one can find the real you. "How's Kate holding up?" He paused long enough for tendrils of fear and anxiety to start crawling around in my stomach.

"Unfortunately, we don't know. She and her husband moved away over a year ago and no one in the family has a forwarding address."

Stunned, I thanked him and said I'd give my new contact info to his secretary. How had I lost touch with Kate?

Late that night, I tossed and turned going over the events of the day. I started thinking about the day Aunt

Nellie stepped in to become the most important person in my life. I turned on the light and brought out the package. I ran my hand over the worn cover of the old journal and went back to 1965 when I'd last read them.

➤➤ ◷ ◳ 1965 ◷ ◳ ◄◄

The small room looked exactly as it had eight years ago when I left for college. Nothing in the room interested me. Then I remembered the journal. I sat on my heels next to the bed I'd slept in as a child. My suitcase lay open with the clothes I'd brought home with me two days ago, repacked and ready to go. I removed the drawers of the bedside table, and reached into the space behind them to retrieve the notebooks.

Mother's heels tapped in the hallway. I shoved the small notebooks into my suitcase. My hands had five thumbs each as I struggled to get the drawers back in place. The door swung open.

"The taxi's here." Her voice was cold and brittle like icicles falling from tree branches, the cold anger of disapproval.

"Thank you, Mother, I'll be right there." The door closed quietly—a lady never slammed doors. I shoved the notebooks into my suitcase and leaned on it until I managed to snap the latches.

That was it. No goodbye kiss, no wave, not even the twitch of a curtain as my taxi pulled away from the curb. Tears blurred the familiar street, but not for me, although I had to admit I'd shed a bucketful of tears feeling sorry for myself these last few months. Now I felt awful for Mother. My father's mercifully brief struggle against an aggressive

4

cancer two years earlier had left only the two of us. I brushed away my tears and clamped my teeth together. Why did I feel like I was deserting her, when she had told me to leave?

Determined not to arrive with tear stains on my face, I focused on Aunt Nellie. She had been magnificent this morning. She'd come right over when Mother called and told her I was home. She came through the door like a breath of fresh air and headed straight for me.

"Charli, welcome back." Her hug was so tight her exotic scent clung to me when she stepped back.

"Charlotte Anne, would you make us some coffee?" I'd been Charli since the fourth grade to everyone except Mother. I went to the kitchen. Their low voices seeped into the room as I moved around. I was in no hurry to sit with them while they discussed my "condition." When the coffee was ready, I picked up the tray and started for the living room. Then Mother raised her voice, and I set it down again. "Why aren't you listening? My plan is perfect. No one else knows she's back. If she disappears for a few months, everyone will assume she's still over there, and no one will ever know." I couldn't hear Nellie's answer, but it ratcheted Mother's volume up another notch. "I called you to help me talk some sense into her, not to scold *me* for wanting her to hide her shame and keep her from ruining her life."

Aunt Nellie exploded. "For God's sake, get your head out of your sanctimonious ass and join the real world." I was stuck between shock and hysterical laughter. Sanctimonious ass? "She's not the first, and she won't be the last. It happens. I can't believe you're ashamed of your own daughter. I'd be pleased and delighted to have her company in my house." Italian stilettos clicked the beat of her march to the kitchen.

"Aunt Nellie..." She stopped my words with another tight hug and thrust a twenty-dollar bill into my hand.

"Call a cab whenever you're ready," and then she was gone. Magnificent. Yes, if I wanted to describe Aunt Nellie in one word, it would definitely be magnificent.

My thoughts turned to the fading notebooks in my suitcase. At an age when most children stumbled through stories about Dick and Jane, I'd concluded that my family must be the victim of a too-many-husbands curse, and it had driven me to write about them. That year I'd read a whole series of books about twins from different countries. Whether it was *The Little Dutch Twins*, or *The Little Chinese Twins*, or even Dick and Jane's family, there was always one father, one mother, and children. My relatives didn't fit that picture. As a child, I'd wanted to know why. So, I'd written down what I saw and heard and searched for a way to break the curse.

My parents had argued constantly, and one time Mother shouted that she was only staying with Daddy because I needed to have a father. As soon as I grew up a little more, she was going to leave him. That's when I started the journal. For years afterward, I'd dreaded each birthday, not knowing how old was old enough for Mother to divorce Daddy. Children don't understand idle threats or heat-of-the-moment remarks.

The taxi stopped in front of Aunt Nellie's house. I paid the fare and added a tip from my dwindling supply of money, which I now considered a non-renewable resource. Aunt Nellie greeted me with another hug and led me inside.

"Coffee?"

"Wonderful. I can't remember the last time I really wanted a cup of coffee."

Aunt Nellie's smile was a ray of sunshine. "Then you're through the hard part. Why don't you sit down and look at the paper while I make us an omelet for lunch?" The paper was sitting by my place, open to the classifieds. Setting a steaming cup of coffee in front of me, Nellie began to do her magic with eggs. "What are you thinking of doing?"

The truth was, I hadn't thought about *doing* anything. I tried to act casual. "I don't know. Nothing too serious, I suppose. Do you have any ideas?"

"Actually, I do. I've circled a few things in the paper, but you can probably do better. Maybe we can talk to a few agencies."

"Aunt Nellie…"

"Yes, dear?"

How do you tell someone she just yanked the wrinkles out of your thinking? "I don't know how to thank you." Not only had she opened her heart and her home to me, but she hadn't asked any questions. I felt as though I was home at last.

"I'm glad you're here. This house has been too empty since Jackie got married. I don't get to see her or my lovely granddaughter as often as I'd like, but I have to step back and let her lead her own life. Just wait until you meet the baby. You'll absolutely adore little Kate."

It was late that night before I opened the notebooks and returned to a time when I was happy playing on the floor with my dolls and listening while the women talked and drank endless cups of coffee.

>> 🕐 🕑 🕒 🕓 <<

JULY 10, 1948: - I may only be an eight-year-old kid, but I know something's wrong with the women in my family. They go through a lot of husbands, and I have to figure out why before I grow up and it hits me, too. Grandmother was widowed three times before she met Grandpa Sam. Auntie Stell was widowed twice, and I don't know what happened to her third husband. Actually, it's her first husband I'm not supposed to ask questions about. Aunt Nellie is different. Mother says Nellie's been in and out of divorce court so often the judge calls her by her first name. I don't know why that surprises Mother—the first name part, I mean. It makes perfect sense because her last name keeps changing.

Aunt Nellie knows more about men than anyone, and all the women come to her with their man problems. If she's in a good mood, she gives them good advice. Sometimes she just says, "Divorce the bastard and find a better one," which might be good advice, too, but no one seems to like hearing it. My mother always shushes her if she remembers I'm in the room. She thinks I don't know the word, but my dad's a sailor. I know all the words—and I know better than to use them.

JULY 17, 1948: - Aunt Nellie sailed into the house like one of those little boats that Daddy says dance on the waves. She had a wake like a boat, too, only hers smelled of dreamy perfume not like Mother's flower perfume. Her flaming red hair lit up her perfect skin and high cheekbones. "Charlotte, wait until you hear the latest," she said as she gave my mother an air kiss. I ran to my room to get my dolls and some doll clothes. I needed to settle into the corner of the living room and become invisible before the story started.

"Poor Nellie. What has that terrible husband of yours done now?"

"You're so unimaginative. Every time I have a story to tell, you assume Willis cheated on me again. What I have to say today is delicious. Is Stella coming?"

"Yes, but she'll be late. She's taking the bus. I'll just put the coffee on." Mother disappeared into the kitchen. Aunt Nellie swung her silk-stockinged leg back and forth and examined her perfect nails. A big toe with matching polish peeked out of her open-toed high-heeled shoes.

The doorbell rang, and a minute later Auntie Stell, flushed and excited, came into the room wearing a bright cotton dress stretched tight over her tummy. Mother hurried in with the coffee tray. The three sisters clustered around the table, poured coffee, and sat back for the main event. Aunt Nellie spooned sugar into her cup and stirred it slowly. She took a careful sip, placed her cup back on the saucer, and reached into her handbag to pull out a small red book.

"Here's the plan," she said, holding out the book. The excitement whooshed out of the room like air from a balloon.

"You found a book with a plan?" asked Stella.

"You read books?" Mother got a dirty look from Nellie.

"This is the first step in my plan to live happily ever after." Nellie put the little book down on the coffee table and reached for her cup.

Mother picked up the book. "*My Diary*? You keep a diary?" Nellie nodded and gave a slow smile. Mother opened the book. "The first entry was six months ago. You started a diary six months ago, and today you're telling us it's big news?"

"No, I started it two days ago and back-dated everything. Read."

"Dear Diary, I am telling you all about my unhappiness because I can't talk to anyone else about it. Willis is acting very strange lately. He seems distant and uninterested. I wore a new dress today and he didn't even notice." Mother looked up. "I get it. This is a record of Willis cheating on you. It starts about the time you began to suspect him of going out with that tart from his office, doesn't it?"

"Yes, but it's not really about Willis. This is my innocent wife documentation. Read some more, but skip the boring pages."

"How will I know if the pages are boring without reading them?"

"Boring pages look boring."

Mother flipped the next few pages. "Did you write this one in the rain?"

"It's just a few artfully placed teardrops. Read it."

"Dear Diary, I am so upset. I had a nice supper all ready for him, but he called saying he had another business meeting. He never used to have business meetings. He came home very late, and he had been drinking. He went straight to sleep." Mother flipped more pages. "Another ruined supper. Something is definitely going on — and it isn't business, unless it's monkey business." Mother frowned. "The part about monkey business is underlined twice."

Why was Mother frowning? Even I had put it all together. If Willis doesn't come home for supper, it means he's cheating, and probably with a tart, which seems to be the same thing as a hussy.

Nellie took the book from Mother. "Here, let's skip to the good part." She thumbed through some pages and stopped.

"Purple ink," said Stella.

Nellie grinned and nodded. She began to read. "This is the night. I've decided to get my husband back any way I can. If seduction is what I have to do, then seduction is what I will do. I'll show that hussy. I bought a new black negligee that is so sheer it almost floats in the air. I fixed his favorite pot roast and apple pie. I set the table with wine glasses and candles. I even went out and bought fresh flowers for the centerpiece. Then I stacked some romantic records on the phonograph. Now I have to put you away, Diary, and be ready to greet him at the door when he comes home." Nellie looked at her sisters with a smile that made me understand what was meant by a cat-that-ate-the-canary look. "Oh, Diary, I waited until ten o'clock and then I blew out the candles and came upstairs. I'm so upset I can't eat. I couldn't bear to put the table settings away because it felt too much like giving up so I left the centerpiece with the wine glasses and candles in place. I just can't write any more tonight."

Auntie Stell's dark brown curls danced as she shook her head. "You shouldn't go to bed without supper."

"Don't worry, I didn't. I had some leftovers in the fridge and ate when I got hungry, then I went up to read the latest issue of *Life*. I was fast asleep by ten." Nellie paused. "Well? What do you think?"

"What else *can* we think? He's a beast," said my mother.

Nellie rolled her eyes. I guess Mother and Stella were

still confused. I know I was, but I'm only a kid.

"Here's my entry for the next day. 'Dear Diary, I woke up this morning still determined to make this marriage work. I got up early and had all the remains of dinner cleared away and a good breakfast ready by the time Willis came downstairs. I never scolded or even mentioned his late night. I was all smiles and sweetness—no trace of the tears I shed into my pillow waiting for him to get home.'" She stopped reading and looked from one sister to the other. "Doesn't that sound like the aggrieved wife?"

"Of course it does; you *are* the aggrieved wife."

Nellie frowned at Mother's answer and kept reading. "I'm going to pull out all the stops tonight. I gave myself a facial and did my nails. When it was almost time for him to come home, I took a bath with scented bath oil and took care of all my little hairy bits so my body would be just perfect." Auntie Stell's eyes widened when Nellie read that part. "Maybe Willis noticed my efforts last night because he came home on time. He hasn't done that in two weeks. Luckily, pot roast tastes even better the second day. The potatoes were a little mushy, but Willis always mushes them with his fork anyway. I was so excited that he was home I could barely eat. My plans were working!

"When it was time to retire for the night, I whispered that I wanted a few minutes before he came upstairs. A little tongue tickling of his ear had the desired effect. I put my best perfume in strategic places, rubbed a little rouge on my nipples, and slipped into the new negligee." Aunt Nellie ran the tip of her tongue over her lips before reading more. She smiled as she continued, "When I looked in the full length mirror, even *I* got a little excited. I just knew Willis was going to want to rip—"

Mother interrupted. "Little pitchers have big ears." That meant me, of course. I was still thinking about the rouge, because I'd thought rouge was for cheeks.

"Nonsense. She's just like my Jackie—absorbed in her play without a thought in her head." I started humming softly and moving my dolls around randomly to show that I was absorbed. She was half wrong. I'm the same size as Jackie, but a year older. The part she was right about was that Jackie didn't have a thought in her head.

The reminder that I was still in the room put an end to the diary read-aloud, but then Nellie outlined her plan. She was preparing her ammunition for the divorce settlement. The diary would document all her unhappiness and sorrow. She called it mental cruelty.

"So were your efforts in vain?" asked Mother.

Nellie looked almost insulted. "My efforts were incredibly successful. You can read about that part later. He begged my forgiveness and promised never to stray again. In fact, he said I should go pick out that mink stole I've been wanting."

"But if he says he'll never stray again, and you get the mink stole, why the diary?" Auntie Stell asked the question I was thinking. "It must have been a lot of work." I almost laughed because I'd been thinking that maybe she just did it for fun. Mother says school was never a happy place for Auntie Stell. She left school at fifteen and got married. That might be why she thinks writing is work. I think it's fun.

"Remember when he cheated on me the first time? After that affair he said the exact same thing—and I got my little Nash convertible. He's getting off cheap this time. Hmmm... Maybe I'll go for a full length mink."

"Maybe he means it this time."

13

"I'm sure he does. He meant it last time, too. A leopard doesn't change his spots." I know Aunt Nellie wasn't talking about Willis's freckles. She meant he'll have supper with the tart again.

Aunt Nellie and Auntie Stell helped themselves to the coffeecake, but Mother had her nose in the diary. She made a choking sound and her face turned bright red, even though she wasn't choking on anything. "You're giving this to a lawyer?"

"Of course." Nellie took the diary out of Mother's hands. "No one will believe the diary's really an account of what happened unless it looks like private confessions. The only way to do that is to include the titillating parts. Besides, that will surely win over the lawyer as well. He'll keep picturing what Willis was giving up for a quickie with a tart."

"So what's next? You just wait?"

"I'll get my mink, drive my car, cook the most amazing meals, and continue to be the perfect wife."

"And if he remains faithful?"

"Sooner or later he'll stray again. He doesn't think I know who it is, and he didn't fire the tart, so I'm guessing it will be sooner rather than later." A clink of coffee cups broke the silence as the women digested that thought. "To paraphrase an old saying, fool me once, shame on you. Fool me twice, and I get ready. The third time, I'll see you in court."

"Three strikes and he's out," said Auntie Stell. Mother nodded.

"Then I told him my first lie."

"What was that?"

"That I believe him."

I realized the curse had struck again. In spite of the fact that Willis wants to do the right thing, Aunt Nellie knows he won't. I don't know how she knows that, but she does. I'm sure Mother and Auntie Stell believe it, too, because Mother never said a word about Aunt Nellie telling a lie. I think Aunt Nellie told Willis that she believed him because he meant what he said, and she didn't want him to know that he was going to cheat again. It's like mothers telling their children that they can grow up to be president. Everyone knows that's not going to happen, but it might make them work harder. Sometimes it might be all right to tell a lie, especially if it's to spare someone else's feelings—like saying you're sorry even if you don't think you did anything wrong, or saying the food is very good, thank you.

All I know is that this is serious and I need to pay attention.

➤➤ ◷ ◶ 2013 ◷ ◷ ◀◀

Sinless lies, the little white lie. How big did a lie have to be before it stopped being white, if it were told to spare feelings? I'd told some whoppers, and Aunt Nellie had been at my side with her support. I closed the journal and turned off the light.

Aunt Nellie was the last of the three sisters. She'd lived well into her nineties, and a way of life died with her. That saddened me more than her death. The last few years had not been kind to Aunt Nellie, but she never lost her pride in her family, especially her beloved granddaughter, Kate. And now I'd lost contact with Kate. Good heavens, little Kate must be fifty. Why do people never age in your mind?

15

Kate was old enough to take care of herself. She knew my penname, and she could find me if she needed me. Still, it was strange that she hadn't contacted any of the family. I could understand her not keeping in touch with me. After all, I was the crazy "aunt" who'd popped in and out of her young life, never staying in one place long enough to put down roots, and finally settling on the other side of the country. Auntie Stell had a boatload of girls, many of whom had children almost Kate's age. There must be a gazillion cousins by now. She hadn't contacted any of them?

The next morning, I pulled myself out of bed after a restless night, determined to do a little detective work on my computer to track down some of those cousins. My list of possible contacts grew slowly but steadily. I glanced at the clock and had a moment of near panic. Noon already?

I rushed upstairs to throw on something more presentable than worn sweats. Today was my writing lunch with Bev and Jean, and I'd nearly missed it. Although ostensibly meeting to discuss our writing, our conversations had no boundaries. The serious writing critique was all done through email. Too bad none of us wrote mysteries. We'd have made great sleuths for a cozy mystery series.

I started down my drive, and saw David's car headed toward his house. He stopped where the two driveways met, blocking my exit. "Hi, Mom, you off to another meeting of the Wednesday Witches?"

"When one of us hits the best seller list, you'll have to show more respect." The joke had become almost a ritual. "We're having lunch at the Grille, and I'm already late."

"I won't stand in your way, then." He already was.

"Can your busy schedule fit in an outing a week from Thursday?"

I jumped like a trout for a fly. It had to be something special for him to take a day away from work. "Sure, what's up?"

"You'll never guess—we found a really great retirement home, and we want you to check it out with us Thursday. The menus sound delicious; the schedule is full of activities going on all the time, *and* not only is there high speed internet in every room, the entire campus is one big wi-fi hot spot. What d'ya think?"

"How much time do you have?" I muttered before raising my voice enough for him to hear. "Can we talk later?" My real answer was the shower of gravel my tires spat in his direction when he cleared my drive.

I tore down the road toward town. My little red car was one thing I could control in my life. The rush of adrenalin at the next corner made me reexamine that thought. I slowed down and forced my grip on the steering wheel to relax. I'd heard stories of kids taking their parents' car keys away from them. The thought made me shudder. A retirement home sounded like hell, but with no car, there'd be no escape. I walked into the restaurant still muttering to myself.

"Who put the bees in your bonnet?" Several heads turned. Jean had asked her question long before I reached the table. "Either your editor said the manuscript stinks, or your internet satellite fell out of the sky."

I slid into the booth. "None of the above. My latest manuscript isn't ready for the editor. My heroine is still in Tangiers, about to find the love of her life. What about you? Find any more interesting ways to kill off the men in your current book?"

"Don't change the subject. You haven't told us what's wrong." Bev wasn't going to let this go. It struck me how much Bev resembled my Auntie Stell, right down to the curly hair. They both were born nurturers and concern about the welfare of others was as natural and necessary as breathing.

"I don't want to spoil a good lunch with a tale of my woes. I'll tell you over coffee and dessert, promise."

By the time coffee arrived, I'd already forgotten what I ate. Eating was the secondary purpose for lunch. Even though I drink my coffee black, I moved my spoon in lazy circles through the dark liquid. I wanted to make sure I had the public part separated from the private part. But as I raised my head, I wasn't really sure which part was which, or why.

I ended up telling it all—the loss of Aunt Nellie, the loss of contact with Kate, my sadness that the last survivor of a wonderful group of women was gone, and lastly, my son's intention to have me put out to pasture. Of course they said all the right things about Aunt Nellie, but they soon arrowed in on the immediate problem.

"So your son's the one that had ya stompin' in here like a bull aimin' for the matador." Jean had spent years of her adult life placating the rich and famous in a big Chicago hotel, but sometimes, just for the hell of it, she threw herself wholeheartedly back to her West Virginia roots. Maybe she was trying to lighten the mood.

"What did they say when you said you didn't want to go?" Bev asked.

"I haven't had the right opportunity to talk."

"Lord love a duck, Charli, what're ya waitin' for?

March right up to their house, plop yerself down and tell 'em to make ya some tea 'cause yall're gonna set a spell and have a good chinwag."

"Jean's right. You don't wait for an opportunity, you make one."

"Why? They've made up their minds that I can't live alone." I knew why I hadn't done it, but I just hadn't put it into words, not even to myself. "To tell the truth, I'm afraid to confront them with a flat refusal. You know, most family disagreements become history and are soon forgotten. But some family disagreements become forks in the road where the two sides are so far apart family never recovers. What if I dig my heels in, and they insist?"

"Don't make me say Lord love a duck again. I almost choked on it the first time. You're an intelligent woman, act like one."

Bev nodded. "Just ask them to explain why they think you need to go to a home, and gently but firmly rebut their arguments. You have logic on your side."

I picked up the check, insisting that it was my turn. Getting the words out there in the open was worth more than a lunch.

"Unless, of course, you *want* to go quietly into that dark night," said Jean as she walked out the door. I gave her a dirty look. I *would* confront David and Susan. Maybe not today, but certainly before next Thursday.

➤➤ TWO ◄◄

With Aunt Nellie's guidance, I spent the next two days on the telephone, and she drove me to a few agencies where I filled out applications and had preliminary interviews. I'm not sure how I would've managed on my own. Even if I'd had a car, I couldn't deal with San Francisco traffic and read maps and street signs at the same time.

Each night I intended to read more of the journal, but by the time the dishes were done and the kitchen clean, I found myself yawning. To my surprise, I almost always fell asleep as soon as my head hit the pillow. I guess the events of the last few months had taken a bigger toll on me than I knew — either that or I was sleeping for two.

The third day a women's organization called and offered me a temporary office job. Of all the openings the agencies had shown me, this was the one that had attracted me the most. My pen flew over the paper as I wrote down the particulars, and the boost in my morale filled me with energy — enough energy to face telling Aunt Nellie the whole story after supper. I hung up the phone and almost collided with her as I rushed to tell her the good news.

"Aunt Nellie, I got the job I wanted, the one with — "

"That's great, Charli. Tell me all about it in the morning." She finished fastening a gold earring with diamond dangles that sparkled every time she moved her head. Her hunter green dress fit like a glove. A simple gold necklace with a diamond pendant sat within the scoop neck, drawing attention to her perfect skin. She would have looked right at home on the cover of a fashion magazine.

"You look fantastic."

"Thanks. Bill's taking me to dinner, and we may go dancing or catch a show afterward. There are leftovers in the fridge. Sorry I didn't warn you, but he can't always predict when he'll be free." She blew me a kiss as she grabbed her purse and a fur stole. I caught sight of a large shiny car at the curb, and a tall man with a touch of gray in his temples coming up the walk. I don't know why it surprised me that she had a date, after all, she was just as beautiful as ever. Her flame red hair might have had some help, but she'd lost neither her figure nor her flair for fashion. Her face looked softer, and the little crow's feet gave her character.

I took off my shoes and dumped little bits of things into a small pan. As one thing heated, I plopped it onto a dish and started eating while heating the next little leftover. I felt like a slob eating in front of the stove in my bare feet, but it was fun. I had no idea what some of the leftovers were, but my taste buds were delighted. Mother would've been horrified. She'd have been horrified at the idea of Aunt Nellie going out on a date, too.

The more I thought about Mother, the more I understood why the date had surprised me. I had this strange idea that only one generation at a time can date. One generation dates, the next one up is the mother and father generation, and above that everyone is neutral or neutered or whatever the right word is for sexless.

Amazing how stereotypes creep up on you from your

upbringing. Thank you Aunt Nellie for tearing down another stereotype. Why shouldn't grandmothers go out and have a good time? I laughed at myself as I got ready for bed, anxious to read more of the journal. Even though I had clear memories of listening to the women talk when I was younger, the journal was full of surprises. I remember being obsessed with the problems that soured marriages. I sat in bed with the journal unopened on my lap. Little Charli had scurried around trying to collect the pearls of wisdom as the women dropped them, hoping to skip the hard part and jump right into the good marriage. Ha! Fat chance! Look where I was now. My enthusiasm for the journal disappeared. I stuck it back in the drawer and turned off the light.

The third time the phone rang, I checked my watch. It was after midnight, and Aunt Nellie still wasn't home. Maybe I should answer. No, whoever it was could call back when Aunt Nellie was home. The next time the phone woke me up, I pulled the covers over my ears.

The sun was bright when I woke up. As I made my way across the hall toward the bathroom, I heard voices. Had Aunt Nellie's date spent the night? That could be awkward. I paused and listened to hear if I should stay in my room or not. At least, that was my intention. Then I heard the last voice I expected—Mother. I stood still and listened.

"I didn't get a wink of sleep. I called again and again, but no one answered."

"I told you, I wasn't home."

I recognized Mother's disapproving hmmmph. "Why didn't Charlotte Anne answer the phone? Or was she out carousing with you?"

"Charli was probably asleep." I heard the scrape of chair legs on the floor and ducked back into my bedroom, leaving the door open a few inches.

"All I have to say is that you two deserve each other." Footsteps moved toward the front door. "Well, I've done my duty and relayed his message. I'm not getting mixed up in this sordid mess." I heard her voice crack. "I don't know where I went wrong...my own daughter—disgraced."

"You didn't go wrong, Charlotte. You raised a delightful young lady who got in a bad situation." I eased the door shut and got dressed.

"Good morning, Aunt Nellie." My voice must not have sounded as confident as I tried to appear because instead of answering, she came over to me and put her arms around me.

"You heard, didn't you?"

"Only the last bit. I didn't mean to eavesdrop, but when I heard Mother's voice, I wasn't sure I wanted to come out of my room. I'm sorry I'm causing problems between you and Mother. I know how close you've always been. I mean, she always says she was your second mother."

Aunt Nellie gave a nice comfortable laugh. "The way I remember it, she was a bossy older sister who wanted the whole house to run by her rules. It often did, too, because your poor grandmother was too exhausted to argue." I had to smile at her description. "Now you just sit here and have some coffee. I'll make hotcakes."

"I don't want to be a bother. I can make the hotcakes."

"Unless you've gone to cooking school since you stopped living with your mother, I'll do the cooking, thank you." Aunt Nellie's laugh helped put me at ease. "So how much did you hear?" she asked as she began moving around the kitchen.

"Aside from her scolding you for staying out late, just that *he* called and she was upset about it."

"That's about the size of it. Let's not spoil a good cup of coffee with serious conversation. Everything looks better with a full stomach. Set the table and get out the butter and syrup. There are fresh strawberries, too." I did as I was told.

I was sure the hotcakes were going to sit in my stomach like a rock, but Aunt Nellie's magic came through and I enjoyed every bite. A fresh pot of coffee was brewing and once the dishes were cleared, Aunt Nellie poured us each a cup.

"I think your mother has good reason to be upset this time. If what she says is true, you might have a bigger problem than we thought. Time to talk, Charli."

"I'm sorry. I should have told you the whole story earlier, but every time I started to talk about it something else came up and..."

Aunt Nellie waved away my words. "I knew you'd tell me when you were ready, and I know the big important part—you're pregnant and you want to keep the baby. Your mother wants to hide the pregnancy, give up the baby, and pretend it never happened. She wants to make you into a duplicate of herself—perfect in every way, especially on the outside."

She sounded as though Mother had some secret of her own, but I didn't want to get sidetracked with questions about Mother. "Yes, that's pretty much it. What could possibly upset my mother even more than my pregnancy?"

"Apparently *he*, who I assume is the father of the child,

called last night. When he found out he was talking to your mother, he said he thought she was dead. He'd seen the telegram saying she was dying, and he'd bought you the ticket because as the only child you needed to take care of things."

"That's true. Wasn't Mother in the hospital last week? The telegram said she was, and she thought she was dying. I showed it to him."

"Oh, yes. I think she had heartburn and was convinced it was a heart attack. They kept her overnight for observation, but she was home before I heard about it." Aunt Nellie shrugged. "Anyway, it upset him to hear she was alive and well enough to answer her own telephone. He said you should have come back if she was well. When your mother said you had no intention of going back, he blew a fuse. He said you were his wife and you were besmirching his honor with your shameless lies. Is that true?"

"Kind of."

"You're married?"

"Kind of. It's complicated."

"If you're married, or even kind of married, what's your mother so upset about? I thought the whole hullabaloo was about you being pregnant without a husband. Now I find out you not only have a husband, but one who wants you back. So why does your mother think you're a disgrace? And why don't you want to go back to him? Does he beat you?"

"It's nothing like that, it's—"

Aunt Nellie held up her hand. "Wait. Start with your mother. It'll be shorter. After that, you can tell me the complicated story. It's Saturday and we have nothing else to do." She lowered her eyebrows and glared at me across the table. "So start singin', Charli, or else." It was a miserable imitation of James Cagney, but I laughed anyway.

"You know Mother. First, she was dead set against me marrying him. Then she was horrified that I left with him before a proper wedding. When I came home and told her I was pregnant, she asked where my ring was, and where was the paper to prove it. I told her I had neither, and she called me a few names. I cried. Then she hugged me and said she'd *fix* it. You know the rest. She's more worried about what the family and neighbors will think than anything else."

"Don't be so hard on her. She still believes that becoming a mother without being a wife is 'a fate worse than death.' The nuns drummed it into her at an early age. She just wants to protect you." I only had angry words, so I kept quiet. "Okay, so let's get on to the complicated story." She got up and poured more coffee. "Why don't we move to the living room, and you can tell it from the beginning. I love stories, especially true stories. Start as far back as you like."

I grinned, sure that it went further back than she imagined. "Once upon a time, there was a little girl with a very active imagination, coupled with a desire to explain what was happening around her." I picked up the cups and Aunt Nellie brought the pot. "Remember when I was a kid and all of you women used to gather for coffee?" By the time I explained about the curse, Aunt Nellie was laughing.

"So my prediction that Willis would cheat again in spite of all his words to the contrary, convinced you."

"Absolutely. I thought we were the only two who

recognized the curse."

"Why didn't you ever talk to me about it?"

"Because I wasn't supposed to know about things like that, much less talk about them. Maybe I was afraid you'd laugh. I don't know." I poured more coffee. "Of course, as I grew older, I knew that the idea of a curse was little girl nonsense, but I was still convinced that a happy marriage was not part of my destiny. I'd never known anyone who lived happily ever after. Whenever I got serious about one of the boys I dated, I'd find some reason to back away from the relationship."

"But if you listened, you'd have heard my feelings on the subject."

"Yes, your 'divorce the bastard' advice."

"Exactly."

"Forgive me, Aunt Nellie, but I'd been taught that divorce is a terrible thing that would condemn you to eternal damnation. Remember the Jesuit thing about 'Give me a child until he is seven?' It's more true than you can imagine. I was afraid—for myself and for any children caught in the middle."

"All right, we'll come back to that later. What made this guy different?"

"Aside from the most beautiful brown eyes I'd ever seen? I can't explain it, but there was an old-fashioned courtesy and correctness that drew me to him. Don't laugh, but it wasn't like dating other guys; he was courting me. He was a gentleman. There aren't many of those left in the world. We went to museums and symphonies and the theater. We sat in the park and talked for hours. Before I knew it, Jamal and I fell head over heels in love with each other. He asked me to marry him, and somehow I blurted

27

out the whole silly story, and said I couldn't marry. He convinced me that the fault was not with the women, but with the American culture and the American men. He said that no one got divorced in his country—and they didn't have mistresses either."

"And you believed him."

"I loved him."

"So you went off to...where was it?"

"The Sultanate of K-something-stan. It's near the Caspian Sea. I can't pronounce it, or even remember how to spell it—too many consonants." I could tell by the crinkles around Aunt Nellie's eyes that her coffee cup was hiding a smile. "It sounds exotic when Jamal says it, but I can't get my tongue and throat to cooperate."

"I've read about culture shock. Is that what happened?"

"My first big shock was on the trip, before we even got there."

"Why? Did you ride camels or elephants or something?"

"Nothing like that, just regular airplanes. The shocking part was what he told me on the plane. He said his father was the Sultan, which means he's the king of the whole Sultanate, and Jamal was the only son."

"You're kidding."

"No." I laughed at Aunt Nellie's expression. "You look as shocked as I was. I knew he had money, but this was so incredible I had trouble believing it at first."

"Why did he wait until you were on the plane to tell you?"

"He wanted to make sure I was in love with him, and not the romantic idea of being the Sultan's wife."

"Judas priest, Charli. Does your mother know this?"

"I tried to tell her, but she said I'd sold my virtue for money." I fought the urge to cry. Mother had said a lot of hurtful things before she decided she could "fix" it. I rushed on with my story. "Hearing that he was a sultan made me so nervous I started shaking, and he had the stewardess bring me tea. I didn't know what to say; I was suddenly shy to even talk to him. I pretended to fall asleep to get time to think. All I could think about were the *Thousand and One Nights*. I thought of all the times I'd played princess as a little girl, and before the plane landed, I had built a fantasy world fit for sugar plum fairies."

"Since you're here, I'm guessing that wasn't what happened."

"*Nothing* could have prepared me for what came next."

Suddenly I was reliving that day. The minute the plane landed, I knew Jamal wasn't just another traveller. Jamal was the first person off the plane, and I followed him. The flight attendants blocked the doorway behind us. Uniformed men stood at the foot of the stairs and took our hand luggage. I don't know when the other passengers deplaned. Tired and hungry, I struggled to catch up with him as he strode toward the small terminal. I had a boatload of questions. Why had the women all gone into the bathroom before we landed and come out wearing things that looked more like black tents than clothes? Why was I the only one in a dress? He lengthened his stride, and the escort stayed in lock step with him. Hampered by my high heels, I remained the caboose of the small parade.

He paused briefly as we entered the building, allowing me to catch up, but the noise level made conversation impossible. The babble of unintelligible sounds washed

29

over me like a wave. My annoyance with Jamal vanished. The excitement of adventure washed it away, along with the exhaustion of the trip. I looked forward to learning the language and the customs, shopping in the markets, and being a part of the vibrancy I saw all around us. Some of the men were wearing long robes, while others were dressed in Western style. The women were anonymous black tents. We didn't go through any of the usual formalities. The crush of people meeting the plane parted before our escort, and Jamal walked right through the crowd, with me trailing along behind.

A woman came forward and threw herself in his arms. I didn't have to see her face to know it wasn't his mother. The embrace was full of passion. The big black car practically blocked the entrance to the terminal. Jamal opened the front door and handed me into the seat next to the driver, and he sat in the back with the other woman.

I turned around and the woman raised a piece of her black covering and gave me a breathtakingly beautiful smile. She put her hand on her chest and said, "Amira."

"Charli, this is my cousin, Amira. We grew up together." The two of them started an animated conversation, and I had no choice but to turn around and look out the heavily tinted windows. I didn't mind too much because I didn't want to miss my first chance to see my new home. I could barely believe my eyes. I'd seen some pretty bad city slums, but this was worse—much worse. The streets were crawling with dirty children of all ages; dusty ragged men bowed under huge bundles of things. Women in dusty black tents scurried to and fro carrying babies and bundles. Donkeys and dogs added to the dusty mix. It looked like an anthill that had been kicked. A yellow haze of dust filled the air, and some of the men had wrapped scarves over their noses. The driver put more pressure on the horn than the gas. This was my first ride in an air-conditioned car, and I said a silent thank you to whoever invented it.

After a short drive through that, we entered a neighborhood that was in such stark contrast that I felt as though I'd stepped through the looking glass in Alice's world. The houses barely peeked above high stone walls and thick, lush vegetation. We stopped and a man in an unusual uniform opened a wrought iron gate for us.

The house met all my expectations. I couldn't see the entire building, but I was surprised a structure so large could look so light and delicate. Once inside, we walked from polished marble floors to deep carpets, past the vaulted entry and intriguing hallways until we reached a massive but delicately carved wooden door. Jamal opened the door, and I caught a faint scent of sandalwood as Amira and I preceded him into a large room, which he said was our private living room. I only had time to take in the general atmosphere of comfortable luxury as we walked through.

Jamal showed me to my room and bath, and said I should refresh myself. He'd come back for me in half an hour and we would join his parents for the evening meal. I opened my suitcase to unpack, and I panicked. What did one wear to dinner with the Sultan? I ran to ask him, and couldn't believe my eyes.

He was in the hallway *kissing* Amira, not a cousinly peck on the cheek either. And then a little boy came running up to Jamal calling him Baba. It didn't take a degree in linguistics to understand that word. He grabbed up the boy and swung him around with a big grin on his face. Then he caught sight of me.

"You said she was your cousin."

"She *is* my cousin. We have a grandmother in common."

"That's not the way cousins kiss."

"Sweetheart, Charli dearest, you've got this all wrong. I can't explain now, but I promise I'll explain everything after dinner when we're alone. Please, Charli, remember I love you. I promise it'll be all right once you understand. Remember, this is a new culture to you. You can't judge by your own standards. Give me the benefit of the doubt, please. My parents are anxious to meet you. Don't start off on the wrong foot."

A silent movie of the dinner played itself out in my mind. Any sound was meaningless. Occasionally Jamal would lean over and explain or translate a remark, but he said most of the talk was catching up about family matters that would have no meaning for me. I kept trying to reconstruct that meal — the looks, the gestures, the glances when they thought I was looking at the food. Was that really memory? Or was my brain making things the way I thought they must have been?

"Here, sweetie, take a break." Startled, I almost spilled the coffee Aunt Nellie was handing me. She'd put a plate of cheese and crackers on the coffee table. How long had I been sitting there? I picked up a cracker and for a few minutes the only sounds were the crunch of the crackers and the clink of coffee cups on saucers.

"What was the explanation?"

The crackers turned to sawdust in my mouth. I took a swallow of hot coffee. "His parents wouldn't let him leave the country without an heir. He'd married Amira," I nearly choked on the words, "and had a son by her before he went to study engineering in the States. It was a marriage of convenience. She was his cousin and they'd grown up together so naturally he was fond of her, but I was the one he really loved. He swore that he loved me more than life itself—and I believed him." I could feel my insides turning in knots. He'd been telling the truth, I was sure of it. Tears rolled down my cheeks. How could love be so wrong?

Nellie put her arm around my shoulders and brushed away my tears. "You still love him, don't you?" How could I still love him? I'd trusted him and he'd let me down.

"Come on, sweetie. Wash your face and let's go shopping. Nothing perks a girl up like a new outfit, especially with a new job on Monday."

"Are you up for the rest of the story this morning?" Oddly enough, I was. Telling Aunt Nellie was such a different experience than telling Mother had been. I knew she was feeling for me as I spoke.

"I didn't think I'd sleep that night, but the exhaustion of the trip caught up to me, and I was down for the count. Amira, Jamal's cousin-wife, woke me up with a knock on the door before she came in with a beautiful smile that brought dimples to her cheeks. I was amazed that she was so friendly, considering that Jamal had told me that I was the one he truly loved."

"Maybe he hadn't told her yet." I acknowledged Aunt Nellie's remark with a small shrug. I couldn't get to that part yet.

"She waited while I cleaned up and dressed, then she led me to breakfast. We were the only ones there. While we

33

ate she got out some index cards that had phrases in both languages. She pointed to the English and I read it out loud. She repeated my words, and read the other part, and I repeated the sounds she made. I couldn't remember them for long, so I got some paper and wrote them down using my own invented spelling. It was actually fun, and we laughed like old friends over our mistakes as we corrected each other."

"So far so good."

"Yes, it was like getting a new college roommate and becoming instant best friends. After breakfast, she came to my room and looked through my clothes. She picked up my very new, very expensive fashionable skirt that was at least four inches above my knees and held it in front of her. She laughed until tears came to her eyes. When she got to the shoes, she wrinkled her nose at the sneakers and laughed again at my high heels. She pantomimed walking in them and not being able to keep her balance. To tell the truth I felt like that myself sometimes."

"Did she say anything about the lacey undies?"

"She didn't open the drawers. When we finished she led me to her room, right next door to mine, and opened her closet."

I was definitely the poor country mouse. My wardrobe had basic pieces of carefully coordinated neutral colors. Hers had all the soft beauty of a double rainbow, and the vibrant colors of jungle parrots—it was all there. Long, flowing dresses of silk and others of velvet with extravagant metallic embroidery. Each one was beautiful; seen together they were breathtaking. Even my wildest dreams of a princess wardrobe could not compare with the beauty before me.

She picked one out and held it toward me. I understood she wanted me to try it on, so I did. It was a dark dusty rose. I loved it, but she shook her head. Then she gave me one that looked like evening sky before a winter storm. When I had it on, she nodded and turned me toward the mirror. I was surprised to see the color matched my eyes. My eyes have always been kind of nondescript blue-gray, but with this dress, they came alive. She didn't let me take it off. Then we looked at her collection of soft leather slippers. She found a pair that was almost a midnight blue and held them out to me. I shook my head. I have a thing about wearing other people's shoes. She insisted and I put them on. She clapped her hands and jumped up and down when they fit me.

"I'm sure you'll laugh, Aunt Nellie, but I turned into a little girl playing dress up." My giggle was cut short when I thought of what happened next. "All morning I'd been wondering where Jamal was, but I didn't know how to ask. Besides, we were having a great time." If I'd had accompanying music, this is where it would've turned ominous.

Aunt Nellie must have sensed my mood change. "More coffee?" I nodded.

"Amira tapped her watch and made running motions. She would have been great at charades. Before I knew what she was doing, she threw one of those black tent thingies over my head. I couldn't see, and I thought I couldn't breathe. I began to flail around, getting more and more tangled in the yards of fabric around me. I felt arms around me, and I got even more panicked. When I finally realized that Amira was rocking me and making shushing baby-soothing noises at me, I calmed down. She turned the

35

thingie around and I could see. Did you know they had a back and front? The woman can see out, but no one can see in because it's dark. Kind of like looking outside from a darkened window."

"To be honest, I never gave it a thought."

"Amira was wearing one, too. I couldn't see her face, but I was sure she was laughing at me. I would have in her place. It felt really strange being led through the house inside a tent, but by this time I trusted Amira. She led me to a room that could only be described as fit for a king, although it was hard to see details through the narrow mesh opening in the tent. I saw everyone I'd met at dinner the night before, and a few new faces. Amira pointed to a chair next to Jamal, who had a silly grin on his face, and she went to sit by his parents." It was all so clear in my mind. "An old man was sitting across from us. He cleared his throat and began to talk. Jamal frowned and squeezed my hand when I tried to whisper a question."

"And then?" I wasn't aware that I'd stopped talking.

"We sat for ages listening to the flow of unintelligible words from the old man. It kept everyone else glued to their seats, but the singsong drone had me nodding before the old graybeard stopped talking. He got up and brought the book he'd been reading and showed it to me. I said it was lovely, and it was. It reminded me of the old bibles you see in pictures that the monks copied by hand. He reached out his hand, and I thought he wanted to shake hands. It felt strange to shake hands after he'd been talking to us for ages, but everything felt strange. I held out my right hand and he grabbed my thumb. Before I could even wonder what he might be doing, he smeared something on it and pressed it into the book. He did the same with

Jamal's thumb. I *really* wanted to know what was going on, but I couldn't make a scene.

Then everyone started crowding around us and talking at the same time. I was beginning to feel claustrophobic, trapped in my tent with people hemming me in on all sides. Amira found my hand and pulled me out of the press of people. She led me to a small room where she helped me take off the tent and rearrange my hair. Then we came out to a larger room filled with women. Jamal's mother hugged me and put an incredible gold necklace around my neck. Before I could remember the word for thank you that Amira taught me, other women started putting gold bracelets on my arm."

"Sounds like you did all right by yourself, kiddo."

"Yeah, except that I dozed off during my own wedding."

"Your *wedding*?" I didn't know why that struck Aunt Nellie so funny. It took me almost a minute before I started laughing too.

"I'll bet you didn't sleep through your wedding night though, did you?" The telephone rang, and Aunt Nellie got up to answer, not waiting to see my cheeks burn with a blush as I shook my head. Her voice was a murmur from the kitchen.

No, I hadn't slept through my wedding night. It had been wonderful. I was living in what amounted to a palace filled with people who wanted me to be happy and showered me with things that outshone any of my princess dreams. To top it off, when prince charming came to my bed on our wedding night, he was as loving and gentle and patient as any girl could hope. The heat of my blush deepened and spread as I remembered how he knew instinctively how to give me pleasure, and he only took his own pleasure when I was ready and panting with desire.

I woke up when he moved my head from his shoulder and started for the door. I heard the musical call for the dawn prayer. "You're not going to pray, are you?"

His low laugh thrilled me as though he'd run his hands over my body. "No, I'm hoping to get back to my room while everyone else is still asleep."

I sat up, fully awake. "Why? If we're married, they must expect you to be here."

"Not exactly."

My heart did flip-flops. "What haven't you told me? We are married, aren't we?" It wasn't as though I could do anything about it at that point.

"Yes, we're married—legally." What other kind of married was there? I didn't even know how to ask another question. He sat on the edge of the bed and explained that the legal marriage was to take all hint of impropriety away from me living under the same roof with him. For him to change his mind now would require a divorce—so it was a marriage. However, society would not expect us to live as husband and wife until the big party when we displayed ourselves as bride and groom for all to see. "I just love you so much I couldn't wait. Don't worry, preparations are underway and the public wedding will be very soon."

"How soon?"

"I have to go now, but when I come back we can talk as long as you like."

"Tonight?"

"Probably not. I'll explain everything later," and with that he was gone.

Aunt Nellie came back and turned her sunshine smile on me. "That was your grandmother on the phone. Guess what?" I tried to smile back. "She and Stella are coming over for lunch. Why don't you go to your room and rest while I whip up something for them?"

I wasn't exactly thrilled at the prospect of sharing my story with Grandmother. I stretched out on the bed, but worrying about how Grandmother might react kept my eyes from closing. What if she agreed with Mother? Grandmother didn't always say much when the women were together, but when she did speak, everyone listened. I hoped I wouldn't disappoint her. I picked up the journal.

➤➤ THREE ◀◀

AUGUST 2, 1948: - We went to visit Grandmother today. I love visiting Grandmother, especially when the weather is nice. Her flower garden is HUGE, and today I pretended I was exploring the Amazon jungle. Once I get past the first row of rose bushes, I can't see any houses. Big trees separate the yard from the neighbors, and the tall fence by the sidewalk is covered with sweet peas and other vines. It's fun to go up and down the rows of bushes and flowers pretending to be chased by wild animals. Today I pretended to be lost and trying to find my way back to civilization. It really is a bit like a jungle. There isn't any lawn, only paths bordered by fluffy grass and short flowers. Set back from that are taller flowers, and the rose bushes are taller than I am. I stay away from the rose bushes. Sometimes I pretend they are enchanted beasts trying to tear my clothes and scratch my arms and legs.

The best part of the garden is the enormous aviary in the middle—a bird kingdom in the garden jungle. Grandfather made lots of birdhouses that cover the one solid wall. The other three walls are made of wire mesh. Bright yellow finches and the less colorful lady finches flutter about the upper area, going in and out of the houses. They always look a lot happier than the chickens scratching around on the ground and the old duck, Clarence. I used to hold fresh grass between the wires and he'd come over and eat from my hand. One day he tried to eat my finger. I screamed and Grandmother put ice on it, but the finger turned purple. No one ever told Clarence not to bite the hand that feeds him; I don't feed him anymore.

After I braved the Amazon jungle and reached the magic bird kingdom, I watched the finches for a long time, trying to tell them apart. Then I walked all the paths between the rose bushes and examined all the flowers before I wandered inside to plink on Grandmother's piano. I always feel special when I do this because none of the other grandchildren are allowed to touch the piano, and I can't touch it if they're around. On special occasions, Uncle Donald puts a roll of paper with little square holes into the piano and sits on the bench and pretends to play. The keys move by themselves. I use one finger and try to make up melodies.

I wasn't paying much attention to the conversation since it was mostly in Spanish. Grandmother is Spanish, even though she was born in Peru, because both of her parents were from Spain. Mother explained it by saying if Daddy had been stationed in Japan when I was born, I'd still be American, not Japanese. That makes sense. I vaguely remember a joke of Daddy's about if a cat had kittens in the oven it wouldn't make them biscuits, but I don't remember what made it funny. Maybe it wasn't funny. I know I'll understand more jokes as I get older, but there are a lot of jokes that Daddy tells that Mother says aren't funny, and she's already older.

All of Grandmother's six children were born in Peru except Uncle Donald. Auntie Stell, or Aunt Estelle, which sounds the same when you say it fast, and Mother are the only ones who still speak Spanish. When the conversation is between any of the three of them, it automatically switches to Spanish when anything comes up that they don't want me or the other young cousins to hear. That's their secret language, but I'm slowly cracking the code. I don't always get it right, but then I don't always get it right in English, either.

I plinked away, letting the sounds of Spanish wash over me. Then I heard Aunt Nellie's name and I started listening. Even paying attention I couldn't figure out what they were saying. I could tell Mother was upset and Grandmother was trying to explain something. I gave up and stopped trying—and suddenly I kind of understood what I was hearing. I just let the words flow without thinking about them, and I surprised myself by putting together enough words to get the idea, or near enough.

Mother said that Nellie shouldn't have been so nice to Willis and the things she did made her no better than a *puta*, which I guessed was a hussy or a tart. I thought that was strange because I remembered that she'd said something different when Aunt Nellie was telling her about it.

Grandmother said that a wife should please her husband, and Mother was arguing. The more she argued, the more she switched to English and Grandmother followed right along, trying to make her pay attention. I don't know if it worked for Mother, but it sure helped me understand a lot better.

"That's what a wife does," said Grandmother. "She pleases her husband. Raise the children and please the husband. That's your job as a wife."

"Not anymore it isn't. Today a wife is independent. Wives aren't chattel that belong to their husbands anymore.

Things have changed. Women do the same work men do. I worked during the war making airplane instruments. It isn't just the men working and the women staying home like it used to be."

Grandmother shook her head. "Oh for goodness sake, stop making it sound as though you were the first woman to put on shoes and leave the kitchen."

Mother sat up straight and looked hurt. "I had a job just like a man. Lots of women did the same work as men, and a lot of them still do. I worked to support the war effort."

"Just because you decided it would be fun to go out and work doesn't mean you're not a wife. You know better than that." Grandmother shook her finger at Mother. "If I hadn't worked, you'd have starved, so don't act like you just invented the idea of a wife going out to work, and don't tell me you don't remember how hard I worked to support you kids when Pop Wulf couldn't do it. Joe used to come home from high school and look out for you kids until I got home."

"Except that Joe was always getting into trouble with the Finnelli boys, and I was the one that had to do all the work. I practically raised Nellie and Harry."

"It was only a couple of hours each afternoon and Mrs. Snyder was right next door if you needed help." Grandmother rolled her eyes. "Besides, that's not what we're talking about. The point is that my work outside the home didn't make me any less a wife. I still tried hard to please my husband. When your husband gets out of the Navy and starts being home every night, you're going to have to learn to please him. Now he's home so seldom he's just happy to be in a warm bed with warm food in his stomach. You'll learn."

"I'm a good cook." Grandmother didn't say her cooking was bad.

"You cook plain healthy food, and lucky for you, that seems to be what your husband likes. Nellie's a gourmet cook. She learned to do that because she found out that was what her husband liked. She also found out what he likes in the bedroom."

"I still think it's disgusting to act like a *puta* with your own husband."

"Maybe you'll be lucky and your husband will continue to like plain meat and potatoes in the bedroom, too. If not, you'll have to learn what he wants."

Why would Daddy want to eat meat and potatoes in bed? Mother never lets me take food to my room.

"Never. My husband respects me too much to expect me to act like a hussy the way Nellie does."

"Listen to me, Charlotte; I was widowed three times and had five children before I was your age. If there's one thing I know about men, it's that they're all different, and each one needs to be treated differently. Some like special food, others like..." Grandmother stopped in mid-sentence, and I could almost feel her eyes turn in my direction, but I was still hunched over the keys and plinking softly. She lowered her voice. "Some like special pleasure in the bedroom. Willis seems to want both and Nellie makes it happen. She's a fantastic cook, and apparently pretty good at the other part, too. It's a wife's job to make her husband happy."

"And what about the wife's happiness? My husband's lucky to have me, and I happen to think it's his job to please me."

"Of course it is, dear. A good marriage is one where

both partners work hard to please each other. Nellie likes expensive things and Willis is giving her a mink coat. She's happy."

Mother huffed, which is more delicate than snorting, but has the same meaning. She tried again. "But you can't believe a wife should write down the intimate details. It's disgusting." She didn't seem to think it was disgusting when she was reading it. In fact, Aunt Nellie had to practically use force to get the diary out of her hands.

"Sometimes a woman does what she must," said Grandmother. "This isn't easy for Nellie. She's been married to Willis for years, and she has a child to provide for." I heard the sound of coffee cups being cleared.

"Would you like some lunch?"

"No, thank you. I have to get home."

Mother huffed and puffed all the way home. I decided it might be a good idea to stay quiet and think about what I'd heard. Grandmother says that no matter what, it's a wife's job to please her husband. She says that it's the husband's job to please the wife, and that's what happens in a good marriage. I'm making a list of things that might ward off the curse. This definitely makes the list.

SEPTEMBER 7, 1948: - School started and I am happy, happy, happy! I love the beginning of the school year. The best part is when I get all my new books and look through them. I saw problems in the arithmetic book that look like little mysteries. I don't understand them now, but by the time we get there I'll know the secret. Third grade's going to be the best year ever.

Mother got out her scissors and some big grocery bags,

and we sat together on the floor making covers to keep the books clean. Too bad grocery bags are all brown. This is the best part of the school year. I got new notebooks and pencils, and every time I open my book bag I smell new pencils.

Even better than getting the new textbooks for the year, I can go to the school library again and get new books.

I haven't heard anything new about Aunt Nellie.

NOVEMBER 19, 1948: - The only trouble with school is that I miss the women's coffee talks, but school is more fun. I've already read all the Bobbsey Twins books in the library. The librarian noticed and started asking me about the books. I told her about all the stories. Maybe she doesn't want to read children's books but still wants to know about them in case other kids asked her advice. I said I like to imagine I'm one of the twins.

Daddy's ship came into port and that makes life more exciting. He's home every night, except when he's on duty. When Daddy's home we get to go places on his days off. Sometimes his buddies come over and they drink beer and tell jokes. Some of the jokes are even funny.

Tonight at dinner Mother announced that we're going to Aunt Nellie's for Thanksgiving. That's great because it means I'm going to find out if Willis is having dinner with the tart again, or if he's keeping his promise not to cheat anymore. If he's keeping his promise, there might not be a curse at all, and I don't have to worry.

After Daddy said he'd be happy to go to Aunt Nellie's for Turkey Day (which is what he calls Thanksgiving), Mother said, "I'm glad, too, because Poor Nellie needs family around her now."

"Poor Nellie? What's poor about Nellie? She lives in a nice house, she has her own car for God's sake, and to top it off, she's a knockout." Daddy sounded as surprised as I was. I must have missed something while I was in school, because I can't figure out why Mother says she's Poor Nellie again. When we were at Grandmother's, she said her behavior was disgusting.

"Don't be crude."

"I'm not being crude—I've seen her. Ask any man who's seen her. She's a knockout."

"Nellie's going through a rough time. Willis was having an affair, and she's worried. He says he's sorry, but she still doesn't trust him. They've been arguing a lot lately, and maybe she thinks he won't argue in front of family, and it'll make the holiday better for Jackie." Then Mother got up to get something from the kitchen.

"It'll make Thanksgiving better for all of us," Daddy muttered under his breath. I knew exactly what he meant. We always spend Thanksgiving morning alternating between offering to help and staying out of the way. Then Daddy makes a big production out of carving the turkey, saying how beautiful it is. Then we eat dry turkey and lumpy mashed potatoes and tell Mother how wonderful it is. The cranberry sauce is the best part, and the pumpkin pie is good, too.

The worst part of Thanksgiving is later, when she says she doesn't know why she bothers because it takes all day to cook a Thanksgiving meal, and it's over in half an hour. It takes more than half an hour to clean up after the meal. No, that isn't the worst part. The really worst part is eating it again the next day, and making happy noises the third day over turkey sandwiches.

NOVEMBER 26, 1948: - Yesterday was Thanksgiving Day. I fell asleep in the car on the way home, but we don't have school today, so I have time to write.

Thanksgiving was just the way a holiday should be. We ate a late breakfast and Mother made pancakes. They weren't like the ones in restaurants, but they were still delicious with lots of syrup. After breakfast, we got all dressed up to go to Aunt Nellie's. Mother brought along her yummy cranberry sauce, which is a little sour even while it's sweet.

I stood behind the front seat, looking out the front windshield. That's the way I always travel because I can hear everything, and I can see out of any window in the car from that position. I stand like that when we go to the drive-in movies, too. We don't go very often, but I love standing and watching the cartoons in the beginning and laughing with Daddy. He always says that Tom is sure to catch those pesky mice next time. He even calls them meeces like Tom does. The last time we went, he teased Mother by telling her that Daisy Duck sure was a looker. Mother pushed out her lips as far as they could go and asked if he liked her as a duck. It was SO funny.

Yesterday was a great day! Jackie and I pretended to be twins all day. The food was good and there was a lot of laughter over things that didn't seem funny at all.

"That's a gorgeous bird," said Uncle Willis when Aunt Nellie brought the turkey to the table.

"Willis has a great eye for gorgeous birds, don't you, honey?" said Aunt Nellie. Everyone laughed. I looked at

Jackie and she kind of shrugged.

When Willis tasted Mother's cranberry sauce, he said it had "just the right amount of sweetness to offset the tart cranberries."

"Believe him, because he's an expert on tarts," said Nellie. I kind of understood that one, but I didn't think it was funny enough for the laugh that followed. That's when I realized they were saying one thing and meaning something different. It can get confusing for a kid, but it must be funny if you understand.

I stopped listening because Jackie and I were playing twins and started synchronizing our eating. We picked up our forks together and took a bite of the same thing, chewed the same, and swallowed together. I nearly spewed a whole mouthful of turkey out by laughing when she swallowed before I did and made a funny face at me.

After the turkey, everyone was too full for dessert, and Aunt Nellie said we could have it later. The women cleared the table, and the men settled down in front of the radio to listen to football. I pulled Jackie into the kitchen so we could listen, but Mother said we were underfoot and we should go to the living room and wait for dessert.

We listened to the men, but it wasn't very interesting. Uncle Willis fiddled with the radio dial. "The first game was Chicago Rockets against the Buffalo Bills. Who do you like in the other games?" I paid special attention to this because Daddy always likes it if I congratulate him about picking a winning team. I ignore the losing picks and pretend I don't know.

"Since I already missed the Rockets, I'll stick with Chicago and root for the Cardinals against the Lions."

"Detroit gives me a pretty good living, so I'll go with

the Lions. What about the last game?"

"I have to pick the Los Angeles Dons against the Cleveland Browns."

"Me, too. As much as I hate L A, it's California against the world."

"I guess that's what we get for living in Frisco," Daddy said.

"Yeah, but on the bright side—we get all the fog," said Uncle Willis and they both laughed. I didn't think that was funny either.

Sitting for a long time being quiet so the men didn't miss any of their boring football made dessert even more welcome. Choosing between pumpkin and apple pie was so hard, Aunt Nellie gave us a little piece of each. I'm glad she did because they were both so good I'd have hated to miss either one. After dessert Jackie and I went to her room and played twins until it was time for us to go home. It was late and I was so tired I just curled up on the back seat and listened.

"So did Willis talk all night about how much trouble Nellie is? Or did the conversation stick to the wonders of his tart?"

"We were listening to the game. When the Dons lost by three points, we started talking cars. That Willis is a joker. He pops out zingers faster than you can say Jack Robinson. Are you sure they're getting a divorce? He seems pretty happy. He took me out and let me drive his Packard Custom Eight. That's one powerful and smooth ride."

"He's a brute and an animal."

"He seems like an all right guy to me."

"You men always stick up for each other. Here's poor Nellie, knocking herself out to make herself attractive so their marriage stays together, and all Willis can talk about is cars. Apparently he loves his car more than he loves his wife."

"Christ, Charlotte, give the guy a break. Of course he talks about cars. That's what he does, he sells cars."

"Did that snake try to sell you a Packard?"

"He didn't have to, that car sells itself. What a beauty!" I heard one of Mother's little hummphs. "I know, I know, we can't afford a Packard, and there's nothing wrong with this car. Don't worry. I like our little car."

"It's not so little."

"No, of course not. It's bigger than Nellie's Nash, but the Packard has a much wider wheel base that makes it more stable on the corners."

"It's probably a menace on the roads. Coming around corners so fast and being so wide can't be safe."

I was just falling asleep when Daddy gave a little laugh that woke me up again. "He did say one thing about Nellie."

"What was it?"

"He said she had a true redhead's temper. She threatened to cut off his balls." I was pretty sure Aunt Nellie wasn't talking about not buying him any more golf balls.

DECEMBER 26, 1948: - Daddy's ship is out again so Mother and I spent Christmas at Grandmother's house. She opened the door dressed up in a swishy taffeta dress. I told her how nice she looked, and she said that dressing in taffeta didn't make her look any less like a cabbage. She laughed when I said that even though her dress was green

I didn't think she looked at all like a cabbage. She said something about being miss five-by-five. Grandpa Sam had on his red suspenders. I don't know why he wears them because his belly is big enough to hold up his pants.

Mother got me a gold necklace of the Immaculate Conception. She wrote on the card that it was from the Virgin Mary. I can deal with Santa Clause because it's kind of a game that parents play with kids, but the Virgin Mary? I think that might be sacrilege or blasphemy. I have to ask the nuns what the difference is between them.

Of course the necklace will go into her jewelry box to be taken out on special occasions along with the watch I've had for two years because Mother says it's real gold. I'd rather have had the Betsy Wetsy doll I asked for, but Mother says they're messy and I'll have enough diapers to change when I grow up.

Christmas dinner was delicious. Grandpa Sam asked if I wanted a drumstick, and I told him yes, please. It tasted great, but I didn't realize how big a turkey leg was. I tried, but I couldn't finish it. Mother said I knew better than to take more than I could eat. I nodded, because I do know better. Luckily, Grandpa Sam interrupted before she got to the part about the starving Armenians who would love to have that food.

"Just calm down, Charlotte. It's my fault for giving her such a big piece."

"But she—"

"No 'but she' about it. It was my fault and that's the end of it."

Mother gave me a look that said, "Wait until we get home, young lady."

I had to look down at my plate to keep from laughing

when Grandpa Sam caught the look. "Charlotte, I *said* that's the end of it." Mother blushed.

After coffee and dessert (I didn't have coffee, of course) Uncle Donald left to go on a date. I wonder if men talk about their dates like women do. Maybe I could learn more about the curse if I listened to the men talk. Of course it would never work because I'm a girl. They'd never talk about women with me around. That's why the women meet for coffee when the men are at work. When the women are there, men only talk about cars and sports. Sometimes they talk about the news.

Grandpa Sam patted his belly and went to the living room to listen to the radio while the women cleared the table. I helped carry things and then I sat at the kitchen table. The women were standing at the sink. Grandmother was washing and Mother was drying and putting away.

"Why don't you go sit with your Grandfather?" asked Mother.

"Because he's smoking his smelly cigar." Of course the cigar was only an excuse. The fact that they were asking me to leave the room meant I wanted to stay. I got my book and started reading. After a few minutes Mother started talking.

"I don't know where he's living, but Nellie kicked him out of the house. She says she's keeping the house and the mink, *and* she wants child support and alimony. She's such a gold digger."

The last time I heard Mother talk about Nellie and Willis, it was Poor Nellie married to that animal. It's hard to figure out what I'm supposed to think about Aunt Nellie. Sometimes Mother calls her Poor Nellie, and then I know I should feel bad that her husband's being mean to her. Other times Mother says things that make me think Aunt Nellie is not a very nice person. Even when Mother says she's not very nice, I still feel bad that Willis is being mean to her.

Right now, I'm pretty sure she's even more of a Poor Nellie than before. It sounds as though the curse has struck her marriage after all. She must have been right about Willis, and they're getting a divorce because that's the only way to get alimony. She said she'd divorce him if he cheated again, so I guess he did. Maybe everyone else knew at Thanksgiving, and that's why the jokes were all about tarts and things like that.

Grandmother said, "A woman does what she must. She's lucky she's getting divorced and not widowed, especially in this country and this time. She's very lucky that there's a man who can provide the money to care for the child, and the law is there to back her up and make sure he does it." Grandmother was widowed three times without alimony or child support. It must have been hard.

"She should let Willis take the mink back to the store like he wants so she'll have money to live on until the divorce goes through."

"If it makes her feel better, she should keep it. A mink can warm the body, but it takes a husband's love to warm the soul. Believe me, a mink is cold comfort in the night when you're up with a sick child and no husband to help you decide if you need to get a doctor, or to help you walk the floor."

"You think I don't know that? My husband's at sea most of the time, and I make do with a good wool coat."

"It's not the same. Believe me, I know. Pop Wulf was at sea most of the time, too, but just knowing he'd be coming back gave me strength to do what I had to do." Grandmother smiled and her eyes had a faraway look. "You have to admit, there's no passion that can match that of a man who's been at sea for a while."

"Yeah, wham, bam, thank you ma'm," Mother said under her breath, but Grandmother wasn't listening. Either that or it didn't make any sense to her either so she didn't answer.

"No matter how bad things got, I always had the comfort of knowing he was out there, still loving me. Once I knew he would never be coming back, it was nearly unbearable."

Mother put down her dishtowel and hugged Grandmother. "I'm sorry, Mama, you're right, of course." I wanted to go and hug Grandmother, too, because she sounded so sad. Hugging Grandmother was kind of like hugging a big pillow that hugged you back. She always smelled of talcum powder, unless she was cooking and then she smelled of good food.

"But now you have Sam."

"Yes, and I thank God and the Virgin Mary every day of my life for Sam. But you missed the point. *Things* can never make up for what she lost. Pop Wulf didn't have to be in the same room to give me comfort, all I needed was to know that somewhere he still loved me with a deep passionate love." Grandmother started sloshing in the dishwater again.

"Oh for goodness sake. Willis cheated on her, and she took the mink and let him stay in her bed. She'd be better off with the money."

"Charlotte, you must stop listening to the green-eyed monster. If Nellie's mink eats at you so much, why don't you save your pennies and buy a mink of your own?"

"I might just do that."

It was all I could do to stay quiet and look at my book. Mother has a green-eyed monster? That tells her to do things she shouldn't do? Does the monster live under her bed? Why does Mother always tell me there aren't any monsters under the bed, if she has her very own monster that *talks* to her? I held my breath and counted to ten, trying to decide what to do. I could break into the conversation and ask about the monster, but that would mean admitting that I was listening. Then they would never let me be in the room when they were talking because they would know I listened. I could never bring it up later either for the same reason. Was it worth it? No. I'd just keep the green-eyed monster as one of my private secrets. I wonder what color the rest of him is. Anyway, as long as I only go in Mother's room when she's there, I should be safe enough. After all, it's *her* monster.

>> FOUR <<

If I was trying to get nostalgic about life with Mother, this was the wrong entry to read. From that moment forward I never had another penny gumball. Mother got her mink, but it took years. By the time she did, pinching pennies had become part of her personality. She transferred the need to save from the mink to something else, like buying a house. Then it was for my education; then it was for "the future." Life was never the same after that. Mother became infamous for being frugal.

A knock on the bedroom door made me jump. I shoved the journal under my pillow. "Are you awake, Charli? Your grandmother and Auntie Stell are here, and lunch is ready."

"Sorry, I didn't hear the doorbell." Grandmother and Auntie Stell's greetings were so sweet with their hugs and kisses that I wondered if they didn't know about my "condition."

Aunt Nellie brought a beautiful soufflé from the kitchen and set it down next to the bowl of crisp salad. I never doubted that she was magic. We ate in near silence, savoring the food. Nellie began the conversation as I cleared the table. "I don't know what Charlotte told you, but I'm pretty sure it wasn't that Charli is a real live princess." They couldn't have looked more shocked if I'd grown a second head. Aunt Nellie gave a quick synopsis of what I'd told her earlier.

Grandmother turned pale. "*Maldición de la bruja.*" The words were barely audible, but the fear in her eyes was unmistakable. I remembered *bruja* meant witch. Putting my linguistics courses to work, I broke *maldición* into two parts, *mal* and *dición*. *Mal* probably meant bad, and *dición*, or diction might mean speech. Maybe she said witch's curse. By the time the others looked in her direction, the moment passed.

"So tell us why any girl in her right mind would leave a handsome prince?"

All eyes were on me. "He isn't a prince, but I guess it's close enough." I felt Grandmother's hand pat my knee under the table. Since Aunt Nellie had caught them up to the wedding, I started from there.

"The next night I couldn't sleep. I'd been surrounded all day by a language I couldn't understand, and my face was sore from forcing a smile every time someone looked my way. I tried to relax, but my head was pounding. I finally got up to ask Amira if she had any aspirin. It didn't occur to me to knock before I opened her door."

"*Mentiroso,*" said Auntie Stell. Liar. Grandmother's hand tightened on my knee. They all knew what was coming. I nodded, relieved that I didn't have to explain my shock and disappointment at finding my new husband in bed with the person I thought was my new friend. Amira had the grace to blush.

"You might as well come in," he said, patting the bed beside him. I couldn't get back to my room fast enough. If he thought I was going to be part of a *ménage a trois*, he had another think coming. I heard him muttering what could only be curses as he followed me to my room, getting into the doorway before I could close the door. "This is supposed to be Amira's night."

"But you said—"

"I said I'd explain. Charli, just try to open your mind to the idea that the entire world doesn't think the way you think, or share what you think are universal values—they aren't. In our religion we are allowed to take more than one wife with the only proviso being that we treat them equally. I said I love you, and I'll love you forever. That's true. Nothing will ever change that."

"But you expect me to get in bed with you and your other wife?" The expression of shock and revulsion on his face made it clear that I was wrong in that, at least.

"I expect you to stay in your own room at night and not go walking into other people's bedrooms."

"I have a headache and was hoping she had an aspirin."

"She doesn't, so get back in bed. I'll get rid of your headache." Again I misunderstood his meaning. He sat on the edge of my bed and massaged my neck and temples until I fell asleep. Of course he was gone in the morning.

"How could he expect to get away with lying like that?"

I was searching for words to explain it to sweet Auntie Stell when Grandmother spoke. "He didn't lie. The first wife is chosen for him, usually for political or financial reasons." I stared at Grandmother. "The second wife is the one he marries for love." How did she know that? "It's no different in Christian countries with similar classes of people—but the second wife has to accept the title of mistress." We were all speechless. "It usually works out.

Go on with the story, Charli."

"Grandmother's right. I began to accept the culture and accept my place as second wife, knowing I was first in his heart. Amira was so sweet and generous that I couldn't hold a grudge. She said we were sisters." I laughed as I remembered the pantomime that went with that statement. "It was only on the long nights in an empty bed that I remembered she was Jamal's wife. After a few weeks I stopped burning with shame at the thought and accepted it."

"Tell us about the wedding party," said Aunt Nellie.

"It kept getting put off because there was trouble at the mines. The workers thought the mines were unsafe because there were a lot of birth defects and sickness in their villages. Jamal said they were so isolated they'd been inbreeding for generations. He went to the mines to try to get them back to work, but the trouble escalated and there were problems in the city, too. Sometimes I could hear gunshots in the middle of the night."

"Were you frightened?"

"No, Auntie Stell. They weren't close enough to worry me, but it emphasized the fact that it wouldn't be safe to leave the compound. I used to take my mind off the troubles by imagining how much fun I'd have later. I pictured Amira and myself shopping. I knew we'd be wearing the black thingies, but we'd take them off in the privacy of the better shops, which were the only ones we'd go into, of course." That got an appreciative chuckle from my audience. "I made a mental list of all the things I wanted to see, and I imagined us giggling together as we sampled perfumes. The sales girls would bring us coffee while they displayed their wares. At the end, we'd go into private dressing rooms and try on our favorites." I took a sip of coffee. "It sounds vain and silly now, but it kept my mind off thoughts of the troubles. Jamal was often gone for days. Amira and I sometimes continued the language lessons far into the night because we were both too worried about Jamal to sleep."

"I don't understand." Auntie Stell looked around to see if she was the only one in the dark. "You went with him intending to marry him, and it sounds like you loved each other. He's fabulously wealthy, and his family is generous. The only reason *not* to go back to him was the second wife part, which would have been enough for me, but you say you even adjusted to that, and the other wife became your best friend. So what's the problem?"

Grandmother started humming, and all eyes turned toward her. Then I recognized the tune, and I threw my arms around her. "You *do* understand!"

"Yes, sweetheart, I do understand. I wasn't always a dumpy gray-haired grandmother, you know. I grew up in a different world, and a lot of things sound similar. Maybe it would help your aunts to understand if you tell more about what your life was like as a princess."

"I wasn't really a princess."

"Close enough. So tell us what you did."

"As I said, Amira and I spent most of our time on language lessons. After all, I had nothing else to do, and it didn't look as though she did either. It felt good to be able to say a few sentences at dinner with the family, but eventually I wanted to see something other than the walls of our house and the enclosed garden. One day I told her that I really wanted to go out."

Amira cocked her head to one side. "Out? In the

garden?"

"No. Out to walk around the town and look in the shops. Maybe we could go to a café or something."

"What is it that you want? Just tell me or Jamal and he will send someone out to buy it." She frowned. "What's a café?"

"It's a place where people go to drink coffee and talk."

Amira could barely speak she was laughing so hard. "Why would we go out to drink coffee and talk? We can do that anywhere — in your room, or our living room, or the guest room, or even out in the garden. If you don't like our coffee, go to the kitchen and show the cook how you like it made."

"Don't you understand? I want to see people, to move around, to do something."

"All right. I'll get the driver and we can go visit a friend." She ran off before I could stop her. Amira made me put on the black tent thingie and the driver took us a few blocks away to visit. It was so close we could easily have walked. Once we were in a room with her friend, we took off the black tents, but it was worse than staying home. It might as well have been the same house for all the differences I could see. The women chatted, and I sat and smiled.

Later that night I asked Amira what she did when there were no troubles in the city. "I do the same things I always do. Trouble in the city never bothers us here."

An arm went around my shoulder and Aunt Nellie's living room came back into focus. "So you see, Grandmother's song was right." I began to sing softly, and Grandmother joined me. "Only a bird in a gilded cage."

"Oh you poor lamb." Auntie Stell's eyes filled with tears.

That was enough. Their expressions of sympathy told me I could spare them the rest of the story. Was it really to spare them? Maybe I was too ashamed of how wrong I'd been about Jamal. Had I been wrong, or was it cultural bias that made me think so?

Aunt Nellie said we all needed something sweet to take away the bad taste that story left behind it. Grateful to be left to my own thoughts for a few minutes, I let them fuss with dessert and fresh coffee. I leaned my head back and went over what had happened next.

After Amira told me that our lives were exactly the same now as they would always be, I asked, "Don't you want to do more?"

She gave me a smile that lit the room. She was both loving and lovely. "Why would I want more? I have everything I want brought to me here, and now that you're here, I even have company." She gave me a mischievous look. "With luck, we may soon have babies to care for. Now that my son is growing up I rarely see him. He spends most of his days with tutors or at the mines."

"He goes to the mines? He's so young."

"He goes with his father. It reassures the workers. In the old days he would already be riding through the mountains, training his own falcon, learning to handle weapons and fight, maybe riding into battle. Now he studies books and learns the business."

"Now that I think about it, I haven't seen him here since the day I arrived. I only see him at an occasional family dinner, but I thought you spent more time with him."

"He was here the day his father came home because it was a special day. He's too big to come to this wing of the house. Jamal is the only man allowed in here."

"Man? He can't be ten years old yet."

"He's eight, but he's a good looking young man, isn't he?" Sadness came through her pride as she spoke. Her son had already passed into the male world. His mother was left behind with me—in the women's wing.

The minute I formed that thought, my world shattered. I'd been living in a house of mirrors and someone had just set off a shotgun blast. Pieces of my princess life lay in sharp shards around my feet. The reality of living within the four walls of that house for the rest of my life settled into place. I felt dizzy and nauseous. The word "harem" screamed in my mind. I gagged and ran for the bathroom.

I'd never been claustrophobic before, but between the black tent and the finality of the four walls, panic clawed at my stomach. I became jittery and snappy and felt like a trapped animal. No, I *was* a trapped animal. I started pushing away food, getting up in the middle of a conversation or a meal and locking myself in my room. Maybe if I became nasty enough they'd send me home to be rid of me.

I thought of Mother. So far my letters home had been carefully superficial. Could I ask Mother for money? Or better yet, for a ticket home? She'd been adamant that I'd burn in Hell forever for running off with an Infidel. Maybe she wouldn't send it. Maybe she'd say I'd made my bed and now I had to lay in it. How could I get Mother to help me? Then it came to me—I had to make her want me there to help *her*. She had to do it for her own reasons. I wrote and rewrote the letter until I was satisfied before I penned it on the blue airmail paper that folded into an envelope. I told her she hadn't sounded like herself in her last letter. I urged her to tell me what was wrong. Was she sick and not telling me? Had she been to a doctor lately? I begged her not to neglect her health just because no one was there to make sure she took care of herself.

I was confident the letter would have her feeling every inch of her body for a lump and scurrying to a doctor at the first gas pain. I was ashamed of manipulating Mother's hypochondria for my own purposes, but I had to get out. Not just out of the house, I had to get out of the country. I wrote every day, escalating my worries over her health. Of course, I couldn't be sure the resulting doctor visit would make her send for me, or how long it might take before it happened. I had to work on Plan B. I had to find another way out on my own.

How? I had no money for an airline ticket, even if I could get out of the house. I thought of the gold bracelets—I could sell one of the gold bracelets and buy a ticket. I needed to get to town. I began to roam the house at odd hours, especially the kitchen. It took days, but I finally caught the driver alone, eating. I sat down and he jumped up, nearly knocking his chair over, and turned his back to me.

"Go. For God's sake, go." His voice trembled.

I knew this might be my only chance. My language skills hadn't exactly prepared me for this, but desperation is the mother of invention. "Sit down, or I'll scream," I said quietly. "God's truth." He turned the chair and sat, facing the wall. "Look at me."

"No. No. Please." He was begging.

It was my face. He couldn't look at my uncovered face.

I scanned the kitchen and saw a rag hanging near the sink. I threw it over my head, nearly gagging on the smell of soap and old grease. "I'm covered, turn around before I wake up everyone." He took a quick peek and turned around, keeping as much distance as he could. I must have looked like a mad woman—maybe I was.

"I need help." I took a bracelet off my wrist and slid it over toward him. "Take it. Help me."

He shook his head. "I can't." The whisper barely carried across the table.

"Why not?"

His answer came out in a torrent of sibilant and guttural sounds that I couldn't even separate into discrete words, but the signs he made were unmistakable. He drew his finger across his throat. I pushed the bracelet closer. He held up his hands, palms outward. Then he rocked an imaginary baby in his arms before slitting its throat as well. He showed the heights of his other children before they, too, were dispatched. His hands were shaking. "For the love of God." The whisper was a prayer.

"Jamal?" He gave a single nod. I took the bracelet and went back to my room. I barely had the door closed behind me when the enormity of what he'd said hit me. I made it to the bathroom, but I couldn't stop puking. I scrubbed my face until it was red and raw, but I still smelled the dishrag. I cried myself to sleep. My only thread of hope had been an illusion.

In the bright sunshine of the next morning, the midnight episode was so bizarre that I doubted its reality. After breakfast Jamal took me out into the garden.

"I can't imagine what you're going through, but all I want is to make your life easier. Whatever you want, I'll get it for you." His arm slipped around my shoulders. I froze at his touch. What if…I couldn't bring myself to finish the thought. "Do you want anything? Anything at all? What about strawberries? I can have them flown in from Paris." Strawberries? What was he talking about?

"Jamal, tell me what's going on. Why can't we go to town? Why did Amira and I have to have the driver take us to visit a friend two blocks away? Amira says it's not safe to walk outside the gate. What is it? Is there a revolution or something?" I was fixated on the need to get to town.

"No. It's just the mines. That's why I'm away so much. I have to keep the workers in line. Outsiders have been stirring up trouble, giving the workers the absurd idea that *they* own the mines. Our family has owned the mines for generations. We give them all jobs, without which they would surely starve. They are ignorant people, and you can't reason with them. They have to be shown." I'd never heard that hard edge in his voice before. I hardly recognized his face. A shiver ran through my body. He felt it and pulled me close. "I'm sorry, darling, I didn't mean to upset you, especially now. We won't talk about it again." I wanted to ask why especially now, but that glimpse of a harder, different Jamal made my stomach churn again. I fled to the safety of my room.

It was days and days before I suspected I was pregnant. Then I burned with humiliation that everyone else had guessed weeks earlier. The knowledge kicked my fear up to terror proportions. If I didn't go right away, I'd never be able to leave. I'd be anchored forever. I drafted dozens of escape plans, each one wilder and less practical than the one before. I even considered poisoning the whole family, and all the while they were smiling and trying to comfort me — chalking it all up to hormones.

My stomach was constantly in knots. I was going nuts by the time the magic telegram arrived. I didn't believe for a minute that Mother was dying, but the tears and hysteria it produced were very real, and had the desired result.

➤➤ FIVE ◄◄

JANUARY 10, 1949: - We visited Auntie Stell today. Auntie Stell looks a lot like Grandmother, but she's not as round and she doesn't have gray hair. Auntie Stell worries about everybody, and is always trying to make people feel better. Her scrumptious cookies always make me feel better. She has high cheekbones like Aunt Nellie, but instead of making her look glamorous, it makes her look like she's smiling all the time. She really *is* smiling most of the time.

Auntie Stell lets Sharon and me use her sewing machine sometimes. Sharon is Auntie Stell's youngest daughter. She's a year younger than Jackie, which makes her two years younger than me, or is it I? Auntie Stell also has a boy and six other girls, but they're much older and don't live at home. Mother says the reason Auntie Stell's tummy is big is because she had so many children it can't shrink back anymore. Sharon's her baby and the only one who calls Uncle Walter "Daddy."

When Sharon and I came to the kitchen for cookies, I heard Auntie Stell say, "Willis won't give Nellie any money until the judge says he has to. In the meantime, she still has to put food on the table. She got a job as a waitress in an Italian restaurant near her house."

"Poor Nellie." I looked at Mother. So it was Poor Nellie again? "Maybe we should go and eat in the restaurant to

69

show support. It can't hurt to give the restaurant some business, can it?"

"It might be embarrassing for her to have to serve us. She's a waitress. More business only means more work for a waitress—except for tips, and we couldn't tip our own sister. More business only makes money for the owner, and she doesn't own the place—yet." Auntie Stell laughed.

"What do you mean?"

"Nellie says the owner is single."

"What's that supposed to mean?"

"She says he's single and attractive."

"But Nellie's not single."

"Almost."

"Hmmmph, you can't be almost single. You're either married or you're not, and Nellie's married." Mother paused to take a breath. "What's she doing with Jackie while she works?"

"My Patsy's staying with them until she gets another job. Poor Patsy was dating her boss, and when they broke up, she lost her job, too. She and Nellie are getting along really well now because they have a lot in common." Auntie Stell shook her head. "Men can be such brutes."

"Come on," said Sharon, holding a double handful of cookies behind her back. I wanted to stay in case they said more, but Sharon was impatient to get back to our game. Why am I the only one who's interested in what the adults are doing and thinking? Isn't that the way we're supposed to learn?

As short as my visit to the kitchen was, I think Aunt Nellie changed from Poor Nellie back to the not-very-nice Nellie. I'm glad she has Patsy to keep her company.

Auntie Stell thinks Patsy is Poor Patsy.

FEBRUARY 14, 1949: - Daddy came home last night. He said he had a big surprise and he wouldn't tell us any more about it. I knew it was really big because he was grinning all night. Every time there was a pause in the conversation, he'd say something else about the surprise. I begged for a hint, but he just said we had to wait until today, which made getting to sleep that night worse than the night before Christmas. When Mother woke me up to go to school, I still felt very tired. Mother felt my head and said I was coming down with something, and I'd better stay home. I didn't argue.

I heard Daddy's voice all the way to my room. "But if we have to stay home with her, what about the surprise?" He'd planned to spring the surprise while I was in school? I would've missed it. I moaned. Last night I'd forgotten that it was Sunday and I had school today. This morning I'd forgotten the surprise until he said that. What now? Was I going to spoil the whole thing?

"Well..." Mother pulled the word out so long it sounded like a whole sentence. My heart leaped. That meant she was thinking of a way to make it work. "Maybe," she said slowly, "we can wrap her up in a blanket to keep her warm and take her with us.

"Great idea!" Daddy said exactly what I thought.

"Of course, I don't know where we're going, so I don't know if we can do that or not."

Daddy laughed. "It's not going to work, Charlotte. I promise she'll be fine, and that's all I'm going to say." After breakfast, Mother brought a blanket and I carried a pillow so I could lie down in the car. Between the excitement and carrying a pillow, I made a mistake I was to regret the rest

71

of the day—I forgot to bring a book. I put my head on the pillow and covered up with the blanket. Maybe I slept a little. I was surprised when the car stopped and we were at a car dealership. I think Mother was surprised, too, because she was unusually quiet.

"I wanted it to be a Christmas present, but it wasn't ready in time. Now it's a Valentine's Day present. You can't imagine how hard it's been to stay quiet and keep it secret. I just *know* you're going to love it." Mother still didn't say anything. I could tell she was even more surprised, or maybe upset, when Uncle Willis came out to meet us. Before she could say anything, Daddy got out of the car and closed the door behind him. He walked over to Willis and shook his hand.

The two of them walked back to the car together. Willis stuck his head in the window to talk to Mother. "Your husband's a pretty great guy. I had a car for him at Christmas, just like he wanted, but he wouldn't take it because it wasn't blue. I had to move heaven and earth to get him a blue one. He says blue's your favorite color. Is that right?"

Mother said it was. I could tell she was uncomfortable. By then Daddy had opened the door for her. I held my breath wondering if she would get out or not. She did, but she was talking to Daddy quietly.

"I can't believe you let him talk you into buying a car. You know we can't afford a Packard." Even though she was upset, Daddy was still grinning.

Willis just kept talking. "Now I know just what you're going to say, Charlotte. You're going to say a chief's pay doesn't stretch to Packards, and I understand that. In fact, part of the bargain I made with Frank was that it had to be affordable. I said I'd find you the perfect car, and I did. Now come on over here and meet your new car." Mother had no choice but to come along. We all followed Willis to the back of the lot. He pointed toward a clump of cars in a back corner. When he stopped, it was in front of a shiny new car that was the most beautiful blue I'd ever seen. I could tell Daddy was in love with it already. I hoped he didn't love it more than he loved Mother, because I didn't want them to divorce. I looked at Mother, hoping she liked it. The color was perfect.

"I thought you only sold Packards," said Mother.

"That's right. That's why your car is tucked away out here. I did a little back fence trading with the GM dealer. His mother-in-law wanted a Packard, and he said he'd never have any peace at home if he didn't get her one. So we made a deal."

"She's a beauty, isn't she?" Uncle Willis didn't wait for an answer. He just kept on selling. "It's a brand new 1948 Pontiac Streamliner. I got a great deal because it's last year's model that didn't sell before the new ones came out, but she's as new as the day she rolled off the assembly line. Eight cylinders will get you up any hill in San Francisco—*and* it has the new hydromatic drive. No more worrying about the clutch and shifting on the hills; no more worrying about rolling back at the stop lights. I tell you she's a beauty." He was looking at Mother the whole time. "Why don't you take it for a spin, Charlotte?" I could tell Daddy was itching to get behind the wheel, but Willis knew Mother was the one he had to sell it to. Daddy was sold before he even saw the car.

We all got in the new car and Mother drove around a few blocks. I could tell she really liked it. She asked questions and paid attention when Willis explained all the great things about it. Even *I* loved the car, and I couldn't even understand half of what Willis said. Finally we all went inside and Willis got out some papers and showed Mother and Daddy the price. He wrote it down on a little piece of paper, and he swore it was what he paid the other dealer for it. Daddy was excited, but Mother said she was sure Willis could come down a little more.

"Your wife drives a hard bargain," Uncle Willis said to Daddy. "Now I know where Nellie gets it." The men laughed. He wrote down another number and said he could afford to take a small loss on the car because he made some money on the Packard he traded. "Besides," he added to Daddy, "if I make any money now Nellie will just screw me out of it anyway."

Later as we were driving home in the new car, Mother said the only reason she agreed was because she knew Willis was stuck with a car he wasn't supposed to sell because he's a Packard dealer, and he had to sell it at a good price. "Making him go below his cost was just my way of getting back at him for being such a beast to my little sister."

Daddy laughed a lot when she said that. "Admit it, Charlotte; you'd have bought the car from Satan himself at that price."

"Well, it *is* my favorite color," said Mother with a grin. "If you get a real bargain, nothing else matters."

"I knew you'd love it." Daddy looked very happy.

"I have an idea," said Mother. "Let's go out and celebrate tonight. There's an Italian restaurant over by Nellie's that I heard about."

"Auntie Stell says Aunt Nellie's working there as a

waitress," I said to be part of the conversation. Car buying means an awful lot of being quiet for a kid.

Mother gave me a look and I sat back, once more wishing I'd brought a book.

"I have a better idea," said Daddy. "Let's go to that Chinese restaurant you like so much. You two can go and visit Nellie at home tomorrow while I'm working."

Daddy doesn't like Chinese food very much, so I think he agreed with Auntie Stell that visiting Aunt Nellie at work was not a good idea. I loved his suggestion of the Chinese restaurant because I'm learning how to use chopsticks. I started eating with the chopsticks, but I switched to a fork half way through the meal. By the way, if your chopsticks slip and the food lands in someone else's plate, don't try to get it back.

FEBRUARY 15, 1949: - Today Mother and I went to Aunt Nellie's in the new car. I got to sit in the front seat for the first time. Aunt Nellie served Jackie and me milk in coffee cups with a few drops of coffee and a spoonful of sugar. We sat on little chairs in the corner of the living room while the women talked.

"Are you really working as a waitress in an Italian restaurant?"

"Yes. It's actually fun. I get good tips and the work isn't hard."

"If you sold the mink, you wouldn't have to work."

"I don't mind. The people at the restaurant are a great bunch, and we have a lot of fun. I may even stay on, after the divorce. I'm enjoying myself and I don't need to sell the mink. Besides, I may never have a chance to get another one."

The women were still on their first cup of coffee when the front door opened and Patsy came in. She said she'd had a swell interview for the perfect job, and she was through going on interviews, at least until she got an answer from this one.

Mother said she was sorry to hear that things weren't going well for Patsy.

"I was upset at first, but Aunt Nellie and I had a long talk about what happened and I'm all right now."

Mother touched Patsy's hand. "You poor dear, it must have been dreadful."

I caught a glimpse of Patsy rolling her eyes at Aunt Nellie before she answered. "No, Aunt Charlotte, I got a lot of benefit from the experience. It was my first real job and now when I apply for another position, I have something on my resume besides school and summer jobs. Aunt Nellie and I worked it out together and I realized that I learned a lot about how the real world works." Patsy and Nellie laughed. "I learned that if a man, especially a boss, asks for a date he usually wants one thing. So...if I accept the first date, I must be willing to make the choice: I either give him what he wants or I break it off and lose my job. If I go into it with my eyes open, it's my choice from the beginning, not his."

"So you're the one in control?" Mother liked that idea.

"Oh, yeah. The other thing Aunt Nellie taught me is to assume the rat is married from the start and make him prove otherwise." She took a sip of coffee. "I guess we both got something out of it. He got to parade around town with a pretty young girl on his arm, but I had a great ride on the merry-go-round. I went to a lot of fancy restaurants, saw a lot of good shows, and went dancing at some great clubs.

He never caught the brass ring, so I think I came out the winner."

"Yes," said Aunt Nellie, "Never let a man use you. However, that doesn't mean you can't let him *think* he's using you. Patsy's boss thought he was using her to show off around town, but she was having a good time, so she let him keep thinking that, at least until he stopped taking no for an answer. Then she stopped the merry-go-round."

"As long as you're the one with your hand on the switch," said Mother.

"By the way, Charlotte," said Aunt Nellie, "Can Jackie spend the weekend with you? I'm off this weekend and Patsy and I want to go out and have some fun."

Jackie and I were both happy when Mother said yes.

FEBRUARY 26, 1949: - Mother's really good at sewing. The weekend Jackie stayed she made us matching dresses on Saturday, and we wore them to church Sunday. We played twins all weekend. Mother took us out and several people actually asked if we *were* twins. We wanted Mother to say we were, but she wouldn't.

About a week later, Patsy got her new job and had to start work right away, so Aunt Nellie called to ask if Jackie could stay with us until she made other arrangements, so we finally got to see the restaurant where Aunt Nellie worked. She took Jackie to the restaurant with her, and we picked her up from there. The owner was very nice; he said our dinner was on the house. I asked Mother what he meant because our food got served on a table like everyone else's. She laughed and said he was giving it to us for free. Mother really enjoyed it. After all, free is the ultimate bargain.

Aunt Nellie washed our table before the food came. I almost spilled my milk because the table wobbled. Jackie and I ordered the same thing. Aunt Nellie looked very smart in her waitress uniform. It was early and there weren't many people, so she got to sit with us while we ate. She and Mother agreed that Jackie would stay with us. On her days off she'd pick Jackie up from school and take her to school the next day before work, but Mother would drive her to school and pick her up on the other days. Jackie and I share my room, and we love being twins.

Today Aunt Nellie came to visit because it's Saturday and she can spend some time with Jackie before she has to go to work. Mother made us coffee milk just like Aunt Nellie and we sat in the living room while they talked.

"Al asked me to stay after the restaurant closed to have dinner with him."

"Did you tell him you were married?"

"I told him I was getting a divorce when I asked for the job."

"Is he married?"

"No, he still lives with his mother in an apartment over the restaurant. Not that he sees much of her with the hours he works."

"So you went?"

"I told him if I was going to eat the restaurant food, he needed to give me ten minutes in the kitchen first. You know that cook just pours tomato sauce over the spaghetti and calls it marinara sauce." I thought it tasted just like what I eat at home.

"I did notice the food was a little..." Mother hesitated.

"Bland is the word," said Nellie. "Al only stays in business because he sells food cheap, and there aren't any

78

other restaurants in the area. Anyway, I made him a meal he said was better than his mother's cooking. He offered me the job of cook. It pays a lot more than waitressing."

"That's great!"

"Not really. I don't want to sling hash in a cheap restaurant."

"Did you tell him that?"

"No. I invited him to dinner the next night at a restaurant of my choice and said we could talk about it then. I took him to a decent restaurant and asked what the difference was between that one and his.

"'Higher prices,' was his first answer. Then I mentioned the tablecloths and good food. I told him that if he spruced his place up a bit, I'd teach the cook how to make a decent spaghetti sauce. Of course he said his customers wouldn't pay more. I suggested that he post new prices that would be effective after six in the evening. Anyone who wanted cheap could come early."

"Did he say he'd do it?"

"I let him kiss me goodnight. Of course he'll do it."

"Nellie, you're still married to Willis."

"It isn't really a marriage any more, but don't worry, I know what I'm doing. 'You must remember this; a kiss is just a kiss.'" Nellie started singing and Mother chimed in.

That's a funny song because even I know that not every kiss is just a kiss. I think the difference is cheek kisses and mouth kisses. Mother says mouth kisses are for married people, but I know that isn't the whole truth. She was telling a half-truth and I caught it. Is the other half of a half-truth a half-lie? Does that make it only a half sin?

⪼⊕ ⊕ 2013 ⊕ ⊕⪻

Melissa looked up into the biggest, deepest, darkest pair of eyes she'd ever seen. Unable to move her gaze from his face, she ignored the hand he was offering.

"S'il vous plaît, mademoiselle."

"Thank you." Better to let him know he had already exhausted her knowledge of French than to say merci *and have him assume she understood. Awkwardly she tried to get her feet under her. Everyone walked around them without a second glance. God, he could bop her on the head and walk off with her over his shoulder and no one would even notice. Why had she thought there was safety on a crowded street? This was Tangiers, the city of spies and*

"Damn it!" I vowed for the umpteenth time to unplug the damned phone when I sat down to write. Then I remembered it could be Robert with news of Kate. "Hello."

"Hi, Charli." It was Jean.

"Oh, it's you."

"Jesus, Charli, you don't have to sound so happy to hear from me. I'll call Bev."

"Sorry, Jean. What's up?"

"It's what isn't up. I can't get Albert out of bed."

"Is he sick?"

"Not physically. My problem is that I have a doctor's appointment tomorrow, and I can't leave him alone that long. He could get out and wander away. I need someone in the house. Can you sit with him? Just keep the front and back doors locked, and don't let him wander off. He won't come downstairs."

"Are you sure?" I prayed she was right. I'd keep my

cell phone clipped to my waist and call 911 if he did. Jean's husband had no memory left, and didn't even talk much anymore. If he really wanted to go out, I couldn't stop him. He outweighed me by at least a hundred pounds. Albert's the one that belongs in a home, not me. Not being able to afford assisted living when you really need it is worse than having to visit a retirement home.

Oh, crap! Tomorrow was the day I was supposed to visit the home. Calling David to cancel the appointment and hearing they only had visitor tours once a month was the first good news of the day. Now I had a whole month to wriggle out of it.

I picked up the phone again. It was late enough for me to call California. First I needed to call Robert and see if he located Kate. If he found her and forgot to call me, I'd give him a piece of my mind. If he hadn't, why hadn't he? Then I needed to get started calling cousins. I could ask what they knew about Kate and her husband, and get more phone numbers to expand my search for people who might know Kate.

After a couple of hours of talking to long lost cousins who tried to sound happy that we connected, I put down the phone and stretched. I had a growing list of phone numbers and a growing list of rumors and maybes. I needed a snack and a walk before I could face another cousin. I tried to track what kind of cousin each one was, but the generations blurred and it didn't matter enough to be worth the effort. The phone rang before I finished my yogurt. I ran to answer, hoping someone remembered something useful. It wasn't a cousin.

"Hey, Mom, I've been trying to call you back all day, but your phone's been busy. You haven't started cooking supper yet, have you?"

"Is Susan inviting?"

"Nope. I am. Susan's visiting her folks for a couple of days."

"I can cook." I tried to sound more enthusiastic than I felt.

"I'm picking up a greasy pizza and a six-pack. Find yourself a bottle of wine. I'll be there about six-thirty."

"Sounds good." We demolished the better part of the pizza laughing over small talk before I decided it was time to do some serious talking. I had to bring up the subject of the retirement home, but David was opening his third beer. He seldom drank more than one. Something was bothering him. It had to be about Susan. "Is one of Susan's parents having a problem?" I barely knew her parents.

"It's just a visit." He didn't seem in a hurry to explain. "You know the trouble with drinking beer out of the bottle?" I shrugged. "You can't stare at the bubbles."

I reached behind me and felt around until I found the beer stein I'd bought in Munich in a former life. "Here, the lid keeps the dust out."

"Do you always have the answer at your fingertips?"

"Sometimes I don't even know there's a question."

"Munich. I remember Munich. It was a cut above the usual places we lived. I used to imagine I was a knight living in the castle."

"So did being headmistress make me the chatelaine of the castle?"

"Yes. Your lord husband had been killed in the Crusades and the science teacher was courting you." He remembered the castle, and I remembered Gregory. "I always wished we'd stayed in Germany longer."

"My publisher wanted another travel book, so we needed a new location."

"The story of my childhood. I'd just get comfortable and you'd drag me off to another country."

"Don't complain. Those books put you through college and the royalties keep your mother from having to live in your basement on crumbs. Speaking of which..."

He swallowed the last of his beer and brought another to pour into the stein. "Oh, yeah, you were asking about Susan's trip." So much for trying to segue into the retirement home topic. "Susan's parents are giving a big party and inviting everyone who's anyone. Susan's gone to press the flesh and get the tip of her wedge back into the right society. Soon they'll just remember which influential family she belongs to and forget that she lived out of state for twenty years."

"Everybody knows Susan enjoys parties and organizing things."

"Yeah, and now that she doesn't have the PTA, school politics, and athletic clubs to dominate she's moving on to bigger things. Sometimes I think the only reason she had kids was to get to the politics."

"Careful, David. The sarcasm will drip into your beer."

He gave me a grin that made him look ten years younger. "Guess I'm just not used to coming home to an empty house. Thanks for the company." I wanted to say that I was always here for him, but I just gave him a quick hug before he left. I'd missed the perfect opportunity to talk about the retirement home, but he was brooding over his own troubles.

I mulled over the strange conversation as I turned off the light. So that's what Susan meant by moving farther south. Why hadn't she come right out and said it was time they moved closer to *her* parents? What would be more natural than her wanting to be there if her parents were giving a big bash? She'd want to help, or more accurately supervise the help. What had David said about politics? I remembered joking to David as he worked the grill at one of Susan's giant cookouts that she moved from group to group working the crowd like a seasoned politician.

Sleep refused to come. David had never, in more than twenty years of marriage, mentioned any disagreements he'd had with Susan. I knew they had their ups and downs like any couple, but it had all been through Susan complaining. Strange, I'd always thought that David and I were very close. I *knew* that he'd tell me if he had problems. Could I be that wrong? It took me one good deep breath to admit that yes, I could be that wrong. My eyes flew open, all traces of sleep gone. What had happened to our relationship?

What a silly goose I was! Nothing had happened to our relationship. It was a blow to my ego—our relationship hadn't changed. Sorting truth from fiction didn't make it any easier to sleep. I reached for the journal.

≫ SIX ≪

APRIL 10, 1949: - Saturday mornings are more exciting now that Aunt Nellie comes every week, but I haven't been able to write in my journal because Jackie shares my room and I don't want her to know where I hide it. Today Aunt Nellie took Jackie out to lunch and a movie. I wanted to go with them, but Mother and Aunt Nellie both said no so fast it was like they were playing twins. Jackie and I laughed at the same time, and it was like two sets of twins, which made us laugh even more. The grownups didn't get it because they didn't laugh.

After they left, Mother took me into the kitchen and gave me a glass of milk. "How would you like it if Jackie moved in with us?" I nodded because my mouth was full. "Your Aunt Nellie was very upset today. She thought the divorce would all be over before this, and Willis would be giving her enough money so she could stay home to take care of Jackie. She can't find anyone to watch Jackie while she's at work. She knows I can't keep driving Jackie to and from school every day, so she's agreed to let her start going to your school with you."

"So now I'll have a twin for real? This is better than Christmas!" I was so excited that I spilled my milk when I jumped up to hug Mother. After we cleaned up the milk, Mother sent me to my room to move my things around so when Aunt Nellie brought Jackie's things over there would be a place to put them. Then she filled the tub with hot water and took a book with her into the bath, so I have time to write.

Since I wrote last, I found out there are two kinds of dating: the kind when you go out to have fun and enjoy the dates, and the kind where you're looking for a husband. If you want to date for fun, you look for someone who's handsome, a good dancer, and preferably has money. Nellie said that if the dating isn't serious, it isn't worth a lot of thought. "If you aren't ready for marriage, enjoy yourself. Just know where to draw the line, and make sure he knows where it is, too." I know it's another time when they don't mean exactly what they say, but I still pictured the cousins going on dates with a crayon tucked into their purses.

One piece of advice she says applies to everyone. "Always try to look your best. If you've just been cleaning house and decide to go to the corner store for a cold one, as sure as God made little green apples someone will see you. Eventually the man of your dreams will hear, 'You should see her without her makeup.' He's supposed to think you always look this good. By the time he sees you without your makeup he should be so besotted he'll still think you're beautiful—which you are, every one of you." She says even the married women should look their best because it's an important part of keeping a husband happy and interested. I'm adding that to my list of things that might keep the curse away.

Aunt Nellie takes the problems with the fiancés very seriously. She says that men are on their best behavior when they're courting, and if the guy's a problem then, he'll be even more of a problem later when he thinks you're his property. According to Aunt Nellie (and Mother), men always think they own their women and that they're entitled to make all the rules.

APRIL 16, 1949: - We spent all morning decorating Easter eggs for tomorrow. After lunch, Al and Aunt Nellie came and took Jackie. They said they'd bring her back tomorrow before the supper rush in the restaurant. I almost cried because I wanted Jackie to be here to look for eggs with me, but Mother said there was no reason we couldn't wait and look for eggs when she came back. It's a dreary damp day and Mother won't let me go outside. She thinks I'm coming down with something.

Grandmother and Auntie Stell came over for coffee. I had a book tucked under my arm and was on my way to the kitchen to grab a slice of the pound cake Mother bought yesterday, when I heard Auntie Stell's voice. "Well, all I can say is that no good can come of it." I sidled into the room so I could sit next to the wall with my book and still see the women over the top of it. Hiding in a book is a lot better than hiding in a closet. It's less scary, more comfortable, and you're almost as invisible.

Grandmother frowned. "Nellie says he's a good Catholic boy."

"Good Catholic my eye. We all know that a good Catholic boy wouldn't marry a divorced woman—and he's not exactly a boy either."

"Estela, how can you say he's not a good man? You never even met him."

"Mark my words. No good can come of marrying an Italian."

"You know better than to judge the man because his

parents came from Italy. Every country has good people and bad people."

"I know about Italians. I married one, remember?"

"I remember," said Mother as she came in with the coffee tray. "I was there one day when he came home and got mad because his dinner wasn't ready. He threw something at your stomach, and you were pregnant with his son at the time, too."

"Don't remind me," said Grandmother with a shudder.

"Mama was incredible," said Auntie Stell with a huge smile. "After you ran home and told her, she marched right into our house and threatened to kill Danicci in his sleep if he ever hurt me. We both believed she'd do it, too. He didn't hit me again until long after Mama had moved out of the neighborhood."

"I believed I'd do it, too." Grandmother wasn't smiling. "That thought haunted me for years. I prayed constantly for forgiveness."

"Oh, Mama, don't make such a big deal about it," said Mother. She says that to me sometimes when someone hurts my feelings. "You were protecting your young. Even animals protect their young."

"But we aren't animals—that's the whole point. We're made in God's image. It was a great sin even to *think* about taking a human life."

"I'm not sure that snake was human," muttered Auntie Stell into her coffee cup. Maybe that's why I'm not supposed to ask about him, because he wasn't a nice person. Why would Auntie Stell marry someone who wasn't nice? Maybe people are like books—you don't always know if you have a good one until you get into the story.

"I haven't thought about him for years," said Mother. "What happened to him? When I came back from boarding school, we didn't see much of you. As I remember, you'd already remarried before our paths came together again." I was so shocked that Mother had been in boarding school that I almost missed the next sentence.

"He died."

"I know that, but how? No one ever talks about it. I remember thinking he died because he was old, but now I realize he couldn't have been that old."

"You thought he was an old man because that's what I said he was," said Grandmother. "He was twice your sister's age, which made him too old for her." She looked at Auntie Stell. "I remember how impressed you were with his jewelry. You didn't believe me when I said that big ring he flashed wasn't a real ruby. You thought he was a good catch."

"Sorry, Mama, I thought you were blowing smoke rings. We were poor as church mice. Where did you ever see real rubies to know the difference?"

"Mother wasn't always poor. She was — "

"Charlotte, pour some more coffee." Grandmother's voice snapped like a slap in the face. I thought Mother would swallow her tongue as she got up to get the coffee pot. I must have missed something.

Auntie Stell never looked up. She gave a funny sounding laugh. "I never told you where he said he got that ring, did I?" Grandmother shook her head, but Auntie Stell wasn't looking. "One day when I was really mad at him, I told him that I didn't think his ring was a real ruby. I was trying to make him mad, but he only laughed. He said he didn't care what it was because the ring was a trophy. He said he took it off the hand of a stiff that wasn't even stiff yet. He said he'd killed him."

Mother nearly dropped the coffee pot. She refilled the cups and I saw her head begin to turn in my direction. I buried my nose in my book, hoping that she'd think I was too engrossed in the story to hear anything. That did happen sometimes, but not nearly as often as she thought it did. When I glanced up, she was sitting as still as a cat watching a bird as Grandmother and Auntie Stell talked.

"Nonsense, he was trying to scare you. It was a different way of making you afraid of him—a way to keep you under his thumb without hitting you. He was afraid to hit you again as long as we lived so close. I was half his size, and if he was that afraid of *me*, you know he couldn't have killed anyone. He was a tailor."

"That's what I thought, too—at first." Auntie Stell's voice dropped to a whisper, and I held my breath so I wouldn't make any noise. I didn't dare look up to see anyone's reactions. This was the best conversation ever! I was so glad Aunt Nellie had Jackie. If Jackie were here, I'd never have heard this. The rattle of cups on saucers let me breathe. "Then one day I came through the back door of the tailor shop with his lunch. I saw a man holding out a wad of money. Danicci took it. When the man pulled back his hand, I saw a gun under his jacket." I peeked up over my book and watched Auntie Stell. "I backed out of the shop and came in again, letting the door slam behind me. By the time I got to the front, the man was gone. I never saw him again. I never saw any of the money, either." I was holding my breath. "After that I believed him about the ring."

Mother broke the next silence. "So how did he die?"

Auntie Stell gave a small shrug when Grandmother

looked at her. Grandmother said, "We didn't want to tell you when it happened because you were so young and impressionable. You had such a vivid imagination." I couldn't believe my ears--there was more? "Go ahead, tell her," Grandmother said to Auntie Stell. The conversation switched to Spanish, and it was harder to understand, but it was worth the effort.

"Mama may have threatened to kill him, but she wasn't the only one that wished him dead."

"You wanted him dead, too?"

Auntie Stell shook her head. "Other people. This was when Mama was living in San Francisco, and you were in boarding school." There it was again—Mother in boarding school. "One day I took little Albert on the ferry to visit Mama. I guess we talked too long and I was late leaving. You know how slow the ferry service can be in the evenings. I knew that by the time I got to Oakland the buses would have stopped running. I was terrified Danicci would beat me for being out all night." She paused, and I held my breath waiting for the next sentence. "He never touched me or anyone else again. His body was in the living room. He had a bullet hole in his head."

It was a good thing Mother gave a loud gasp because it covered my own gasp. So *that* was what happened to Auntie Stell's first husband.

"Oh, how awful," Mother said. From the look on her face, I think what she really meant was "how exciting."

"What happened next? Who did it? Was there a big trial?"

"There was an investigation, but they never found anything. I don't think the police tried very hard. I can still picture these two detectives talking to each other as clear as if it happened yesterday. They were standing on the front steps and didn't see, or maybe didn't care, that I was on the other side of the screen door. The guy talking had a cigarette stuck in the corner of his mouth, and it bobbled around when he talked. I can still remember the smell of his cheap tobacco blowing through the door. He said, 'You know these Eyetalians, they're always killin' each other off.' Then he spat out the cigarette and ground it into the stoop. 'Good riddance,' he said. Then they got in their car and drove off." Grandmother took Auntie Stell's hand.

"So they just let it go?" Auntie Stell nodded. On the radio, The Shadow always catches the bad guy. I was surprised that real detectives don't always catch the murderers, and sometimes they don't care.

"They never came back to talk to me again. He wasn't a very good husband, but he kept a roof over our heads and there was always food on the table. I was so young…" Her voice trailed off, and I barely heard the rest. "I'd never even seen a dead person before…there was so much blood…and that cop just said 'good riddance' like he was a bug or something."

"Estela, querida." Grandmother's voice held so much love it filled the room like pink fog. Mother said something too quiet for me to hear.

"And that brings us back to Nellie thinking about marrying an Italian." Auntie Stell's voice sounded loud after the quiet of the talk before it. "Even the police know they're bad news. Where did he get the money to buy the restaurant in the first place? He's probably up to no good."

I didn't listen to the rest of the conversation. I ran to my room to write everything down before Aunt Nellie brought Jackie back. If she was going to have an Italian for a new father, she didn't need to know what Auntie Stell thought of Italians.

I was certain Grandmother was right about there being a lot of good Italians. After all, Christopher Columbus was Italian, and so was Marconi who invented the radio. And what about the Italians who make the shoes Aunt Nellie likes so much?

Then I thought about Mother being in boarding school. That was a totally different puzzle. Whenever Mother thinks I'm being difficult, she threatens me with boarding school. She keeps telling me that bad children get sent to boarding school, yet she always tells me how good she'd been as a child and how much help she was to her mother. I can't imagine Grandmother sending Mother to boarding school for being bad. Maybe girls in boarding schools are like Italians—only some of them are bad. There must be more to this story, too.

I thought about Auntie Stell's first husband again. She must have loved him a lot because she left school to marry him. How could anyone be mean to Auntie Stell? Mother says Auntie Stell doesn't have a mean bone in her body, but that's silly because bones aren't mean—it's usually tongues.

Auntie Stell's not as pillowy as Grandmother, but she's still very huggable. So, if her husband was mean to her, then he must have been a bad person. All I can think about is The Unsolved Murder. Maybe instead of just making a list of things that might help me avoid the curse, I can read about being a detective.

MAY 6, 1949: - It's getting hard to remember all the things that happen until I get a chance to write them down, so I wasn't disappointed when Mother felt my forehead this morning and decided I needed to stay home from school. Now I really do feel hot because she put a ton of blankets on my bed.

First, I have to say that things around here have been pretty dull lately. The cousins aren't having any boyfriend problems so they don't come for coffee. The older women have been talking about boring things, and I'm happier reading a book than listening to them. The trouble is that Jackie always wants to play. I love playing and sewing doll clothes, but sometimes I just want to read. One of my favorite places to read is in the car, but Jackie and Mother keep wanting me to play games when we're in the car, games like going down the alphabet and finding words on road signs that begin with each letter, or "I went to Grandma's house and I brought her..." where we take turns adding things.

I always wanted a little sister, but now that I have one (more or less), it isn't as much fun as I thought it would be. We aren't interested in many of the same things, and it's hard to get her to sit still very long. Mother says it's because she's young, but I don't think so. I read a lot of books when I was her age.

The other night I got up for a drink of water, and I heard Mother talking to Daddy. "I can't get over the idea that Nellie's going to hire a stranger to raise her child so she can work. You know Jackie would be *so* much better off with us. I'm always here, ready to do anything for the girls. She'd always have a mother here, and a father, too. I mean you're at sea a lot, but your next tour should be shore duty, shouldn't it? At least she wouldn't have a new father every time she turned around. If she just stayed with us, it would be a perfect solution, don't you think? Jackie would have a stable home, and the girls would always have each other for company. Neither one would have to grow up all alone."

What? She wanted Jackie to stay with us *forever*? I'd be stuck with her for the rest of my life! I'd always have somebody in my room, and I'd never be sure my things would be where I put them. When would I have time alone to read and draw and do quiet things?

"Don't be silly. Nellie won't agree to let her stay."

"We'll see. If I get Mama on my side, I bet we could persuade her."

"Don't put money on it."

I heard the bedsprings creak, so I scurried back to bed. They both had sisters and brothers. They couldn't possibly know how nice it was to be alone after a whole day in school with other kids. Of course I don't want to be alone *all* the time. I'd love to have a best friend, but Jackie's a younger cousin. It's not the same. I don't think Aunt Nellie will do it, but it worries me just the same.

When Aunt Nellie came over last weekend, she was very excited. She was wearing a black dress with big white polka dots and a big full skirt, but what I noticed first was her bright red lipstick that exactly matched her red patent leather shoes and her wide matching belt. The shoes caught my eye because when I wanted some red shoes Mother wouldn't let me get them. She said nice girls don't wear red shoes. I asked why not and she said I'd understand when I got older. I'm guessing Aunt Nellie and Mother disagree about that, too. Aunt Nellie looked gorgeous as she rushed in and hugged Jackie very tight, and then she hugged Mother. When she stepped back from Mother, she twirled around like a dancer, and her skirt flared out and showed her frilly petticoat. She was beautiful. "The divorce is final—at last."

"So Willis will be paying you alimony. Will you quit work?" Aunt Nellie talked right over Mother's questions.

"Al was very happy, and he's giving a big party at the restaurant. I'm inviting everyone in the family. Not just you and Frank, but especially the girls." Jackie started jumping up and down. I was afraid Mother would say I couldn't go. I never get to go with them when they go out at night. Usually Mother has one of the older cousins stay overnight, but sometimes the neighbor girl comes. I held my breath and looked at Mother, hoping she'd accept. "There'll be dancing after dinner."

"We'd love to come." Mother loved dancing.

"Wouldn't miss it for the world," Daddy said when he came home and she told him. "Italians know how to throw a party." Mother gave him the raised eyebrow that usually meant "I don't believe that for a minute," but this time I think it meant, "How do you know?" Mother made Jackie and me take a nap, but it was worth it to be able to go to a grown-up party.

When we got there, Aunt Nellie greeted us at the door. She was wearing a black lace dress with long skinny sleeves that let her white skin show through. Under the black lace was a strapless dress of bright red. She was smiling really hard and kissed us all as we came in. Al looked very handsome in his black suit with tiny white stripes, and a stiff white shirt. His black hair was slicked back with something shiny. He hugged Mother and then he hugged Daddy. Daddy looked surprised, but he slapped Al on the back and gave a funny laugh. When Al was slapping

Daddy on the back, I saw a ring on his pinky finger. It had a red stone. Was it a real ruby? I shuddered to think he might have gotten it the same way Auntie Stell's husband got his. I hoped not. Al patted my head. He picked Jackie up and twirled her around, then he held her hand as he led us to a table.

I thought everybody at the party was going to be from our family because it was about Aunt Nellie's divorce, but there were a lot of people I didn't know. They all seemed to be named Lombardi.

Mother leaned over to Daddy and said, "I thought we were celebrating Nellie's divorce, although I'm not sure anyone ought to celebrate a divorce."

"Charlotte, it's a party. Any excuse for a party is a good excuse." All of the men wore suits with tiny little white stripes woven into the material. Some of them wore pink shirts! I'd never seen a man wearing pink before. They all had rings on their little fingers. They couldn't *all* have taken rings from dead men.

I started to tell Jackie that it looked like the men were playing twins, but somebody shouted, "Stella, baby, what're you doing here?" I was surprised to see Auntie Stell there, considering her opinion of Italians, but in she walked with Uncle Walter. Auntie Stell looked pretty, but Uncle Walter looked like his tie was too tight. One of the Lombardi men waved at her.

Auntie Stell jumped, and her face got so pale her rouge stood out like two bright spots on her cheeks. "Hello, Guido, meet my husband, Walter." Auntie Stell grabbed Uncle Walter's arm and pulled him close.

"It's a pleasure." Guido shook Walter's hand and turned back to Auntie Stell. "Damn! The years have sure been good to you. You're looking better than ever. How's little Albert doing?"

Auntie Stell hung on Uncle Walter like a barnacle on the bottom of a boat. "Little Albert is all grown up with a family of his own."

"Has it been that long? How time flies when you're having fun, eh? So what're you doing here? You know Nellie?"

"She's my sister."

"Hey, ain't that a kick. We could be kissin' cousins when those two—" Guido slapped his hand over his mouth. "Oops. Me and my big mouth. I'd better shut up."

"That would probably be a good idea," said Auntie Stell with a funny smile. She had recovered her color and she pulled Walter in our direction. Guido said he'd catch them later, and walked toward a group of men who were standing together talking. That's when I saw how different the two families were. It wasn't just that their men had stripes in their suits and ours didn't. We were all sitting at our tables like we were in a restaurant, which we were of course. They were acting like they were at home. The men were standing around talking, and the women were sitting at a few tables talking and laughing. They were all moving around. It looked like they were having a lot more fun.

Al started opening bottles of wine and putting them on tables. The men who'd been standing around moved to tables, and some of the women moved from one table to another. Once they all got sorted out, Aunt Nellie stood up and gave a toast, "To my ex, the cheating bastard, for finally letting go." If I hadn't been sitting right next to Mother I'd never have heard her remark about ladies using profanity, because everyone else was laughing so hard.

Then the food started coming. We each got a dish with salad that was so colorful it made me think of eating flowers. It tasted good, too. We almost never have salad at home. Daddy calls it rabbit food. Vegetables come out of a can in our house, just like in all of our friends' houses. Salad was a real treat.

After the salad we had pasta. I'm glad they didn't call it spaghetti, because it didn't taste anything like the spaghetti Mother makes. I couldn't eat another bite after that. Even Daddy slowed down before the end.

When the dishes had been taken to the kitchen, the waiter came around with glasses with a different kind of wine.

Clink. Clink. Clink. Everyone got quiet and looked at Al, who was banging the side of his glass with a fork. He gestured toward the door to the kitchen and Aunt Nellie wheeled out the most amazing cake I ever saw! It looked like an enormous castle, bigger than my dollhouse. It was so beautiful that everyone in the room just froze in place and stared. The oooohs and aaaaahs came a second or two later. I knew Aunt Nellie had made it herself, and I was very proud of her. Jackie's face was pink with excitement.

Al put his arm around Aunt Nellie. "I want you all to share in my good news. Nellie promised to marry me as soon as her divorce was finalized." The cheers from the Lombardi family were so loud I'm sure no one heard Mother's surprised squeak. People started banging on their glasses with their forks and Al kissed Aunt Nellie on the mouth right there in front of everyone.

Jackie grinned like a jack o lantern. She knew all the time, and she never told me? After all, we were practically sisters now. After everyone stopped cheering and laughing, Al finished his speech. "So I want everyone to congratulate me on getting engaged to the most wonderful woman in the world. Nellie's the best thing that ever happened to me. No offense to you, Mama, but she's also the best cook on the West Coast. No, she's probably the best cook on either coast, even if she isn't Italian." Everyone laughed again.

"Jackie, come here and drink a toast," Al's voice boomed out over the laughter. Jackie ran to them and Al lifted her up and sat her on his shoulder. "Everyone, this is my beautiful new daughter, Jackie." Everyone clapped and shouted, and somebody gave a really loud whistle. The next sound was popping corks and suddenly everyone had a glass of champagne—even me! I barely got the glass to my face when Mother snatched it out of my hand saying that they should have had more sense than to serve champagne to a child. When Jackie came back to our table, she told me that it didn't taste as good as soda, and the bubbles tickled her nose so much she almost sneezed.

After we ate dessert, they moved the tables and there was dancing. Mama Lombardi, that was Al's mother, danced a lot. Mother said it was indecent for a woman who was still wearing widow's weeds to dance. Later, when Mama Lombardi came to our table to hug Jackie, I looked at her really close. I didn't see any weeds, just a regular black dress. After she hugged Jackie, she hugged me. She was wearing a lot of perfume. I thought she'd be pillowy like Grandmother, but she wasn't. When I told Mother, she said Mama Lombardi was wearing a corset. Daddy said women didn't wear corsets anymore, and Mother rolled her eyes at him.

Daddy danced with Mother, and then he danced with

me standing on his shoes. It was fun. Then he started dancing with Jackie, but Al cut in and Daddy came back to the table. When I saw Jackie again she was dancing on the shoes of Guido. I wonder how Auntie Stell knew Guido and why she didn't seem as happy to see him as he was to see her. Guido brought Jackie back to the table, and I noticed that the stripes on his suit were wider than the stripes on the other suits. His ring was bigger, too. More bottles of wine came out of the kitchen, and the party kept getting louder.

The party was still going strong when we left, but Mother said I needed my sleep. Jackie stayed, and Aunt Nellie said they'd drop her off at our house on the way to Vegas the next day. We were going to keep Jackie for another week until Al and Nellie got back from their honeymoon. The restaurant was closing for a week. When they got back from their honeymoon, Jackie would live with them. She'd stay upstairs with Mama Lombardi while Nellie worked, and they'd take her home when the restaurant closed at night. They had it all planned out, and they'd kept it all a secret. I was a little hurt that Jackie hadn't told me, but I was mostly relieved that she wouldn't be staying with us forever.

I curled up on the back seat on the way home trying not to fall asleep.

"Can you imagine that?" My mother's outraged voice floated back to me. "She's getting married not twenty-four hours after her divorce is final. She should at least wait a decent interval."

"What's a decent interval? That divorce has been dragging out for months now. It isn't as though she was really married when she started dating Al."

"Of course she was really married. You can't be kind of married. You're either married or you're not. She was married until yesterday."

"That was only a piece of paper. The marriage was over long before Nellie walked into the office of the divorce lawyer. The real marriage has nothing to do with paper; it has to do with two people and their feelings for each other. Even you have to admit there hadn't been much of that for a long time." That was something new, there are two kinds of marriages: one kind is on paper and the other kind is about two people and their feelings.

"In the eyes of God and the Church, they were still married."

Daddy sighed. "I can't speak for the eyes of God, but was she ever married in the eyes of the Church? The Church probably thinks she should still be with her first husband, whoever that was, and however miserable it would have made them both. Whether she marries Al tomorrow or after twenty years, that won't change. Just relax and let your sister enjoy her new love without seeing your disapproval every time she looks at you."

Mother huffed and Daddy kept talking. "Did you see how happy she looked? She was positively glowing. Of course Nellie always glows. That cake was a real labor of love, wasn't it?" Mother didn't answer. If she answered later, I missed it because I fell asleep. When Mother and Daddy kind of argue, one of them ends it by not answering. When they really argue, I don't know how it ends because I go to my room and try not to hear them.

▷▷ SEVEN ◁◁

Why hadn't I seen it earlier? Nellie's marriage to Al hot on the heels of the divorce was her way of doing what she had to do to keep Jackie with her. Like Grandmother said, "A woman does what she must." My sympathy for Aunt Nellie was so strong it brought tears to my eyes. No wonder the marriage had been short lived. Maybe the curse wasn't so much a question of making poor choices as it was running out of options. I knew that feeling.

I heard a car start and the crunch of tires on the gravel drive. "You can stop playing possum, Charli. He's gone." I tucked the journal away and poked my head out of the room. Aunt Nellie was standing there smiling. "I appreciate you trying to be discreet, but I never do anything I'm ashamed of. He seldom stays over, but it's no big deal—just don't tell your mother, I don't hold up well under scolding."

"Neither do I." I grinned and headed for the bathroom.

Her voice followed me. "The ladies are coming for coffee this morning."

After the perfect Saturday breakfast, I vacuumed and dusted while Aunt Nellie cleaned the kitchen and made a tart for later. Grandmother and Auntie Stell arrived and were just pouring the first round of coffee when the doorbell rang again. I froze, ready to retreat to my room if Mother showed up and started ranting.

"Look who's here." Aunt Nellie came in with her arm

around Jackie, who was holding a pink bundle. I saw a tiny fist wave above the folds of pink flannel.

I flew across the space between us. "How can I hug you?"

"Hug us both, just be careful."

"So this is the beautiful Kate I've heard so much about."

She placed the little pink bundle in my arms and uncovered the face. "Kate, meet your mommy's twin, Aunt Charli." We both burst into laughter. "We had so much fun pretending to be twins."

"Except that we're a little out of synch on this one." I gave the baby a peck on the cheek and put her into Grandmother's outstretched arms. "Now I can give you a proper hug. Remember snorting milk through your nose when I swallowed first and made you laugh?"

"How can I forget? I don't think your mother has forgiven me yet. But we're not very far out of synch with the babies, from what I hear."

It was another hour before we got down to what Grandmother called the Business of the Day. It was partly because everyone had to fuss over the baby and partly because I had to crow about my success at work. "I started stuffing fund raising envelopes and found a mistake in the letter. I pointed it out to the supervisor, and I also told her how she could make the letter more effective. So guess what? I got promoted already. I'll be working directly with Janice, the supervisor, on the fund raising campaigns. She's really nice."

"That's wonderful, Charli, but it's time for you to begin planning for the future." Grandmother said.

"I *have* been planning. Aunt Nellie says I can stay here,

so I'll be able to save all my salary."

"That's not what I'm talking about. Your baby needs a name. It's all very well to say you can support him, but you have to consider the stigma of illegitimacy he'll have to deal with as he gets older."

"But he's not illegitimate."

"We believe you, dear, but will anyone else? Your mother doesn't." I kept my mouth shut, but it wasn't easy. "You don't have any *proof* of a marriage. Forgive me, child, but you must admit your story sounds like a fairy tale. Without something official to substantiate it, your mother won't be the only one to dismiss it as the ramblings of a desperate girl in trouble. You have questions to answer. Whose name will he carry? Yours? What will you tell him when he grows up and asks about his father?" I didn't have answers. "Even if he believes you, and he probably will, what will you tell him about his father? At some point in his life, he'll want to know more and more. You need to have answers, and this is the time to make those decisions."

Aunt Nellie clapped her hands. "All right, ladies. Let's get some ideas on the table."

The afternoon was pleasant enough. No ideas worth having came out of it, but the company was wonderful. Jackie and I had so much to talk about that we didn't hear much of the women's talk. Holding Kate gave me the shivers. I'm looking forward to having a baby of my own to hold. It wasn't until I climbed into bed that I realized I had a host of problems I'd never even considered—and I had no idea how to solve them.

I woke up early Sunday morning and stripped the bed, gathering all my laundry into a bundle. I had just started the washer when Aunt Nellie opened the door.

"You'd better come. Your mother's here, and she's foaming at the mouth." My expression must have shown her how much I'd rather stay in the laundry room. "Grow up, honey. You have to face your problems." Her soft tone of voice didn't take the sting out of the rebuke. She was right—about me facing my problems and about Mother's foaming. By the time I reached the kitchen, Nellie had poured coffee and placed a leftover tart in front of Mother.

"Your so-called husband phoned again. He says you have to come back because you're carrying his baby and he wants it."

"He's not a so-called husband. We're married."

"Was there a priest there?" I started to answer, but Aunt Nellie's outrage got there first.

"Charlotte, how can you of all people say that? You'd better rethink your opinion on this."

Mother chose to ignore her. "*And* he said if you refused, he'd press charges."

"Charges for what?"

"Oh, Charlotte Anne, how could you? We've never had a criminal in the family."

"It's Charli, and I don't know what you're talking about."

Mother buried her face in her hands. "I've never been so ashamed in my life. What have I done to deserve this?"

"What?"

"He says you stole jewelry that's been in his family for generations."

My hands flew to my ears. "I never—"

"See? I've never seen such a guilty reaction in my life."

"These earrings belonged to Amira. She took them off her ears and gave them to me. She said they had belonged to her mother, and she wanted me to have them. I never took a single thing from him, even when Amira said they'd never miss a couple of the gold bracelets, and I might need the money."

"Either you stole the earrings, or your friend planted stolen goods on you before you left. What kind of people have you gotten yourself mixed up with?"

"Mother, I—"

She grabbed my hand and looked at me with tear-filled eyes. "Just give him the baby, sweetheart. I'm begging you. Can't you see that's all he really wants? It's the perfect solution. Raising a child on your own is hard. You won't be getting any child support or alimony to help you. You'll struggle financially the rest of your life. You'll need to buy food and clothes, pay the rent, pay for a sitter when you go to work. You'll both be poor the rest of your life. He, on the other hand, can give the child everything. If you give him his baby, you get your life back. You can come home like nothing happened. No one will know."

I got my hand back from Mother's grasp. "I can't give up my baby. Mother, a child isn't something that goes to the most convenient family. This is my child, and it's my duty to protect and care for it. It's my duty to look out for all aspects of its life, not just the material aspects."

"Hummph. You won't even be raising him. Some stranger will be raising your child while you're at work."

"Charli, may I say something?"

"Sure, Aunt Nellie."

"I understand that you don't think you can live under the restrictions you would have there, but like you just said, it's not about you anymore. You have to do what's best for the child. Take some time and think about what your mother said." I saw Mother relax and reach for her coffee. "He has money to burn. He can give him everything."

"Except a mother."

"Be fair, Charli. You can't give him a father."

"You could ensure that he has both if you go back like he wants." Mother overused her pronouns but I got the idea. "And don't forget the earrings."

"We're all saying he, he, he, but what if it's a girl? She'll grow up thinking life within four walls is natural. Since her father's important, she'll be married off to someone for political reasons, and have to share her husband with a woman he probably married for love. Could I do that to my daughter? Could you?"

"You say Amira was cheerful and happy. It's a question of how you're raised. Think of the advantages. She'd be secure. She'd never have to worry about a thing."

"Except displeasing her husband."

"So what else is new? That doesn't change."

"The stakes are higher," I whispered.

Mother wasn't listening. She swallowed the last of the tart and picked up her purse. "He said he'll call back in three days to talk to you and make the arrangements." The front door banged shut and Mother's car pulled out of the driveway.

"She already agreed for me, didn't she? She already decided for me and told him I'd go—money trumps everything."

"What did you mean the stakes are higher?"

"When I told Amira I wasn't coming back, I asked her not to tell Jamal. Her eyes got really big and she turned very pale. She shuddered and said that if he found out she knew before I left that I wasn't coming back, he'd...he'd..."

"He'd what? Beat her?"

I shook my head. "He'd slit her throat."

"Oh, Charli, she didn't mean it literally. It's like the kid who says his mom will kill him if she finds out he nicked a candy bar or something. It's just an expression."

"You wouldn't say that if you'd seen her face. She meant it literally." I could almost smell the stale grease of the dishrag as I pictured the driver shoving the bracelet back at me; sweat beading on his forehead, his skin a sickly gray. He'd certainly meant every word he said. "I can't let a child of mine grow up like that—boy or girl."

"Oh, my God, Charli." She came over and put her arms around me while tears rolled down my cheeks.

"Aunt Nellie, what can I do? I think he means it about criminal charges. Of course he'd get the baby if the mother were a convicted felon. Maybe my choice isn't between going back or staying and raising my child alone. Maybe my choice is between a prison with marble floors and beautiful gardens or a prison with iron bars and shared toilets. Maybe Mother's right and I don't have a real choice at all." I could feel hysteria building. What could I do?

"You go lie down and I'll bring you some breakfast. I'll call the women and we'll do some real brainstorming."

I lay on the bed staring at the ceiling. Aunt Nellie was right about one thing; I had to confront my problems. I had to be there when he called and tell him myself. I had to be very clear about what I wanted to say before I picked up the phone. In spite of what I knew about him from Amira and the driver, I couldn't believe he was a monster. His love was deep and genuine, I was sure of it. It was the Jesuit thing about "give me a child until he's seven" again.

He was raised to be the Sultan, the absolute ruler of his people. He thought he owned them. In his eyes, disloyalty to him was the same as treason—a capital crime. I felt sick. Would he judge me by the same standard?

I reached for my journal like a baby clutching a favorite blanket.

>> ⏰ ⏰ ⏰ ⏰ <<

AUGUST 27, 1949: - Auntie Stell says bad things come in threes. Mother says that's nonsense, but three bad things happened to me this summer. I've been so miserable I haven't been able to write a word. First Jackie left to live with her mother again. I thought that would be a good thing, but it wasn't. I really miss her. Without her, I don't have anyone to talk to about the really terrible thing—Daddy got transferred to San Diego, but we're going to stay in San Francisco.

He was expecting shore duty, but he's on another ship. It was awful when he told us. Mother said if he's on a ship he won't be home enough to be worth moving, and San Diego's close enough that he can come and see us when he has liberty. Daddy said he can't—he has to accumulate leave. He said with liberty he has to stay close to the ship in case they need him back. He can't travel far away unless he has leave. It's like when I go outside and play. I have to be close enough to answer if Mother calls. Leave is like when I go to a friend's house. I just have to be home on time. Daddy only gets a little leave every month. It's like getting an allowance.

Mother said no one would know if he popped on a bus and came home. What Daddy said started with "God damn it" and I ran to my room.

I thought Daddy living in San Diego with us still living in San Francisco meant they were separated, and separated is half divorced. I was afraid this meant I was finally old enough for Mother to leave Daddy, or maybe almost old enough since they aren't actually getting a divorce yet. I cried a lot, hoping that would convince her I was still too little not to have a Daddy. One night I even wet the bed. I really didn't mean to do that, and I was embarrassed.

Then I tried to convince her it would be better for me if we moved. I stopped reading books and said I didn't like school anymore because I'd read all the books in my library. Every morning I cried about going to school. Then I said, "I bet the schools in San Diego have different books, and I'll like school again." I was sure it would work because I *have* read all the books for my age. It didn't. She brought me books from the public library and the librarian got me books from another school.

I wrote to Daddy every day and told him how much we miss him. I told him that Mother loved him a lot. I don't know what Mother wrote.

He came home one weekend, but he slept most of the time. He said riding five hundred miles on a bus was more miserable than standing on deck all night in the rain.

The final disaster was summer camp. The camp wasn't the disaster. The disaster was that since Daddy was in San Diego, Mother decided to be one of the camp counselors. To top it off, I got glandular fever a few weeks before we left. It was too late for them to find another counselor who could do the arts and crafts stuff, so I went off to camp still feeling yucky. I had to share a cabin with my mother—at summer camp.

The only person in camp who was more pathetic than I was the swimming instructor who swam through poison ivy the week before camp started. She spent the entire time in the infirmary. She couldn't even read because her eyes were swollen shut. I, on the other hand, had to take a nap every afternoon to build up my strength. My activities were limited—no hiking, no games involving strenuous effort. I had to go to bed early so I never got to sit around the campfires or tell scary stories after lights out to my cabin mates. I didn't even have cabin mates—I had Mother.

Whenever my group was doing anything Mother thought was strenuous, I was in the arts and crafts room. Almost the only time I was away from Mother was when I was taking swimming lessons. Too bad I wasn't any good at swimming. It took me both camp sessions to do a splashy dog paddle. It was miserable. The camp didn't even have a library.

But today I can write because my three bad things are getting better. I'm going to Auntie Stell's tomorrow and staying until next Tuesday. Jackie is coming Friday morning and Uncle Walter and Auntie Stell are taking us all to a cabin by a river for the weekend. This makes all the bad things better.

1. I'll be with Jackie again, at least for a few days. I can't wait.
2. I'm going for more days than the river trip because Mother's going to San Diego to spend Daddy's liberty weekend with him. They aren't separated!
3. The miserable camp taught me to swim so I can go in the river and have fun.

It's going to be the best weekend ever!

SEPTEMBER 3, 1949: - The weekend at the river was so much fun! There weren't enough beds for everyone, so Jackie and I shared. We whispered together after Sharon fell asleep. She misses me as much as I miss her.

Mother was tired when she came home from San Diego. She says driving five hundred miles is exhausting. That's why I was surprised when she said we were going to Auntie Stell's today. When we got there we had to park in the next block because there were so many cars. "What's going on?"

"I'm not sure. Your Auntie Stell called this morning and told me to come right over. It looks like all the girls are here. There's Patsy's little car. I hope it isn't anything too awful." Mother sounded worried, and I began to worry, too. What if there was another Unsolved Murder? It made me shudder to think about it, but I walked faster.

I'd given up on learning any more about the Unsolved Murder. Reading more detective stories won't help because all the clues are gone by now. I don't even know exactly where the scene of the crime was. Maybe when I get as old as Nancy Drew and have my own car I can find the scene of the crime, but I don't think there'll be any clues to find. It's not even likely to come up in conversation again.

The minute we stepped in Auntie Stell's house, Sharon pulled me into her room. "Guess what? Rita's getting married! It's the most exciting thing ever." She was so wound up that she kept hopping around the room. Exciting? What's so exciting about it? Weddings are really boring. You sit in church for a long time. The bride looks nice in a big white dress, and the groom looks all stiff in a black suit. Mother never lets me bring a book, so I sit there and look at the funny hats the ladies wear.

Rita set the date for next September because she wants a fall wedding. That's almost a year away, but according to Sharon, it's barely enough time to plan everything.

"How hard can it be? Buy a white dress and make a big cake—done." Sharon found this comment too funny for words. Doubling over with laughter, she crossed and uncrossed her legs and made a beeline for the bathroom. I was left standing in her room feeling more than slightly offended.

"Wow, that's funny." Sharon still had a silly grin on her face. "This is the first time I know something really big that you don't. First you have to find the right church, and then a place for the reception. Rita wants to be married in the cathedral and it's booked months and sometimes more than a year in advance." Sharon blathered on and on about invitations and guest lists and seating arrangements until I was overwhelmed. Seating arrangements? It's not school, they're all adults, why do they have to be told where to sit?

I thought the hard part was finding the right man. Now I find out there's still another year of work before getting the pretty dress. It's depressing.

Sharon finally ran out of things to say about planning a wedding and we headed toward the kitchen for cookies. I love Auntie Stell's cookies, but more important, her kitchen is right off the living room and we could hear what the women were saying, although I'd probably already missed the best part.

"So did you get the job?" That was Mother. Why were they talking about a job?

"No. That's the best part." Rita stopped and I found myself holding my breath, waiting to hear about the best part. "He said he liked me too much to give me the job. He said there was a hotel policy that managers couldn't go out with their employees, and he wanted to take me to dinner that night."

"So you gave up the job for a dinner?"

"Well, I thought, if I said I'd rather have the job, he might feel rejected and give it to someone else anyway. What did I have to lose?"

"And the story has a happy ending." I heard the same thing out of both ears. Sharon had swallowed her cookies and started talking again, and one of the other sisters in the other room said pretty much the same thing.

I might not even get married. There's more work to a wedding than I ever imagined. All that just to get a man who earns money to buy you food and clothes. Oh, yes, and you need someone to be the father. Is it worth it? I'm going to college when I grow up, so maybe I can just earn my own money. It sounds a lot easier and there'd be lots less laundry and cooking and arguing.

➤➤ ⏱ ⏲ 2013 ⏲ ⏰ ◂◂

I laughed. How many women have wondered if having a husband is really worth the hassle? There might be a lot of men out there who had similar opinions about wives. I guess it all depends on love. Any relationship requires work, and love provides the motivation to keep working on it.

Thinking of marriage and relationships made me think of David and the thoughts that had been gnawing at me ever since we shared the pizza. There was definitely something more behind his words. I glanced at my watch. Susan should be here any minute. Maybe I'd learn something while she drove me to the eye doctor. I heard her car and opened the door before she turned off the engine.

"So sorry to disrupt your busy schedule, Susan."

"No problem, Mom. I wouldn't want you driving while your eyes are dilated."

"How was your visit? Are your folks both doing well?"

"They're fine, thanks. It was a great visit. Did David tell you they were giving a big party to open the campaign season?" I didn't have to say another word as she described the party in excruciating detail, from the caterers to each individual guest. I was more impressed by her memory of each person, their pedigree, and their political stance than I was by the event itself. The woman had a mind like the La Brea tar pits.

On the way home, I started the conversation. "So you plan to move to South Carolina to be near your folks?"

"In a way. It's more about starting a new life. I don't suppose you'd understand because you've always worked and had a life, but sometimes a stay-at-home mom feels like she's only there to take care of the people around her and has no life of her own. Now that the kids are out of the house, I figure it's my turn to spread my wings."

"Is David selling the business?" He hadn't mentioned it to me, but apparently there were a lot of things he hadn't mentioned to me.

"He can't make up his mind. Sometimes it's hard to get your son off his butt and moving. Even if he doesn't sell it, he can just come up for a few days a month and make sure everything's running smoothly. A lot of his work is done by phone and internet anyway." She gave a short laugh. "After all, what's the use of being the boss if you have to do the actual work? That's what you hire people for."

116

After Susan dropped me off at home, I lay on my bed fretting. My eyes were still too cloudy to do much else. When the phone rang, I grabbed it, hoping one of my more talkative friends would help me get through the afternoon.

"Hi, Mom. Just thought I'd call and see how the eye exam went."

"Fine. It was a routine checkup. My prescription didn't even change." I started to tell him about Susan's chatter, but changed my mind. It felt like tattling. Why had he called in the middle of a workday? Surely not to talk about my eyes.

"Have you heard from Kate since Aunt Nellie passed?"

Hadn't I told him? "No one's heard from her."

"*What?*" Too late I held the receiver away from my ear.

"I was sure I told you. According to the cousins, she and her current husband sold Jackie's house after the accident and moved away. She'd been 'keeping herself to herself,' to use a British expression, since she remarried. After they sold the house, they just dropped out of sight."

"How could you let that happen?"

"How could *I* let it happen? David, she's a grown woman on the other side of the continent. If she wants to move, she doesn't ask my permission. Anyway, Aunt Nellie's lawyer's looking for her."

"But you could have written more often, let her know that people cared about her." Maybe I could have. "Can you give me the lawyer's name so I can keep on top of it? Something like this can get shelved in a busy law office if no one seems interested."

I started to tell him about my own efforts, but after his scolding it would sound like an excuse. "Sure, hang on." I went to my desk to find Bob's letter. "Here it is." I squinted at the telephone number. "I'll text it to you when the dilation wears off and I can see."

"Don't forget."

I hung up feeling worse than I had before. Now on top of my worry about David and Susan, he had rekindled the guilt of letting Kate disappear from my life. I made myself a cup of tea and called Bev.

"Well, did you have your chat?"

"What chat?"

"About the retirement home."

"No. I forgot."

"How could you forget?"

"I cancelled the visit to help Jean and when it was rescheduled a month out, it lost its priority."

"What could be more important than your independence?"

"David."

"What's wrong?"

"I'm not sure, but it seems the curse can hit men as well as women."

"What are you talking about?"

"Nothing. My eyes are all fuzzy, and I can't think straight. It takes my eyes damned near forever to recover from dilation. Can you come over for a glass of wine?"

"You know you're crazy, don't you?"

"I've had my suspicions for years."

"All right. I'm totally stressed over getting ready for the family reunion, but since we won't be meeting Wednesday, I'll be fine.

"What about Wednesday?

"I was just talking to Jean. She decided she can't take care of her husband by herself anymore. She's moving to be near her son. Between that and my family reunion, I guess our little group is up a creek."

That was a blow. Maybe Auntie Stell was right. Bad things do come in threes. First Kate, then David and Susan, now this. My two best friends going different ways.

The wine with Bev cheered me considerably. I took the evening off and watched some mindless television shows. The next morning I threw myself into my manuscript. The words flowed through my fingertips to the keyboard, and I was feeling smug by lunchtime. A quick sandwich and a walk would refocus my energies for the afternoon calls to California.

I decided to walk down the road to David's. It's only half a mile of unused country road—just long enough for a quick break. I hadn't expected to stop, but when I saw both cars in the drive, I changed my mind. This might be the perfect opportunity to have that chinwag about the home. The longer I put it off, the more I was giving my implicit consent to the plan. My quick decision left me no time to get cold feet.

I raised my hand to knock on the door. My arm froze in midair. Susan wasn't exactly yelling, but she sure wasn't whispering. I knew I should turn around and walk away, but my feet were glued in place.

"For God's sake, David, you're a grown man; act like one. You have to cut the umbilical cord sometime." I felt as though someone had kicked me in the stomach. I couldn't breathe. My knees felt weak, and I had to grab the doorjamb to stay upright. "I've always admired the fact that you were attentive to your mother. I thought it set a fine example for the children, but good God, you have to draw the line. Remember your *wife* is your next of kin. It's time to move on." My eyes blurred as I turned for home. I wanted to run, but my breath was already ragged.

I'd fooled myself into thinking I was being useful, staying with the children for their occasional vacations or long weekends alone, helping with the kid taxi duty when needed, or staying with a sick child when Susan had something else to do. Now I was the wedge driving my son from his wife.

No. My knees and brain began to work again. Susan was the one who asked me to move here. Susan had practically begged me to come and live next to them. It sure wasn't my idea to live out in the middle of nowhere, although I *had* grown to love it. I gave up a perfectly happy life on my own to come here. It was always Susan's voice I heard. "I'm running late. Can you meet the school bus?" or "Can the kids have dinner and a DVD with you tonight? David's working late and one of my friends is having a wine party." or "Can you sit in our house today and wait for a repairman? I have a meeting." The mental pictures went on and on like flipping pages of a book. It was always Susan wanting something.

Anger gave me strength. I turned around. I wasn't going to let her use me for years and then throw me out with the rubbish. I was going to march right in and give her a piece of my mind.

Two steps later I realized that would be the wrong thing to do. I'd be putting David in the untenable position of having to choose between his mother and his wife. No, I had to calm down and deal with this like a responsible mother. I had to think of David first. I had to step away and let them do whatever they had to do for their marriage.

If David didn't want to move because of me, I had to

let him go. If I resisted the retirement home, it would keep him here and quite possibly split his marriage like an overripe tomato.

➤➤ EIGHT ◀◀

Aunt Nellie took Mother to the kitchen so I'd have some privacy during my talk with Jamal. The seconds ticked by with all the speed of water running uphill. The three days waiting for Jamal's call had been an eternity of anxiety and indecision. No matter what happened, I knew the ending would be anything but happy. I'd been so jumpy at work that Janice asked me more than once if anything was wrong. If I were the type to gnaw my fingernails, I'd be up to the elbows by now.

The telephone rang, jolting my heart into overdrive. My hands shook as I reached for the receiver. "Hello?"

"Charli, my love, it's so good to hear your voice. I miss you more than you can imagine. How is the love of my life?" Even over the static and crackle of the international call, I heard the emotion in his voice and the husky overtones I associated with his passion. My eyes filled with tears and a lump rose to my throat, blocking any words I might have said. "Is your mother trying to keep you there?" I shook my head. "She's been telling me you want to stay. I almost had to threaten her to get you to the phone."

"Jamal..." I had to tell him I wasn't going back.

"I understand. She's probably sitting right next to you, listening to every word. You don't have to say anything. I miss you so much. I'll have a car come for you Thursday about one-thirty. I can't wait to see you again."

I closed my eyes. My heart was thudding in my chest. His words overwhelmed me with memories of his love. It would be so easy. All I had to do was get in the car when it came for me. I'd be back in his arms again. I'd be pampered and granted my slightest wish. I'd never have to worry about anything. I didn't have to say a word; it would just happen. It took all my strength to get out the word. "No." I needed more time. I grabbed the first thing I could pull out of the fog in my head. "I have a doctor's appointment Thursday."

"Doctor's appointment? What's wrong? Is something wrong with our baby? Charli, you've got to come home. I'll get the best obstetrician in the country and move him into the guesthouse so he'll be within calling distance until you deliver. I'll get a nurse to stay in the room with you. You'll have the best medical care in the world. I can arrange for your own doctor to travel with you, if it makes you more comfortable. I'll have him stay as long as you like."

Absolute power, wielded with a casual wave of the hand, a dictated letter, or a telephone call. The thought loosened my tongue. "It's just a checkup to make sure nothing's wrong."

"How could I be so thoughtless? Of course you don't want to rush back. You've just had a scare about your mother's health. I'm so sorry." I could hear his sincerity. "You're such an angel to worry about your mother and be willing to sacrifice your own comfort. I have a great idea! She can come with you. You'll never have to worry about her being taken care of in her old age, and she'll be company for you. Charli, you have to learn to ask me for what you want. I'll never deny you anything." Again his voice dipped into the lower register that loosed butterflies in my insides. "I'll call Friday and you can tell me how the doctor's appointment went. That'll give your mother time to make arrangements."

"Jamal, I—"

"Shhhh. You don't have to say it in front of your mother. I love you, too. Talk to you Friday." Click.

I sat frozen and stunned with the receiver in my hand.

"Well? You didn't say much." Mother was standing in the kitchen doorway. Aunt Nellie walked up behind Mother and shrugged—she'd tried.

"No, we didn't say much. He's going to call again on Friday."

"Friday?"

"Yes, I have a doctor's appointment on Thursday, and he wants me to tell him about it." I picked up my purse. "Ready, Aunt Nellie?"

Aunt Nellie began to talk almost before the car doors were closed. "Why didn't you tell him?"

That released a flood of tears. We drove several blocks before I could speak. "He really loves me. I heard it in his voice, and I turned to jelly." It took the rest of the trip home to tell her about the short conversation between my tears.

"Are you going to tell your mother?" I shook my head. "Why not?"

"There are two ways that might turn out. She might be indignant and tell me that if I thought she was going to spend the rest of her life among heathens, I have another think coming." Aunt Nellie smiled and nodded. "The other possibility is that she'd like the idea of being Queen Mother and she'd do it. Think of it. She'd live with me forever in a world where I was the only person she could talk to."

"No. She'd learn the language, if only to complain." I

giggled in spite of my tears. "Do you have a doctor's appointment?"

"No, but I'm going to make some calls as soon as I get home. I'll have to have something to say on Friday or he'll be on the next plane." I saw Nellie's eyebrow lift.

Aunt Nellie drove me to my appointment on Thursday. She waited in a nearby coffee shop until I finished.

"That was more humiliating and embarrassing than I imagined it would be," I said as I sat on the cute but uncomfortable chair opposite her.

"So what did he say?"

"Nothing I didn't know. I'm pregnant. Everything looks normal. I have to take vitamins. He gave me a booklet written for five-year-olds about how the fetus grows."

"I wonder how many pregnant five-year-olds he gets."

"You know what I mean, small words and big pictures."

"Glad you went?"

"I'm glad I don't have to lie to Jamal because I'm a miserable liar. I'm pleased the doctor didn't find any problems, although how he could tell is a mystery to me, but I'm darned near broke. Do you know how expensive that visit was?"

"I think I do. What're you going to do next?"

"If you don't mind driving me back to work, I'd appreciate it. Maybe we can stop at a drugstore and get the right vitamins. The regular ones I've been taking are missing things the baby needs."

"You know what I mean. You can't keep waffling between letting your child grow up in the lap of luxury and raising him alone. If you stay, it won't be easy. If it's a girl, she won't have the latest fad in clothes, for example. Hell, you'll be lucky to feed, clothe, and keep a roof over your heads. This is an important decision."

"I know, and once I commit, I can't go back and change my mind." I'd said the same things to myself night after night, day after day. I'd been thinking along the same path until I thought there might be an actual rut worn into my brain, or maybe a pool of butter like the tigers who chased each other around the tree so fast they'd blurred and melted. "Aunt Nellie, how do you always know whether or not to say yes when a man asks you to marry him?"

"I don't. Sometimes it takes a long time to make up my mind, other times I do what I have to do."

"You've never had to get married."

"I've never been pregnant when I got married, if that's what you mean, but an unborn child is not the only reason one might have to get married." I was curious but didn't want to ask. "Do you remember Willis?"

"Sure. Always laughing, freckles, cars, the mink, and..." I hesitated, but decided I could say it, "tarts."

That made her laugh. "You remember very well. But I barely got out of that marriage in time." At the next light, she looked at me and held my eyes long enough to make me uncomfortable. "No one else knows this." The look was a question. I nodded. She looked back at the road as the light turned green. "He'd transferred title of the house to me, but before we could get a final ruling on the alimony and child support, his business collapsed. It seems the tart wasn't his only sub rosa interest. Maybe I should have suspected that, too, but I didn't."

"That's when Jackie came to live with us. You know, I was never lonely before Jackie lived with us, but when you married Al and she went back to live with you... I really missed her. I already thought of her as my real sister." I hadn't known Willis wasn't paying her, but that must have added a layer of desperation. Funny. I'd just figured out for myself that she'd probably married Al to keep Jackie.

"Jackie felt the same way about you, but it also made her feel disloyal to me. It took a long time for her to get over it."

"The experience must have been dreadful for you, but it made two only children into siblings. We still love each other like sisters."

"I'm glad something good came of it, but that's not the point of the story."

"So you're telling me a mother sacrifices her own comfort for the sake of the child, and maybe I should go back to Jamal so my child won't have to live in less than comfortable circumstances."

"No, I don't want to tell you what to do. I only want you to think of it from as many different angles as possible."

Sometime in the early hours of Friday morning I made a decision. Aunt Nellie was right. I had to be realistic. No matter how much education I had, there was no way I could provide all the things I wanted for my child. Even if I could afford decent care, it would still be someone else taking care of my baby. I'd be working when he took his first steps. I'd be working when he needed someone to kiss a skinned knee and make it better. I'd be depriving my child of more than material things.

And what about Mother? We may never be best friends, but at some point she would become my responsibility. Aunt Nellie was right there, too. Mother would love to have servants. She would probably complain about the food, but I'm sure she'd love the idea of never having to cook another meal. To give her credit, she always tried to do what was best for me. Did I have the right to refuse a better life on her behalf?

It would be incredibly selfish to refuse wealth and comfort for three people just because I'd be bored. I could probably find a million ways to occupy myself if I really tried. Jamal would be delighted to get me books to read. I could take correspondence courses. I just had to stop being so insular in my thinking. It would be a different life, but I'd always known that.

Once I'd made the decision, I had trouble understanding why I'd felt so strongly that I couldn't live as Jamal's wife. It must have been the early pregnancy. Everyone knows pregnant women have wacky hormones. They must be settling down now, and I can think clearly and make a rational decision.

Of course the driver had to exaggerate so I'd understand the seriousness of him being caught alone with me. I'm sure it would have cost him his job. And Amira was giving me her version of the my-husband-will-kill-me-if-he-finds-out that must be the same all over the world.

That night I felt at peace for the first time in ages. I picked up the journal, and decided that a Christmas entry must be an omen that I was going to be happy. After all, Christmas is always a happy time.

➤➤ ⊕ ⊕ ⊕ ⊕ ◄◄

DECEMBER 26, 1949: - Daddy got leave to come home for

two whole weeks. I hope he was kidding when he told Mother he had to sell his soul to get it. A couple of days before Christmas, he took me to a big toy store and said his ship was buying toys for an orphanage. He asked me to help by picking out things the children might like. I thought that was surprisingly nice of his shipmates. I picked out some things I thought the orphans might like. Yesterday I unwrapped my presents and recognized them immediately. If I'd known they were going to be for me, I wouldn't have picked two different young artist sets. Both sets are really nice, but now I have enough paints and crayons to color a house — a real one. Daddy always finds nice presents. I still remember the best Christmas present ever — my dollhouse.

I got my dollhouse long before I started keeping the journal, and it's still my all-time favorite present. It wasn't as pretty as the dollhouse that Willis bought Jackie, but it's very special because Daddy made it himself. When I heard the story of him painting the roof on Christmas Eve, it made the dollhouse even more special.

He went up to the attic where he had hidden the project. It was all finished except for the paint on the roof. We were stationed in Rhode Island at the time, and it was an especially cold Christmas. He said his hands were shaking from the cold, so he got a bottle of brandy to keep him warm. According to him, he had to drink quite a bit to get warm, and by then the dollhouse decided not to be painted. It began to go around in circles. Every time it came by, he'd give it a swipe with the paintbrush. Mother said half the attic was black and he was almost out of paint before the dollhouse roof was finished. I can still close my eyes and picture Daddy standing in the middle of the attic, holding out his paintbrush, hoping to hit the dollhouse as it flew by in its orbit around the room.

JANUARY 27, 1949: - It's been really quiet since Daddy's leave ended. The women still have coffee, but I'm always in school. The only good thing about Daddy's not being home much is that Mother talks to me a lot more at supper. Since there isn't usually much to say about school, she tells me about the coffee talks. Of course, she leaves out all the stuff I really want to hear, and I just get the boring part, but I listen anyway. Sometimes I get good parts.

I learned that Rita's fiancé is very handsome and his father owns part of the big hotel where Rita had applied for the job. He owns parts of a lot of other hotels in other cities, too. I wonder which part of the hotel Richard's father owns. If he owns the kitchen, he could eat there any time he wants to without paying. But what if the person who owns the front door got mad at him and didn't let him in? I can't imagine how it would work having a lot of people own the same thing. It's hard enough for two people to cooperate enough to get through a three-legged race without falling.

Mother said that Rita caught the brass ring and was marrying Prince Charming—handsome *and* rich. I'm not sure why she said it was a brass ring, because all the women agreed it's the biggest diamond they'd ever seen.

It took me a few minutes, but when I remembered the last time the women had talked about getting the brass ring, it wasn't a good thing. It was what the man was not supposed to get. I knew they were talking about something other than real brass rings. I woke up in the night and realized they were actually talking about good luck. I don't know why it took me so long.

130

A couple of weeks ago, Auntie Stell announced she was inviting all the women to Wedding Wednesdays. Each Wednesday everybody goes to Auntie Stell's for coffee. Actually, Mother, Grandmother, and the married cousins go for coffee. Patsy and the single cousins usually have to work, so they don't come. I was disappointed they picked Wednesdays because I'm in school, but since Daddy's in San Diego, Mother tells me all about it at supper. She said I wasn't missing much except the cookies, because they do the same thing every Wednesday.

Rita brings out *The Guide to the Perfect Wedding* and goes through each section, telling everyone what she did that week and what she still needs to do. While she talks, the others start working. It turns out the real reason for Wedding Wednesdays is that Auntie Stell needs people to help sew the wedding gown. Each woman gets a bunch of seed pearls to sew. The women on one couch sew their pearls on the dress, and the women on the other couch sew their pearls on the lace of the veil. After they sew on the pearls, the dress gets put away and everyone has coffee and some of Auntie Stell's yummy cookies. Mother says that Rita drew an elaborate pattern that looks like flowers and butterflies, and it's all going to be drawn with pearls. It sounds like a fairy tale come to life, and I'm waiting for summer so I can go to the Wednesdays, too.

FEBRUARY 22, 1950: - Today was Ash Wednesday and Mother said I looked peaked. I looked in the mirror to see what peaked meant, but I didn't see anything different. Looking peaked must not be as sick as feeling hot because she took me to church. I was surprised when we drove to a church near Auntie Stell's house. Auntie Stell and Sharon were there! Sharon goes to public school so her class doesn't go to mass.

I was excited that Wedding Wednesday wasn't cancelled for Ash Wednesday. I should have known better. Very often when I wait and wait for something to happen, it isn't as wonderful as I thought it was going to be. Wedding Wednesdays are like that. Mother had been right when she said the only part I was really missing was the cookies, although the book itself was something worth seeing.

The Guide to the Perfect Wedding is a huge book—larger than our dictionary. When Sharon asked if we could look at it, Rita set the book in our laps as gently as if it had been a baby.

We opened the book and looked at the names of the sections. There were so many sections it made my head spin to think of all that went into a wedding. Since Rita was talking about the reception, we decided to look at that section as we listened to the conversation. The book gave suggestions about arranging the tables, how to set the tables, rules about seating, and step-by-step instructions. I never knew there could be so many rules. At the end of the section, there was a checklist and blank spaces for the bride to make notes about each step. There were cutout silhouettes of chairs and different shaped tables drawn to scale just like the maps in our geography books. We made scale maps of our classroom last year and I came home and made a scale map of my room.

The bride was supposed to cut out paper tables and chairs. Then she was supposed to write all the names of the wedding guests on the paper chairs and place them around the paper tables. She could rearrange the names until she had each table just the way she wanted it. It sounded like a game with a lot of complicated rules.

Rita was saying that some people couldn't sit at the same table. For example, her fiancé's Aunt Matilda wouldn't sit with his cousin Harold because he'd broken one of her antique Chinese vases when he was a little boy, and she'd never forgiven him. The business clients had to be dealt with separately. Some were rivals and could not sit together, and some were friends and would enjoy sitting together. It got too complicated and boring, so Sharon and I flipped to another section.

The section on wedding cakes was beautiful, but it made Sharon hungry again. She went to the kitchen and got us more cookies. We ate the cookies and then turned to the section on wedding gowns. Sharon pointed out the gown that Rita had used to design her dress, and when she took her hand away, there was a big spot of chocolate on the picture of the perfect dress for the perfect wedding. She tried to wipe it off, but it just smeared and turned into an even bigger spot of chocolate.

"What do we do?" Sharon whispered. I saw her eyes fill with tears. "Mama will kill me, and Rita will never speak to me again." Her tears spilled over and I panicked as her voice got louder. "She might not even let me be in the wedding."

I had to think of something before Sharon burst into a full-throated wail. Then I remembered what Mother did when I got chocolate on my white blouse. "We could get some bleach from the laundry room and bleach the spot white."

"Okay. How do we do that?"

"Get some cotton and put bleach on it." Sharon hugged

me and ran off to get the bleach-soaked cotton. I concentrated on keeping the book tilted toward me so no one would see the page.

When Sharon got back, she plopped down next to me. "I got it." She raised her hand and showed me a soggy blob of cotton. Suddenly everything was moving in slow motion.

"Watch out!" I intended the warning to come out as a whisper, but it didn't. I jumped to get my hand under hers and form a second line of defense to catch the bleach that was dripping between her fingers. The precious book tumbled off my lap, landing awkwardly in a heap of bent pages. Somewhere in the background I heard Rita scream. Sharon was so startled by Rita's scream and my lunge toward her that she screeched and threw up her hands.

The cotton ball rose slowly in the air, sparkling drops of bleach flying off in a fascinating pattern that will probably remain in my memory forever. My mind was racing as I tried to judge the path of the cotton and each of the drops. Carpet, dress, book—all were in danger. In a flash of insight, I realized the carpet was the most important. I was still moving toward Sharon, and I pushed off as hard as I could and tried to twist myself to get under the cotton ball.

Something went wrong with my calculations. I hadn't counted on Sharon trying to catch the cotton ball too. Our heads collided with a crack and an explosion of pain.

The next thing I knew, my throbbing head was battered by Sharon's loud wailing, Rita's shrill laments over the condition of her book, and a torrent of excited Spanish between my mother and Auntie Stell. Mother was saying something about her daughter bleeding to death, and

Auntie Stell was upset about something else. Mother lapsed into English long enough for me to hear, "Stop worrying about your damned carpet and get me some ice and a wet towel." I closed my eyes and tried not to move so as not to call any more attention to myself, although I now think that was a big mistake. Not only is it impossible to avoid attention when blood is pouring out of your nose, but one of the cousins told Mother to give me a good slap on the face to wake me up. I opened my eyes just in time to see the hand on its downward path to my face. I didn't have to pretend the yelp and tears that followed. "See, Aunt Charlotte? I told you it would work." Mother was so upset she couldn't get a word out in either language. Still sputtering, she grabbed the wet towel from an open-mouthed Auntie Stell and half led, half carried me out the front door. The wet towel made it difficult to breathe and impossible to talk.

The trip home was strangely silent. I wasn't sure if Mother was mad at me or at Auntie Stell or at Sharon, or all three of us. I wanted to explain, but it didn't feel like the right time. I went over the happenings of the day in my mind, trying to get my story organized for the time when it was right to tell Mother what happened. It was Sharon's fault, of course. I mean she was the one who got chocolate on the book in the first place, and she was the one who brought the cotton ball dripping with bleach, and she was the one who threw it into the air. It was definitely Sharon's fault.

I thought about Auntie Stell's carpet, Rita's book, and the bruise I glimpsed around Sharon's eye before Mother clapped the wet towel over my face. I'll bet Sharon has told the story in a way to make it sound like my fault. No matter whose fault it was, they are all sure to be mad at me because it was my blood all over everything.

What if they never forgive me? Will we have to sit at different tables at family weddings from now on? Will Mother and Auntie Stell not sit together because of Sharon and me? That would be very sad because they have loved each other their whole lives. I think if I had a sister, I'd be able to forgive her no matter what she did. When Jackie lived with us, she was annoying sometimes, but I always forgave her.

Is it possible to stay mad at someone forever? Sometimes I tell one of my friends that I'll never talk to her again, but it doesn't last very long. Never is a long time. Forever is a long time, too. I wonder why Never and Forever are the same sometimes.

➤➤ NINE ◄◄

JUNE 18, 1950: - I'm glad it's summer. Even though I love school, I miss being around when the women meet. I'm not sure I'll ever be invited to Wedding Wednesdays again, but it's going to be a great summer.

I couldn't believe my good luck when Mother told me that even though Daddy's in San Diego, she's not going to camp with me. She's too busy helping Auntie Stell to be a counselor. They still have to sew thousands of little pearls onto Rita's dress and her veil. I'm not exaggerating—thousands. The dress has a train so long it should have its own caboose, and the veil has to be the same length. It's a good thing she's getting married in the cathedral because the dress wouldn't fit in a small church. I was almost afraid to ask why it was taking so long for fear Mother would change her mind and go to camp after all, but I finally asked because it didn't make sense. "Why do you only sew for an hour or so every week? You could sew for three or four hours, and the dress would be done in no time."

"Because the pearls are very expensive and Uncle Walter can't buy them all at once. Each Wednesday we sew on all the ones we have."

"So why doesn't Richard's father buy them? You said he was rich."

"He's already doing more than he ought to be doing for

the wedding. The bride's family's supposed to pay for it."

"Then why doesn't Rita plan a wedding Uncle Walter can afford?"

"Why can't you stop asking questions and make a last check to make sure you have everything you need to take to camp?"

I knew it wasn't a question, so I did as I was told. Camp isn't for two more weeks, but there is a lot to do. I have to sew on my own nametags this year. We're also packing for a vacation!

We're going to San Diego the week before I go to camp. I'm so excited! We're going to stay in a hotel for a whole week, and eat in restaurants. Daddy says his ship is going to be in port for a while having maintenance. He gets weekends off, and he wangled a three-day liberty so he'll be with us almost the whole time.

The best part is we get to take Jackie with us so I'll have someone to play with when we go to the beach, and it's going to be so much fun! Mother promised to make us new matching dresses to wear in San Diego.

➢➢ ⊕ ⊕ 2013 ⊕ ⊕ ◄◄

The telephone rang, and I looked at the clock. It was earlier than I'd thought. "Hello?"

"Mom, do you have any of those energy-saving light bulbs? Our outside light is burned out, and I want to replace it while I think of it."

"Yes, but I'm—"

"Great. I'll be right there."

"—in my pajamas," I said to a dead telephone. On second thought, it was better not to let him know I was in bed this early. I slipped on my sweats and rooted through the cupboard for light bulbs. By the time I got downstairs, his headlights were in sight. "I don't suppose you have time for a cuppa?"

"I thought you'd never ask." He grabbed an apple out of the fruit basket and wandered toward the couch. "What have you been up to?"

"Nothing much. I spent another couple of hours on the phone today. What a zoo my family is."

"Did you locate Kate? I mean, that *is* what you were trying to do, isn't it?"

"It's what I'm trying to do, but I didn't get very far. There are a couple of generations of cousins that I never met. Half of them don't talk to the other half, but they all seem to enjoy spreading gossip."

"What did you learn?"

"Leaving out the more sordid details, I *finally* learned the name of Kate's husband. One cousin thinks they moved to Arizona, but it could be New Mexico or Texas. She only remembered thinking there'd be a lot of Mexican workers. It's all very vague. Someone else thought she remembered that they moved because he got a job with a company that was building a hospital."

"Do you think you can find her?"

"I don't know, but I'm going to try. I think the hospital bit narrows it to cities, and I know about when they moved. Tomorrow morning I'll look for hospitals being built at that time and see where I go from there."

"It's more progress than the lawyer's making. Let me know how it goes. I might be able to spare one of the girls in my office to make calls, if you think it'll help."

"I'll manage." The teakettle was calling. "How's Susan?"

"Fine, but I think she's determined to get to the end of the internet tonight." It was an old ad we'd adopted as a family joke. Usually I was the one being accused. I brought two steaming mugs of tea. "Can I ask you a personal question?"

"No guaranteed answer, but ask away."

"Are you happy here?"

Where had that come from? "Of course I am. I might be happier if my broadband were a little broader, but I don't have any complaints worth mentioning." He was staring into his tea. He was being serious. I changed my tone to match. "I've always considered myself to be in at least the top five percent when it comes to happiness. I've lived a long and reasonably successful life; I am well fed and have good medical care. I have a small but loving family. Yes. I'm happy."

"I mean here, in this house."

"Oh. Yes, I like the house. It's comfortable for me. I'm happy with my stuff and clutter."

"Then why are you so hot on moving to a retirement home?"

"What?" Hot tea sloshed over the side of my mug, causing my hand to jerk and spill more tea. By the time I cleaned up the mess, I had what I hoped was a neutral answer. "I'm not looking forward to moving. Given my druthers, I'd stay in the house, but I don't want to be a roadblock to you moving on with your life. Susan said you wanted to make sure I was taken care of before you moved. I can't stay here if it means you're anchored here as well.

Of course I'll move if it gives you peace of mind and lets you get on with your own life."

"That malicious, treacherous, mendacious, scheming bitch."

I couldn't believe my ears. "David, in all the years you've been married I've never heard you say anything bad about Susan, and you start off on the top rung? I don't know what's going on between you two, but I'll be in that retirement home tomorrow if it solves the problem."

"You've never heard me say anything about our marital disagreements because I never like to worry you about things you can't control, not to mention that I firmly believe troubles with a marriage should be solved within the marriage."

"And are none of my business."

"Pretty much. The truth is, the trouble's been there for a long time, but this just broke the dam or the camel's back, or whatever it is that breaks. Anyway, Susan, my once beloved wife, told me that you were falling apart, crushed under the load of managing the property and keeping up the house on your own. She said you wanted a place where you didn't have to worry about anything, a place where you'd always have company and feel safe." He set his empty tea mug down a little harder than necessary. "If you can find a beer, I'll explain. I have to buy you a bottle of decent scotch."

I blinked away my shock and got up to find a cold beer for him and a large glass of wine for me. "David, this is wrong with a capital R. You don't leave a wife of more than twenty years just because she wants you without your mother. No matter how hard I try, there's no escaping the fact that I'm her mother-in-law. It's no coincidence that mothers-in-law have a bad rep everywhere."

"Don't mean to burst your bubble, Mom, but this has nothing to do with you — except in a very peripheral way." He grinned, trying to calm me down, but it wasn't working. "You remember all the parties she used to give?"

"Of course."

"They had nothing to do with the PTA, or the sports teams, or school, or anything else like that."

"What was it?"

"It was to get me in front of as many people as she could find."

"You? Why?"

"Because she wanted me to get into local politics."

I felt cold. "I put that into her head. I mean, I said something like that once."

"Yeah, Mom. I remember, too, because I was so surprised you hit the nail so squarely. Don't worry; it was there long before you said anything. I think she was born with it. It's been a bone of contention between us for years. It never goes away. Always the guilt trip, how I never do anything she wants me to do."

"Getting into politics isn't just something she wants you to do like mowing the grass on Sunday. It's a change in your way of life. Politicians, even local politicians have no private lives."

"That's what I said. She said she'd spent years preparing the groundwork."

"Did she ever discuss this with you before she started those preparations?"

"She thinks she did. She'd occasionally read something out loud from the local paper and make a remark like 'you could do a better job than that guy,' and I'd nod because I usually thought they were idiots and *anyone* could do a better job. I didn't mean I wanted to do it, but she heard what she wanted to hear. When she finally understood that I meant it when I said I wasn't interested, she didn't speak to me for weeks. Then she said she'd do it herself."

"It still doesn't make sense. If she prepared the so-called groundwork here, why move?"

David shrugged. "She said if she started in her home town, she'd begin on the third or fourth rung of the ladder. Her grandfather and her father were both in politics. Apparently the whole family is entrenched in party machinery, and her father still wields a lot of clout." That fit with what she'd said about her recent trip. "We've been going round and round about it for over a year, but we finally reached a compromise, or I *thought* we did."

"But?"

"Now I find out that she's not playing fair." He got up and walked to the kitchen. "Guess that means she's a politician already." I was afraid he was going to leave me with a cliffhanger. He came back with another beer and the wine bottle. "My business is doing well, and I have some good people working for me that I can trust to run things when I'm out of the office, but I'm not ready to trust them to run it entirely—and I'm not ready to be a house husband smiling at all her political rallies. The compromise was that I'd spend two weeks a month with her, two weeks of her choosing so she could schedule events where she thought my presence would be useful. The rest of the month I'd be up here working."

"That doesn't sound too comfortable."

143

"That's where you come in. I said I wasn't willing to spend half my life in hotels, but I'd ask if you were willing to have a house guest when I was in town."

I opened my mouth to say something like, "of course," but it came out, "Ohh," as I connected the dots to the retirement home.

"She didn't like the idea because she said it would show lack of a commitment on my part. She said people would think I didn't support her endeavors as wholeheartedly as I should. We argued a lot about that, too, before she agreed."

"I wish I could get out of the middle of your problem."

"You aren't in the middle; you were supposed to be my lifeline to sanity. How else could I get through it?" He looked around at nothing in particular. "God, I wish I'd brought some scotch."

"Well, since I didn't want to move in the first place, and I'd love to have you around sometimes, doesn't that solve your problem?" I hoped so, because it would sure solve mine.

"It would've, but not now. This was the last straw. She poisoned the well. She lied to me about something big. This isn't just about how much she paid for her shoes, or who she's really with when she has those endless meetings. *This* is a life altering lie — and she almost got away with it."

I didn't miss the little red light about the meetings, but I shoved it into the not-my-business drawer. I had trouble swallowing the retirement home story. "How could she think she'd get away with it? She had to know we'd find out, and probably sooner rather than later."

"I guess it was my fault. I was gullible. I never expected her to lie about something so big or so easily refuted. She had me convinced that you were so anxious to get moved, that you were close to a breakdown. Thinking about it now, I don't know how I believed it, but I did. If we'd gone last Thursday and you'd said positive things, I was prepared to put down the money for your unit. She already had a moving company ready to pack your stuff so you wouldn't have to lift a finger. She was so 'concerned' about your feelings that she had it all planned, and she'd already rented a storage unit for all your precious relics from around the world so you could visit them, or cull them at your leisure."

"But it had to come to light eventually. What then?"

"By then it would be a fait accompli. We'd be angry and outraged, but what could we do? The house would have been sold and there'd be no going back."

"Sounds like she thought of everything."

"Except that you put a monkey wrench in the visit and it gave me time to think. Her story just didn't hold water. The very idea that you wanted a place where you'd always have people around you was absurd. You value your privacy too much for that. I couldn't picture you wanting to live in a home. Maybe some day, but not yet."

"Thank God."

"By the way, tonight she's searching the internet for suitable houses. She's going for another visit next week to look with a real estate agent. She plans to put our house on the market as soon as she locates the perfect place."

I heard the bitterness in his voice and my eyes stung with tears. "I thought it was only the women." I blinked and a tear escaped.

"What was only the women? What're you talking about?" He handed me my wine glass.

I took a gulp of wine. Too late to pretend I hadn't said anything. "You know that after your father died I lived with my grandmother until you were big enough for me to start teaching." He nodded. "Grandmother had been widowed four times and we talked a lot as I tried to get over things. I moaned that the women in our family had extraordinarily bad luck with marriages. She confided that we were cursed."

David couldn't suppress a laugh. "You aren't serious."

"She said that she'd once threatened her stepmother, and the stepmother cursed her marriages and those of all her progeny."

"Come on, Mom. You can't believe in an actual curse."

"No, of course not. But Grandmother believed it, and not one of the women in the family had what I'd call a happy marriage until she'd gone through several unhappy ones. I sometimes thought it was a genetic tendency to pick the wrong mate, but that didn't explain the deaths. I've never been able to come up with a good explanation. It never entered my mind that it would touch you because you're a man."

"Look around you. Divorce is the new norm. Women didn't have any option in the old days, no matter how bad the marriage. Things have changed. Maybe our family was just ahead of the curve on this."

"Maybe so." I managed to laugh with him. "I guess it was just the shock of hearing that what I thought was your happy marriage wasn't."

He gave me a hug and talked over the top of my head. "Maybe Susan wasn't the right woman, but we had a pretty good run of it, and raised some great kids. Maybe the right woman was someone I couldn't have."

It was only after I locked the door behind him that I saw the light bulbs still sitting on the table. I was far too upset to sleep, so I sought refuge in my computer. I started searching for new hospital construction. To my surprise, there were companies that specialized in building hospitals. That was as good a place as any to start looking for Kate. What next? I wrote a little script about trying to find Kate for purposes of an inheritance. When I read it over, even I thought it smelled of scam. If I were an H.R. person, I wouldn't release information like that.

I sent an email to Aldeman's office asking if I could speak in Bob's name. I was surprised when an answer came almost immediately. His whole office was working late on a big case, but he'd have someone draft a letter and he'd scan and email it within the hour. He suggested that I ask for a fax number and fax his letter. He also said he'd take care of any legal documents they requested if they had any record of Kate's husband. I compiled a list with as much information as I could find about each company's recent projects and looked for contact information. By the time I went to bed I had a respectable list of telephone numbers; some direct to the personnel department.

Satisfied that I was making progress, I pulled out the journal.

➤➤ 🕐 🕑 🕒 🕓 ◀◀

AUGUST 18, 1950: - Summer camp was a lot better this year than it was last year. It would have been even better if Mother hadn't sent a letter telling them not to let me do anything too strenuous. I discovered a new section of the library with biographies, and I've been reading a lot of those. Between biographies I read all the Black Beauty books and found the Red Stallion books. Having a horse must be the most wonderful thing in the world.

So that was my summer in a nutshell — nothing new, nothing to write about, until today.

I was just settling down to read the next Red Stallion book when Mother told me to get ready to go to Auntie Stell's. I'd forgotten it was Wednesday. Summer vacation does that sometimes. I was happy to go. Spending time with Sharon isn't a bad way to pass a summer day, and the cookies are always delicious. The best part of the trip is driving over the bridge. I don't know why it scares Auntie Stell so much.

As soon as we walked in the door, Auntie Stell turned me toward Sharon's room. "Go play with Sharon. I'll bring you some cookies later." Then her fingers tightened on my shoulder. "Oh, no. One of Sharon's friends took her on a picnic today." She paused and I thought she was going to send me to Sharon's room anyway, so I held up my book and grabbed Mother's arm. "All right, come on in — just stay out of trouble."

The living room was a lot noisier than usual. The older cousins, Patsy and Mary Lou, were sitting with their heads together chattering and laughing the kind of laugh I was beginning to associate with jokes I didn't always get. It was a little higher and louder than regular laughter. I was surprised to see Jean there as well. Jean is Auntie Stell's oldest daughter and she almost never comes to the coffee time because her children don't go to school yet.

The coffee table had been moved in front of the picture window to leave a big space in the middle of the room. That part of the floor was covered with clean white sheets and The Dress was in a heap on the sheets with Grandmother holding the top close to her face. She was doing something to the inside.

"*No se puede.*" Grandmother must have been upset because she was speaking Spanish and there were people there (other than me) who didn't understand. Something was up. I took one of the small pillows from the couch and my book over to a corner and willed myself to be invisible. A book is the best invisibility cloak available to non-magic people.

"*Ay Dios mío.*" Auntie Stell looked as though she was about to cry. Mother was practically sweating question marks. "Two weeks until the wedding, and Rita can't fit into it." The cousins burst into gales of laughter, which stopped abruptly when both Grandmother and Auntie Stell glared at them. They couldn't have made a mistake about the size. Grandmother used to make money by sewing fancy dresses for other women. If they made the dress the wrong size, how could they not have noticed sooner? Why was it funny?

"Where's Rita?" Mother looked around the room, as though she thought Rita was hiding behind a chair or something. Auntie Stell bustled off toward the kitchen.

It was Patsy who answered. "She went to Napa Valley with Prince Charming for the week. They're picking the right wines for the wedding." The cousins thought that was hilarious, too, and the giggles started again.

Mother's eyebrows went up so high they disappear under her bangs. I buried my face in my book. It was like dominoes falling over as I made connections. There were still some key pieces missing, but I had learned that babies were made by a man and a woman in bed or the back seat of a car. Only married people are supposed to make babies, and women get too big to fit into their clothes when they grow the baby. Uh-oh. Even though some parts of the process are a little foggy, I know that Rita and Prince Charming are in big trouble. Good thing the wedding is in two weeks.

"I thought the wines were chosen months ago. In fact, I distinctly remember the discussion over when to serve what. Besides, aren't they choosing wines from the cellar of the fancy hotel he runs?" Mother's voice was almost normal.

"Apparently, they're also looking for new wines to include on the hotel wine list. That makes it a business trip." The laughter could not be stopped with a simple glare this time.

"If all you girls can do is laugh, you can go home. It's not as though you've been all that helpful through this. Your sister's fiancé is everything any girl could want in a husband." Auntie Stell banged the tray with the stacks of cups and saucers down on the end table so hard the cups rattled.

"Stop giggling like schoolgirls and listen to me." Grandmother's quiet voice cut through the anger and the laughter like a hot knife through butter. "You should be ashamed of yourselves, treating your sister like a dirty joke. I'm disappointed that you older girls don't know better. Don't you know anything about love?" When Grandmother said the word "love," her face lost its stern expression and she seemed to be looking at something far away. The room got so quiet I'm sure I could hear our hearts beating. "I mean real love between a man and a woman. There are times in a woman's life when love becomes such an overwhelming force that nothing can stand in its way — regardless of the possible consequences." Seconds passed in silence. "Sometimes it's the high point of the woman's life, and sometimes it's the worst thing that ever happens to her. Either way, she is changed forever." All eyes were on Grandmother, and I was holding my breath, waiting for her to say more. Instead, she shook her head and she looked up at her oldest daughter. "I'd love to have some coffee, Estela." The silence stretched for a few really long seconds before everyone took a deep breath. I could almost see the curtains move. No one was laughing.

"I'll get the coffee," said Patsy.

"I'll get the cookies."

"I'll help."

Jean kissed Grandmother on the cheek before disappearing into the kitchen with her sisters. Mother dragged the sheet with The Dress over to one side out of the way of any possible coffee mishap, and the coffee table was put back in operation. I kept my eyes on my book, but my ears were open in case any more was said about Grandmother's remark. Even I could tell she was speaking Truth from Experience.

Auntie Stell said I could have some cookies, but if I wanted milk I'd have to eat in the kitchen. Once I'd finished my milk and cookies, I came back to my place in the living room. I don't think they noticed me. I sat and watched Grandmother. She didn't say a word, and it looked like she was daydreaming. After a while she sat up straight and tapped her spoon on her coffee cup until everyone stopped talking. "This is the answer." I could hardly breathe. I was sure she was going to tell us all about her experience with real love. I think the women felt the same way. You could have heard a pin drop—even on the carpet.

"There isn't enough material to let the seams out, and we don't have time to sew an entirely new dress, or even just a new bodice. Bring it here and I'll show you how we'll fix it." I had totally forgotten the problem of The Dress. The cousins cleared away the coffee things while Mother and Auntie Stell put the coffee table back by the window and pulled the sheet with The Dress back to its place in front of Grandmother. "We open the side seams and add an insert of lace on either side that matches the veil."

"Oh, no, not more pearls." I knew Auntie Stell was worried about the money.

Mother said, "An insert will spoil the pattern on the skirt. We worked so hard to get the pattern to come out exactly right, and now we have to break it up for inserts?" Mother was searching for perfection. She always criticized clothes where the plaids didn't match, or had stripes that looked uneven at the seams.

"No to both of you. First, pearls will be very uncomfortable on the sides where her arms will brush against them as she moves, so we embroider French knots that will look similar and be softer. Second, the skirt is very full. We can easily adjust the skirt."

"Mama, you're a genius." Auntie Stell actually shoved The Dress out of the way with her foot to get to Grandmother and give her a big hug. Even though we never heard any more about Grandmother's Great Love, everybody was smiling when we left.

I thought of adding Grandmother's experience to my list of mysteries to solve, but I don't think I'll solve it. Usually the family would be all over a remark like that, wanting to know all the delicious details. This time no one asked any questions. Grandmother's voice had been so serious and sad that it made me shiver. Sometimes people need to keep their secrets secret.

➤➤ TEN ◄◄

The telephone rang and my heart started racing. I snatched the receiver off the hook. "Jamal?"

"What did the doctor say?"

It made my heart swell that he was so concerned that he asked about the doctor before even saying he loved me and missed me. "He said exactly what you'd want him to say. Mother and child are doing well. Don't worry; everything's fine."

"Everything's fine here, too. Finally solved the situation at the mines."

"I'm so glad you reached a settlement."

"Settlement? I guess you could call it that. It's all settled. I brought in some Russians and blocked the roads to the mining area. When they got hungry enough, they saw my point of view. Then I began evicting the malcontents and replacing them with Russians. After the ringleaders got tossed out with their families and had to slink off into the mountains with their tails between their legs, the others lined up like sheep to get their jobs back."

"You starved them into submission?"

"Don't exaggerate, Charli. Only a couple of sickly kids and old people died. I was a lot gentler than the old union busters in your country. At least I didn't arm the Russians with machine guns. They only had defensive weapons, and they didn't shoot to kill."

"People were shot?"

"Not many. The point is that now I don't have to spend days at a time at the mines. The Russians will be there, and they'll let me know about any unpleasantness before it reaches the level it was when I came home. Things are quieter, and I can't wait for our wedding party to present you to our friends."

I was confused. My thinking was getting turned around again. How could my sweet thoughtful husband talk this way about his own people? "Jamal, I'm sorry."

"Sorry?"

"About the earrings." I was babbling to buy time while I scrabbled around to find a rational explanation. I felt my foundations shake, and I needed something I could hold and believe. He withheld food from people to get them to work on his terms. "Amira let me try the earrings on, and I guess I forgot I was still wearing them in the rush to get packed."

"The earrings are meaningless." They weren't meaningless to Amira, or to me either. "Amira didn't even miss them until I asked why she wasn't wearing them. I only mentioned it to make your mother bring you to the phone. Keep them. Consider them my gift." They weren't his to give. "There'll be no more talk of earrings."

"I'll send them back."

"How long will it take your mother to settle her affairs? She is coming, isn't she?"

"No, Jamal, we're not coming. I'm sorry. I realize now that I made a mistake. I can never adapt to your way of thinking. I can't go back." I may have been as surprised as he was by the words coming out of my mouth.

"You don't know what you're saying." He sounded as though he was explaining something to a small child. "We are legally married, and under the laws of my country any children of the union belong to the husband's family." He paused, but I said nothing. "You are violating the laws of my country by stealing my child. I can and will get you extradited."

"Jamal, please try to understand." I wasn't sure he even heard me. My mouth was so dry my tongue stuck to my teeth.

"I don't want to create an international incident, but if you persist in this silly notion, I will have no choice." His voice became hard and brittle. "If that happens, you will seriously damage your reputation and standing with my family, which will make your life less comfortable." The threat was thinly veiled. "I'll give you one more chance. Let's consider this one more incident of your hormone imbalance, and I will mention it to no one for...two weeks. You have two weeks to change your mind with no consequences." I didn't even hear a click, just a dial tone.

"Charli, are you all right? You look like you've seen a ghost."

"I...no, I'm not all right." I didn't have the strength to talk.

"She doesn't look good. Maybe she's having a miscarriage. That would solve everything, wouldn't it?" Mother was talking in a low voice, but she was only a few feet away, and there was nothing wrong with my ears. I leaned forward, covering my abdomen as though to protect my unborn child. I was lightheaded. Cold fingers of dread made my stomach crawl with nausea. Jamal, the man I once loved, murdered his own people for profit, threatened me with a lifetime of God knew what kind of treatment, and now Mother wished my child dead? My breath came in short gasps, just like the time I'd caught my finger in the car door and it hurt so bad I couldn't breathe, let alone scream or cry.

Mother offered to let me spend the night, but I declined, pleading lack of pajamas and toothbrush. How could I stay with her? She wanted my baby to die. What if she put something in my tea? Aunt Nellie helped me to the car and made me lie down in the back. Mother brought out my old quilt and covered me.

It was a couple of hours and at least as many cups of tea later before I could tell Aunt Nellie about the call.

"I have two weeks." I felt like a prisoner on death row. In two weeks he'd take me back kicking and screaming and I'd be disgraced forever, or else I'd go against every value I ever held and go back as a willing bride. I got through the rest of the day like an automaton. My body did all the things it had to do, but my mind kept playing the tape of Jamal's conversation over and over. Even after I fell into an exhausted sleep, I couldn't escape the thoughts of the village of mine workers cut off from food and threatened with slow starvation.

I stumbled out of bed the next morning and paused on my way to the bathroom. A man's voice came from the direction of the kitchen.

"I'm sure he's right. The government will do whatever's necessary to avoid an international incident. Things are tense enough without having a brouhaha over something like this."

"You mean to tell me they won't lift a finger to prevent

a kidnapping?"

"I'm telling you it isn't considered a kidnapping if the right papers are filed for the extradition of a criminal."

"Don't give me that lawyer crap. She's not a criminal and you know it."

"You saw the earrings."

"But he said she could keep them."

"In writing? Did you hear him say it?"

"No, but—"

"Then it never happened. No writing, no witnesses, no proof. Sorry, Nellie, but you asked my opinion as a lawyer."

I slowly closed my door and flopped back down on the bed. For a few minutes I'd been thinking of a hot shower instead of my status as a condemned criminal, but the overheard conversation brought it all crashing back down on me. I lay spread-eagle across the bed with neither the will nor the energy to move.

I gasped. "Aunt Nellie!" Her footsteps came running, and the door flew open. "I felt it! I felt the baby move. He's like a little butterfly inside me." My spirits soared, and my resolve strengthened. I *had* to keep this tiny helpless being from growing up with a father who could thoughtlessly kill people for his own financial gain. I would find a way somehow.

"Is she all right?" The man's voice followed Aunt Nellie.

"She's fine, love. We'll be out in a minute." She gave me a big hug and whispered in my ear. "I'm so happy for you. It's a wonderful feeling, isn't it? Get dressed; come and meet my friend, Bill. He's the one you've been tiptoeing around." She gave me a final squeeze before leaving the room.

So Aunt Nellie's gentleman friend was a lawyer. Suddenly ravenous, I dressed quickly. The shower could wait. "Am I too late for breakfast?"

"Have some cereal. We'll be having lunch with the ladies in an hour."

"Hi, Charli, nice to meet you at last. Nellie told me about your situation. Unfortunately, he's probably right that the government will help him."

"Why would they bother? The Sultanate is such a tiny country they don't even have a proper airport. His father doesn't rule like a president or king, he *owns* the country. We didn't even have to go through customs."

"The reason you didn't go through customs is because it isn't a real country. It's just one of the many small republics that make up the Soviet Union. The USSR will likely help him get what he wants for the same reason they haven't gone in and nationalized the mines—they don't want to deal with the radioactivity themselves, and it's making them a lot of money. They might just enjoy embarrassing the US by saying that US operatives are criminals and thieves." I nodded as the facts tried to settle into a meaningful pattern in my brain. "Call me any time." The name on the card was William R. Aldeman. "I have to run, Nellie. I'll do whatever I can, but you might want to look for a different solution."

Aunt Nellie walked him to the door, and came back with a smile on her face. "Why don't you take that cereal into your room so I can get to work on lunch? The ladies will be here soon."

Although it bothered me that Aunt Nellie thought I was more trouble than help in the kitchen, I was happy to read while I ate my cereal.

>> 🕐 🕑 🕒 🕓 <<

SEPTEMBER 9, 1950: - Yesterday was Rita's wedding. It was an amazing event, but by the time we got home it was too late to write. I couldn't wait to see what The Dress looked like on Rita. I was so excited I could barely stand still while Mother wound my watch and put it on my wrist. I even skipped the usual "Why can't I wear my watch to school?" conversation. I once asked for a Mickey Mouse watch that I could wear to school, but Mother was so shocked by my extravagant request for a second watch that I never asked again. Anyway, today I was happy to have it because a gold watch was perfect with my new fancy dress.

At last we were in the car and on our way. I could see from where I stood in the back seat that the hair that usually sticks straight up on the top of Daddy's head was slicked down today. He looked very handsome in his suit, and Mother looked as pretty as a bride herself with her new dress and hat.

As we drove toward the cathedral, I started thinking about all the work that went into the wedding, and one thought led to another. "When is Rita going to have her baby?" I asked. Daddy's head whipped around so fast he swerved the car and I sat down hard as he put on the brakes. Mother turned bright red.

"What made you say such a dreadful thing?"

"I...I thought..." Flustered by their reactions, I didn't think before I blurted out, "Isn't that why people get married? To have babies and make a family?"

Daddy laughed. "Let's just get through the wedding

first. Babies come later, after the man and woman get to know each other."

"Oh, Rita and her boyfriend already know each other. They spent a week in Napa Valley drinking wine together."

"What?" At least Daddy didn't swerve the car this time.

"It was a business trip and Rita was being helpful." Mother's explanation came out a little too rushed and a little too loud.

"I bet she was."

"Frank, don't be crude. And they weren't *drinking* wine, they were *tasting* it. Richard wanted to stock some new California wines for the hotel, and he took Rita along because she studied about wine as part of the wedding planning." Mother turned her head to look at me. "I don't want you to mention that ever again—to anyone." I think she was talking to both of us. "She's been planning this wedding for a year. She's probably lived it in her mind so many times and dreamed about it so many times that she already felt married."

"I've dreamed of having my own command, but I know better than to march to the bridge and start giving orders." Mother didn't answer that. Daddy was right about the dreaming thing. I've dreamed I could fly, but I know better than to jump off a bridge and try it.

Daddy said, "Out of the mouths of babes." I didn't think that was a nice thing to say because I'm not a baby, and I'm too young to be the other kind of babe.

"It's a good thing she didn't say that during the reception." Mother was still upset. I sat back and kept very quiet. I'd slipped up and showed that I could listen with a book in front of me. Maybe with the excitement of the wedding she'll forget.

161

The cathedral was humungous. I tripped over an old woman's cane that was sticking out in the aisle and hurt my knee because I couldn't stop staring at the stained glass windows. They made the air itself look like rainbows. I smelled incense, even before the mass started. The organ was playing softly and everyone was all dressed up. I saw Jackie and we waved at each other.

The organ began to play "Here Comes the Bride" and everyone stood up and there was Sharon, wearing something that looked very much like The Dress, throwing flower petals on the floor.

Rita came down the aisle looking exactly like a fairy tale princess. I wouldn't have been surprised if her foot peeked out and she had on glass slippers. Even though I'd seen The Dress from the time it was just rolls of material and packages of other stuff, it looked different with Rita inside. It was like magic. Richard, her new husband, was grinning very hard. His white teeth almost sparkled against his tan face. I could see why the cousins call him Prince Charming. He'd be perfect on horseback with a cape and sword. The wedding was lovely, but it did go on for a long time.

Everybody followed the long white limousine from the cathedral to the big hotel for the reception. It was like a parade. We even drove through red lights. Policemen stopped traffic and waved us through. That was exciting. Once inside the ballroom, I got a little dizzy looking up at the chandeliers. There must have been as many little bits of crystal in the chandeliers as there were pearls on Rita's dress.

We had to look for the table with our names, but they were all so beautiful that it was fun to walk around. Each centerpiece was different. Some had tiny tree branches with leaves of yellow, orange, or even deep red; they all had big fluffy flowers that Mother said were chrysanthemums. That's a wonderful word to say. It fills your whole mouth and you can almost chew it. There were so many different kinds of flowers that even Mother didn't know all the names.

Mother had told me that Sharon and Jackie would sit with us. Jackie was already at our table and waving to us. A long time later Sharon came and joined us. I asked her what took her so long because she was in the first car. She said the wedding party was having pictures taken. She sounded so smug about being in the wedding party that I didn't ask her any more questions.

Rita and Prince Charming came in and the music started. Rita wasn't wearing the veil and she'd done something with the dress because it didn't have a train anymore. Mother said the train was a separate piece that she could take off for the reception so she could dance. It made me think of the little lizards I tried to catch that left me with a bit of tail between my fingers. Sometimes the tail wriggled even without the lizard. It made me laugh to imagine the train dancing alone in another room.

Our table was near the edge of the room, so the three of us girls got up and danced around to the music. When the food was served, Mother brought us things to eat from the buffet, and she took the champagne glasses away from our places.

Then came the best part of the whole party — the cake. I think the cake was even more beautiful than The Dress. There were two cakes, not just one, and each one was perfect. The surprise wasn't just the cake; the surprise was that Aunt Nellie was the one pushing the cart into the room. I heard the oooooh's and aaaaaah's even over the sound of the music. Daddy muttered, "Hot damn! Ain't that something." Mother didn't even scold him for saying ain't and damn. Jackie jumped up and down clapping her hands. She said this was their wedding present to Rita. Rita and Richard posed next to the cakes for pictures. Then there was a picture of Aunt Nellie and the cakes. After all the pictures, the bride and groom cut the first piece and fed each other a bite of cake. They must have been nervous because they were a little messy about it.

It took a long time for the waiters to get to our table with our little pieces of cake, but it was worth the wait. I still remember the feeling I had when that cake sat on my tongue. I didn't want to swallow — ever. I closed my eyes and let the pleasure spread from my tongue through my whole body. I wonder what Aunt Nellie put in that cake to make it so wonderful. Imagine being a chemist and capturing that taste in a bottle. You could put it on vegetables or add it to nasty medicines.

I did hear one strange conversation at the reception. I was near Auntie Stell's table waiting to ask if Sharon could come and spend the night. I was under strict orders not to interrupt, or even stand around looking impatient if someone else was talking. As the mother of the bride, Auntie Stell was nearly as important as the bride, and a lot of people were talking to her. Just before I reached the table, a man sort of merged in front of me. I didn't mean to eavesdrop, but it happened.

"Hey, Stella, how ya doin'?"

"Guido, I don't remember sending you an invitation."

"My feelings is hurt, Stella. You know I always liked

you. You was always one of my favorite people. Even though I once did you a really big favor, I still didn't get no invitation."

"As I remember it, I did you the favor."

"You don't understand yet? I swear I didn't do nothin'."

"Whatever. It still doesn't explain why you're here."

"I was helpin' Nellie haul the cakes and thought I'd drop by and say hello, maybe get a chance to kiss the bride."

"Guido, you keep your hands off my daughter."

"—or the mother of the bride, know what I mean?" Everybody had been kissing the bride and Auntie Stell, too, so I don't know why her face got so red. Guido winked and grinned. "Don't get your knickers twisted, I'm just kiddin'." He looked over at Uncle Walter, who was talking with some other people. "He givin' you any trouble?"

"Certainly not."

"'Cause if he is...you know I can deal with it."

"Guido, I'd appreciate it if you'd just leave now."

"Sure thing, Stella Baby." I could see Auntie Stell wanted to say something else, but Guido walked away and disappeared into the swirl of dancers.

Guido and Auntie Stell must have been friends a long time ago. He wanted to kiss her, so maybe he was her boyfriend before she married her first husband, the Italian. I know they didn't get married, and she's mad at him after all those years. Maybe they had a big fight and she never forgave him for whatever he did. She was upset to see him at Aunt Nellie's engagement party, too.

I'm surprised Auntie Stell stayed mad at him for so long. I guess when Auntie Stell says she'll never forgive you, she means never. I'm glad she forgave me for bleeding on her carpet, especially now that I know how long she can stay mad. Even so, I don't think she should still be mad at Guido.

SEPTEMBER 11, 1950: - I've been thinking about Guido ever since the wedding. He likes Auntie Stell a lot, and he said he did her a really big favor. It must have been when she was married to her first husband because Albert was little. Then he asked if Uncle Walter was giving her any trouble because he could "take care of it." What if, what if, what if — and when I thought of this my whole body shivered. What if he "took care of" Auntie Stell's first husband? That would explain why she was still mad at him, because no matter what that's a really bad thing to do. It almost fits. The part that's wrong is that Auntie Stell says she did Guido a favor, too. Auntie Stell could never hurt anyone. I'll have to think about this.

➤➤ ☾ ☾ 1965 ☽ ☽ ◀◀

The germ of an idea popped into my head. I closed the journal and thought about it. If Mr. Aldeman was right about the government helping Jamal, there was no escape. My social security number would follow me around wherever I worked, and my passport would show up if I left the country. I had to disappear.

The more I thought about it, the more my mind split into two voices that disagreed. Voice One said, "You read too many mysteries and watch too much TV." Voice Two said, "If Guido runs in the same circles as Stella's first husband, he would know what to do. On TV the Italian mobsters make people disappear all the time, and not always with cement overshoes. The mobsters sometimes had plastic surgery and started somewhere else with a different name. I could probably skip the surgery." Voice One said I was crazy but I might as well run it by Aunt Nellie. I went to the kitchen.

"Aunt Nellie, do you remember a man named Guido Lombardi?" When she nodded I asked if she knew how to contact him.

"I haven't talked to Guido for years and years, but I guess I could find him. What's on your mind, Charli?" I explained my crazy idea. She laughed and said, "You're right, it *is* crazy—but it just might work. Actually, Guido was the only Lombardi that thought I was doing the right thing when I left Al. I think I have his number somewhere, unless he's moved."

"So you don't think I'm totally insane?"

"Not *totally*." She dropped what she was doing and said she'd be right back. "Found it." Her muffled voice came from the other room. "I have a box of old papers in my closet. The number was in an old address book."

I practically held my breath as she dialed. When she said hello, my heart started thumping. What was I doing getting involved with organized crime? Nellie laughed as she hung up. "What's funny? Did you tell him?"

"I told him we had a little problem, and that Stella would be here. He won't make it for lunch, but he should show up soon after." She gave another little laugh. "Now go get ready for company."

Still feeling ambivalent about what I was doing, I went to my room. I began to put the journal away, but the next entry was so short I decided to read it, hoping to find some humor in my early life.

>> ⊕ ⊕ ⊕ ⊕ <<

SEPTEMBER 15, 1950: - School is a lot more fun now because I have a new friend, Betty. Betty is nice, and she's really funny, too. The best part is that we like the same things, and we both really hate dodge ball. I don't know why they call it physical education. The only education I get from it is the knowledge that being hit by a ball hurts.

Betty and I eat lunch together, and we found out we even like the same books. We talk about all sorts of interesting things. We started sharing things we'd never tell anyone else. She told me about her dog, and what happened when she (the dog) got out one day and the neighbor's dog...you know. (Actually, I didn't know a lot of it, but Betty filled in some of the blanks.) Her father turned the hose on them, but her dog is still going to have puppies. I'm going to ask Mother if I can have one.

I didn't know dogs got stuck sometimes. I wonder if people ever get stuck? If they do, and the bedroom door is closed, who will turn a hose on them?

I didn't have anything that interesting to share, so I told her about how Guido still likes Auntie Stell after years and years apart. I made Betty swear never to tell anyone, even though I didn't say anything about the murder.

I bet when I fall in love it will be like having a best friend—only better.

>> ⊕ ⊕ 2013 ⊕ ⊕ <<

"Bev, I was thinking about best friends and thought I'd

give you a call. Can you come over for a chat and some of my homemade potato soup?" I hoped that she'd accept. I'd spent all day on the phone with various human resource people. I had emailed or faxed Bob's legalese request for the information to every one of them—a feat of Herculean proportions since most of them wanted to hang up when they heard my story. In one case I resorted to tears before they agreed to search for his name. How hard could it be in today's world of computerized everything? I was mentally exhausted and needed a break before tackling the smaller companies.

"Can't. I'm running late for a dental appointment. I probably won't be able to eat after she's done with me." I stopped short of begging.

"All the more reason to come. Cream of potato soup'll be just the thing. I haven't started cooking, so while you're sitting in the chair you can think of me slaving over a hot stove making soup for you."

"All right. I'll pick up something soft and sweet for dessert. See you in an hour or so, I can't promise a definite time."

"Soup waits." I hung up the phone and it rang again. Maybe Bev remembered something else she had to do.

"Charli? Bob Aldeman. I can't believe it, but you got a hit."

"You found Kate?"

"Maybe." He gave a chuckle. "The man I talked to said he was going to hang up on you, but when you started crying he said you reminded him of his favorite aunt and he looked it up right away. You're still a charmer, Charli." I didn't consider tears charming. "I got a number, but no one answered. It might belong to someone else by now, so don't pin too many hopes on it. It was a canned message just reading the number I'd reached, but I left a message saying you needed to talk to Kate and left your number. Sorry to dump it back in your lap, but I'm up to my ears right now."

"That's perfect. Thanks, Bob, and good luck on your big case." I went back to making soup, but my mind was a couple of thousand miles away. I snapped into focus when I chopped the end of my fingernail into the onions. I couldn't find it because when I got close enough to distinguish fingernail from onion my eyes teared up from the onions. I threw the whole thing away and started with a new onion. I tried not to get too excited. The number was old, and they could have moved. Where would I go next? I didn't have any ideas.

The knife clattered from my nerveless fingers, scattering bits of minced onion across the black granite counter top. What if she didn't want to be found? What if she had a reason to disappear? The thought made my knees weak. What might she be running from? She and her husband disappeared at the same time, so it couldn't be her husband. I remembered she'd had an unfortunate marriage while David was in college. Hadn't she had a child? How could I be so neglectful? I realized I didn't even know the names of any of the cousins' children. I'd been so paranoid about someone finding my new identity, that I had avoided all contact with family. Aunt Nellie and her immediate family were the exceptions—and now I'd lost even that thread of a connection to family.

If nothing came of this phone number, I'd make the rounds of the cousins again, looking for information about her child. A plan of action helped. I went back to the comforting task of cooking, but I couldn't stop my mind from running in hamster circles wondering why she (or they) might be hiding. As soon as the soup was on the stove, I went to my computer to see where the phone number Richard gave me was located. Houston. I'd heard about reverse directories and was trying to find an address to go with the number when the phone rang again. I jumped to answer.

"Auntie, it's Kate."

I nearly dropped the phone in my excitement. "Kate! Am I glad to hear your voice!"

"Damn, he's back already. I'll call late tonight." I heard something in the background and then Kate's voice, muffled as though she had her hand over the receiver. She said, "Just some jerk selling life insurance," and hung up.

When Bev came, I told her I'd sorted out the retirement home thing with David. I spent the rest of the afternoon half listening to her hilarious accounts of the family reunion. Bev has a real flair for humor. I was sorry when she left because I knew I'd do nothing but fret over Kate until the phone rang again.

➢➢ ELEVEN ◁◁

I hadn't seen Guido in years, but I knew him the minute he stepped through the door. He was getting gray, and bigger around the middle, but essentially unchanged. Auntie Stell didn't sit next to him. I outlined the situation to him over coffee.

"I don't know why Mr. Aldeman thinks he'll have me extradited over the earrings. Jamal said they were meaningless. It's the baby he wants."

"Bill explained it before you joined us. Jamal knows that if he tries to get the baby, you could claim it wasn't his."

"But we both know that's not possible."

"This whole thing is an affront to his honor. That's probably why he's giving you two weeks to think it over—he can't let people think that his wife left him. Having even one person doubt that the baby is his would make him a laughing stock. If you don't go back willingly, he *has* to present you as a scheming criminal who was after money from the beginning."

"But I left a drawer full of gold and jewelry that his family gave me. I only took the earrings because Amira wanted me to have them. They were never part of his family jewels."

"You said they were cousins. That's family."

"I'm sorry I ever took the earrings."

"Don't be. He'd probably have accused you of theft anyway." It made him sound like a monster, but I knew it was plausible. This was the most innocuous of the possibilities. My stomach churned. He *was* a monster, by my values at least.

"Excuse me." I pushed my chair back and escaped to the bathroom before I lost my lunch. I had come so close. If he had started the last conversation with a declaration of undying love, I'd probably be on my way back already. If he'd never bragged about getting the miners under control, I'd be packing today. It was only the faint flutter of movement in my womb that gave me the strength to resist.

"Are you all right, Charli?"

"Yes, I'll be out in a minute."

"Okay, I'll make you some herb tea."

"You're in a real fix, honey." Guido wasn't kidding. "So what you need's a change of name, right? Then he can't find you. Change your hair style and bingo—you're somebody else."

I had to smile. "You make it sound so easy."

"Yeah, well it ain't easy, not in today's world. Used to be that a driver's license was enough, but now there's social security cards and stuff like that to consider. The system's all connected and complicated."

"You make people disappear all the time, don't you? You've been doing it for years," said Auntie Stell.

"Stella Baby, I never made nobody disappear, but I know people who know people, that's all." Auntie Stell stared at him so long I don't think she even noticed that Aunt Nellie and Grandmother were clearing the table. I picked up my cup and followed them, but as soon as I was out of sight Auntie Stell began talking, and my feet stopped moving.

"Guido, don't come any closer. I still have nightmares about finding Leonard face down in a pool of his own blood. You had to do it in my own house? I wouldn't have come today if I'd known you were going to be here."

"Jesus, Stella, that's what's been buggin' you all these years? You think I offed Leonard?"

"Who else? You told me to miss the last ferry home that night. Why didn't you do it somewhere else? You knew I'd discover the body. I had Albert with me, too."

"I swear to God, Stella, it wasn't me. It wasn't even our family. I just heard it was going down 'cause he'd been skimmin' and I didn't want you around when it happened. I swear that's the truth." Guido paused, and I tried to get my feet to move. "If you thought it was me, why didn't you tell the cops?"

"They never asked me. They just blew smoke in my face, and said, 'Good riddance, one less Eyetalian,' or something like that. I guess it made me so mad that I decided not to give them another Eyetalian. If they'd been more concerned, I might've told them I thought you did it."

"I always knew you was sweet on me."

"Charli, either take the tray, or move and let me through."

"Sorry, Grandmother, I'll take the tray." In the time it took to serve the dessert and pour more coffee, Auntie Stell recovered her composure.

"So you want me to get new papers from the ground up—birth certificate, driver's license, social security card, passport? That'll run you an arm and a leg. Wouldn't it be easier to find her a husband? Then she could just change her name on the other things."

"But I'm already married."

Guido waved his hand in dismissal. "Easy. I heard that you could just say 'I divorce you' three times and bingo—no more marriage."

"Not exactly," said Grandmother. "First, it has to have witnesses, and second, I don't think it works for women." How did she know things like that?

"I'll be damned." Guido must have thought the same thing. "Anyway, the marriage ain't recorded over here, so it don't count. Hell, if I wasn't such an old fart, I'd marry you myself. No, I gotta keep myself pure in case Stella's old man takes a powder." Auntie Stell smiled, but the rest of us laughed. "All right, if you don't want a husband, what about a marriage license with no husband?"

I thought about it for a minute. "That might work, except at some point I'd also need divorce papers. I mean eventually the child will ask about Daddy."

"And what will you tell him?"

"That's no problem. I'll borrow a story from one of Aunt Nellie's divorces."

Guido jumped. "That's it! Nellie, you must have a whole collection of marriage licenses you aren't using no more, unless you threw them away."

"I've kept them all, because I learned from each of them."

"Can I borrow them?" Aunt Nellie nodded and soon produced a large envelope. "Give me a little time to see a guy I know. I think I figured out a way to make Charli a widow."

"Guido, even if you could get to Jamal, which I doubt, I

175

can't let you kill him."

Guido laughed so hard he had to wipe his eyes. "Sweetheart, like I told your Auntie here, I ain't never killed nobody, and I ain't about to start now." He got up and gave me a peck on the cheek. "Gotta run, ladies. I'll call soon."

That night, unable to sleep, I remembered what Aunt Nellie had said about Guido agreeing with her decision to leave Al. Unless my memory was wrong, it was Rita's wedding cake that had started the events leading to that divorce. I couldn't remember the details, but it had something to do with baking for the hotel. I pulled out the journal again.

>> ⏱ ⏲ ⏰ ⏱ <<

SEPTEMBER 25, 1950: - Aunt Nellie came to see Mother today. She was terribly upset and I was sent to my room. I waited until they were talking in the living room before going to the kitchen for chocolate milk and cookies. I clinked the spoon on the glass while stirring in the chocolate syrup so they could hear me and wouldn't think I was sneaky, but after that I was very quiet and slow about eating.

"This is a career for me." Aunt Nellie was talking.

"But is having a career worth the price?"

"It's not like I can sit home reading novels and eating bonbons all day. I work in that restaurant every single night and a lot of the days, too. It isn't easy supervising the kitchen all day and being a charming hostess in the evenings. By the time I get home at night, I'm exhausted."

"I don't sit home reading and eating bonbons." I knew

176

that was coming. "I cook and clean and do laundry and volunteer in the school, and I—"

"—cook for two or three people. I clean the house and do laundry *and* cook for hundreds of people and still have to make sure the homework is done. Besides, this is not about you." I didn't hear Mother's reply. "How can he expect me to keep slinging hash in his restaurant when I have such a wonderful opportunity? Do you know what I have to look forward to if I work my ass off to be the best cook that ever walked the earth as long as I'm working in that restaurant?"

"You'd be—"

"I'd be a good cook in a neighborhood restaurant, working herself into an early grave. A restaurant like that doesn't even have a chef. I'd always be a cook at a local restaurant. The best I could ever hope for would be a write-up in a local paper I could frame and hang on the wall."

"But it must give you satisfaction to be good at what you do and to work with your husband every day. Sharing your life with your loving husband, who only wants you to stay near him, would be its own reward."

"Oh my God, Charlotte. Is your entire thought process just stringing one platitude after the other." I ran to the drawer where Mother keeps her notepad. I wrote down "platitude" so I could look it up later. "If I take this job I'll be a pastry chef in the best hotel in the Bay Area. I'd cater weddings of famous people; I'd have assistants to work with me; I'd become a name in the industry. Do you know how much money I could make? Instead, Al says it's my duty as a wife to support his efforts."

"You know, Nellie, money isn't everything. Your

wifely duty doesn't stop at the bedroom door."

"You don't think I know that? I'm the one that became a gourmet cook when my husband wanted gourmet cooking. I'm the one who brought Al's miserable diner up to restaurant standards. I'm the one who taught his cook how to cook, and I still have to spend most of my time preparing the seasonings and overseeing what he does."

"You just proved my point. You've always done things to please your husband. Why're you upset about not accepting a job offer?"

"Because this is a life-changing opportunity. Learning gourmet cooking for Willis was fun, and I was acquiring a skill I wanted to have. Working as a cook for Al was fun because I got to use my skills. Improving his restaurant was good for both of us. This is different. If I stay, it will be good for him but bad for me. If I leave, he might make a little less money because his stupid cook can't remember my instructions from one day to the next, but his restaurant will still be better than it was when he met me. I don't think this has anything to do with him needing me in the restaurant. I think it's all about him wanting me under his thumb."

"I'm sure you're wrong. He wants you near him because he loves you."

"That's a load of crap and you know it. If he really loved me, he'd want me to do what makes *me* happy, not what puts a couple more bucks in *his* pocket. This is *my* decision. Listen, Charlotte, making a decision because someone else wants you to do it is fine when you're choosing a menu for supper, but when you're choosing a life path, it's never a good idea. This is a major decision in my life, and it must be right for me."

"But Nellie—"

"Don't 'but Nellie' me. There's nothing in the marriage vows about being an eternal doormat. Al thinks he can control my every move. I understand that attitude in the restaurant, although I often manage to talk him around. I don't like it, but I understand it. This one is my life decision, not his."

"But—"

"Oh, Charlotte, I came here for some support, and all I'm getting is the same old lecture about wifely duty. For that I could've stayed home."

Then Aunt Nellie started crying. I'd never heard her cry before, and it kind of scared me. I gulped the last of my milk and tiptoed back to my room.

OCTOBER 16, 1950: - Something awful is happening. I catch the murmur of low-voiced conversations, and Mother walks around looking worried. I know it's about Aunt Nellie because I caught her name a couple of times when I walked into the room unexpectedly. While I'm at school Mother goes to see Auntie Stell and Grandmother every other day or so. I always know when things are serious because she mutters to herself in Spanish.

Last night I woke up and Jackie was in my bed, crying into my pillow. She whispered, "Are you awake?" as she reached over and put an arm around me.

"I am now." Of course I was awake. Did she think I could sleep through her crying? "What's wrong, Jackie?" She started sniveling and snuffling something fierce and I had to get up and find some tissues before she could talk. "What happened?"

"I don't know." Her face crumpled into the red crying

face again.

"Why are you crying if you don't know what happened?"

"I know he hit her, I just don't know what made him so mad. He was yelling at her about doing what he told her to do, and she yelled back that she was a wife, not a slave. Then he hit her."

I remembered all the mysteries I'd read where someone got hit and fell, knocking their head on something hard and died. "Did she hit her head? Is she all right?"

Jackie shrugged. "She says she is, but one eye looks puffed up almost shut and her cheek is turning black and blue. Aunt Charlotte said she should see a doctor, but Mommy said no."

"If Mother said she should see a doctor, she must be hurt."

"You know your mother always makes a big deal about everything. Look at you—she drags you to doctors all the time."

"But I'm..." I started to say I was really sick, but I don't feel sick. The thought that Mother might just be making a big deal over my health was something that never occurred to me. Jackie was busy blowing her nose again and trying to control her sniveling. I patted her shoulder as I thought about the possibility of not being sick.

I know that when I was little I was in the hospital for a long time with rheumatic fever. Daddy even came home on emergency leave to see me, but that was years ago. Now I feel fine. Mother says you never really get over rheumatic fever. She says I'll always have to be careful to get enough sleep and not over-exert myself. Could it be Mother making a big deal?

If Jackie didn't know what happened, I wasn't going to learn any more about it until morning. I gently eased Jackie back down on the pillow, making it'll-be-all-right sounds. Crying takes its toll. She was soon snoring softly; her nose was still a bit stuffed. I lay back on my own pillow and tried to think and remember. I was excited by the thought that I might be just a regular skinny kid instead of a sickly one.

I vowed to pay close attention from now on to find out if the doctor said anything about me being sick or if it was just Mother telling the doctor, and him nodding. After all, rheumatic fever is invisible, not like the measles, I don't have a rash or cough or anything like that. Wouldn't it be nice not to be sick and have to be treated special all the time? Nothing more I can do about it now, but I'm sure I'll be at the doctor again soon and be able to test out the new theory.

Meanwhile, I have something exciting to share with Betty. An aunt with a black eye is even better than a dog that got pregnant. I'll have to make her swear not to tell anyone, because if this means Jackie will live with us and go to my school again, I don't want everyone to know. I'm sure Jackie would get mad at me if everyone in her class knew her mother was afraid to go home.

The next morning I got dressed very quietly because Jackie was still sleeping. I smelled coffee before I reached the kitchen. Mother and Aunt Nellie were sitting at the table. Mother's back was to me and Nellie was looking into her coffee cup so I couldn't see her face. I took a quiet step backward out of the doorway and into the hall. I know it was shameless eavesdropping, but what's a girl to do? No one ever tells me anything, and I had to know what was going on.

"Maybe you should just give up on the whole hotel job thing. Go back to Al and say you were wrong. You know he's not a real wife beater."

"Not a real wife beater?" I jumped when Nellie's hand slammed the table. "Jesus, Charlotte, what the hell do you call this? An accident? For someone so smart, you're really thick-headed sometimes." I backed up another step. I'd never heard anyone talk to Mother that way. Even when Daddy was mad, he never said anything like that, but mostly he didn't say anything.

"How can you..." Mother was practically sputtering.

"Oh, shut up and listen." I clapped my hand over my mouth to keep any sound from coming out. *No one* told Mother to shut up—ever. "I will *not* be shackled to the gas range in that miserable restaurant the rest of my life just to make his life easier. If he thinks I will, he's got another think coming. The way I see it, if I take the hotel job he'll be unhappy. If I don't take the hotel job, I'll be unhappy. If one of us is going to be unhappy, it might as well be him." Aunt Nellie slammed her mug down on the table and shoved her chair back. It was time to become visible.

"Good morning. Should I wake Jackie up?" Nellie stormed out of the kitchen. "Good morning, Aunt Nellie." I didn't expect an answer, and I didn't get one.

"Come and get your breakfast. Your aunt Nellie will take care of Jackie. I'm not sure what their plans are today." That was that. I ate breakfast and went out to catch the bus to school. That's why I stoop to eavesdropping—no one tells me anything.

I love school, and now that I have a best friend, I even love the recess part. Today was different. I was itching to tell Betty all about what was happening with Aunt Nellie, but I wasn't sure about it. After all, what if she thought my family had wife-beaters in it. Well, strictly speaking it did. How did that reflect on the rest of us? Mother always said that whenever I misbehaved, people thought that she must not know how to raise a child because the child misbehaved. If that's true, then the ripples spread from there. If Mother didn't know how to raise a child that behaved, it was because *her* mother never taught her. So...it made Grandmother look bad, and all the aunts and uncles could be bad, too.

How far might the ripples go out if one person does bad things? The theory doesn't make sense, but if people *believe* it, then they *will* think it's my mother's fault if I do something wrong, and her mother's fault, etc. I didn't even open my book on the way to school. I thought I'd discovered something important. The truth isn't always as important as what people *believe* is true. So, even if it makes no sense, my behavior does reflect on my entire family. That's a lot of responsibility.

I'm going to wait before I tell Betty. After all, telling about a dog is one thing, but family members are something different. Besides, I don't know the end of the story yet. I'll wait until I know what happens next.

When I got home, Mother didn't even ask what I learned in school today. She told me to go to my room and do homework. I didn't argue because she had that tight-lipped look that meant she was in a bad mood.

I don't have any homework today, so I'm using the time to write.

I've decided to change my name to Charli. First of all, Charlotte Anne is too long. All the people I like the best have shorter names like Betty and Jackie and Nellie. Secondly, I know mother gave me her name so I'd be just like her, but I'd rather be me.

OCTOBER 22, 1950: - Yesterday was Saturday, and I thought nothing much was going to happen until I saw Aunt Nellie in the kitchen working on something I just knew would be delicious. Jackie and I were shooed out of the kitchen. Mother was busy putting out her good China cups, but we followed her around asking questions until we learned that all the women of the family were coming for coffee.

"Is Auntie Stell driving?" When she has to take the bus, she's always late. I don't know why Auntie Stell hates driving over the bridge from Oakland to San Francisco. It seems to me that driving is a lot like coloring. Once you get old enough to stay in the lines, it should be easy. Besides, I can swim. Summer camp had to be good for something.

"Yes, Stell's driving." Mother gave a short laugh. "She wasn't going to come at all until Nellie promised to make a cake." I'd drive over the bridge for Aunt Nellie's cake, too. In fact, Jackie and I offered to dust—just to make sure Mother noticed how good we were. It didn't pay to take chances when something as good as Aunt Nellie's cake was at stake.

When the doorbell rang, Jackie and I were hustled into my room with promises of cake later. We sat and played cards. Jackie said she was too nervous to read, and I was sympathetic. I told Jackie that I thought her mother should find a way to do her pastry thing in the hotel in the mornings and work in the restaurant in the evenings when most of the customers come to eat. "That way she can bake her cake and eat it too." I thought that was terribly clever, but I don't think Jackie got it.

The cake was delicious, but not nearly as good as the wedding cake. Maybe Mother didn't have all the ingredients, and Aunt Nellie had other things on her mind. I was sorry to miss all the discussion going on in the living room, but it was worth it to be with Jackie again. I can see this whole thing is hard on her. Her mother and Al argue all the time, and she never knows from one day to the next if they're getting a divorce.

Aunt Nellie decided to go back to Al and try to work things out. I was astonished when I heard that the women suggested the same compromise I'd thought of, but none of them said anything clever about it.

➤➤ 🕐 🕑 2013 🕒 🕓 ◄◄

It was almost dawn before the phone rang, but I still caught it on the first ring. "Kate, what's wrong?"

"Everything." Her voice was so low I had to strain to make out the words. "George lost his job, and the doctor I was working for fired me when I came in with a black eye. We're living on credit cards, and he won't stay sober long enough to get another job." She started crying, which made it even harder to understand her.

"Do you want me to send money?" I knew it was the wrong thing to do even as I offered, but it was all that came to mind. I don't care what David thinks, how else can he explain that the women in the family attract all the drunks, and deadbeats? Kate deserved better than that.

"No, he'll find it and drink it up." Smart girl. "I need to

leave, but I don't know how."

"I'll send you a ticket."

"No. If he knows I called you, he'll be furious, and God knows what he'll do."

"Do you have anyone you can trust? A neighbor, a priest?"

"No."

"Give me your address and I'll come and get you."

"Oh, Auntie, I can't let you do that."

"Of course you can, sweetheart. Just hang in there for a couple more days." I took down her address and was starting to give her my cell number when she interrupted.

"I hear his footsteps. Bye."

I packed quickly and began to research flights to Houston. I'd already missed check-in time for the first flight out. The next one was late afternoon. I called David to tell him where I was going.

"Kate's in Houston, and she needs my help."

"How'd you find her?"

"Dumb luck and tears. She called me at five this morning. She sounds desperate."

"Have you bought your ticket?"

"No, I can't decide if I want to arrive tonight or tomorrow morning. When's her husband less likely to be violent? When he's drunk or when he's hung over?"

"Oh, I see. Hold off for an hour or so. Let me check my appointments, and I'll let you know when I can pick you up."

I'd been hoping he'd offer to drive me to the airport. "Thanks, David."

≫ TWELVE ≪

NOVEMBER 23, 1950: - Today is Thanksgiving. We were going to go to San Diego, but the trip was cancelled at the last minute because Daddy's on duty all weekend. The good news is that he's saving up his leave and we're going on a trip for Christmas. I was afraid we'd be all alone on Thanksgiving, but we went to see Grandmother and Grandpa Sam.

I'd been hearing bits of phone conversation, and got the idea that Aunt Nellie and Al aren't doing so well trying to work it out. Today while the women were cleaning the kitchen Grandmother was talking to Mother, and I found out that Al told Nellie that if she didn't want to share in the work of the restaurant, that meant she didn't want to share her life with him because the restaurant *is* his life. She said that if all there was to his life was his restaurant, then he was right and she'd help him pack up his things. When Mother asked if he'd gone back to live with his mother, Grandmother laughed and said that Al was so surprised by Nellie's reaction that he'd tried to pretend he was joking. They're still living together.

Then Grandpa Sam came in and turned on the radio, and we all started listening to the radio news. There's a huge storm that's dumping tons of snow all over the east coast. The news is calling it the Great Thanksgiving Storm. It's blocking roads and everything, and they expect it to keep snowing.

When I was in the first grade we spent a year in Rhode Island, and there was a lot of snow. I remember how it looked, but I can't remember making a snowman. Too bad it doesn't snow here.

➤➤ ⏱ ⏲ 1965 ⏲ ⏱ ◄◄

It wasn't much of a journal entry, but I wasn't much in the mood to read. I was trying not to think about Jamal. It's hard *not* to think about something. Guido still hadn't called. Just as I thought about it, the phone rang. I jammed the journal into a drawer and went running. Of course Aunt Nellie had already answered and was talking, or rather listening. She kept nodding her head. Then she said we'd be ready, and hung up.

"Ready for what?"

"We're going to a funeral. Let's go find something suitable to wear."

"Who died?"

"Your husband." I was shocked. I couldn't say a word. "Guido says he'll explain when he picks us up." He didn't. We were hustled into a black car, and Guido handed me a handkerchief. He shook his head and motioned toward the driver, so I figured the driver wasn't part of the plan. Thinking of my own bleak future, it was easy to shed tears. I didn't think Guido would want his handkerchief back.

We drove to a church. The service was almost over when we slipped in and joined the worshippers. We blended into the somber congregation, and the coffin covered with wreaths and flowers left no doubt that this was a funeral mass. When mass was over, the priest and altar boys walked down the aisle followed by a matched set of young men carrying the coffin, and finally the rest of us left. Guido took my elbow and moved us out of the stream of mourners for a few steps after we exited the front door. We got back into the car and joined the procession to the cemetery. I haven't been to many funerals, and being surrounded by all the grief-stricken family members kept my tears flowing.

After the funeral, Guido came to the house with us and dismissed the car. I kicked off my high heels as soon as I got through the door. "I'm lucky I didn't sprain an ankle trying to walk through that cemetery in these."

"You did fine, Charli." Guido loosened his tie and sat on the sofa. I hurried to my room to take off the borrowed hat and dress before I spilled something on it. Aunt Nellie disappeared into the kitchen. By the time I came back, the smell of coffee was beckoning.

"How does it feel to be a widow, Charli?"

"A little confusing since I still don't know who my husband is, I mean was."

"I don't know who was in the box. My friend only said it would be a nice funeral with a lot of Italians, and…" He handed me an envelope from his inside pocket. "if you're going to bury your Lombardi husband, you gotta expect lots of Italians at the funeral."

I opened the envelope and pulled out its contents. "Aunt Nellie, come and look. It's a marriage license for Nellie B. Forast and Alberto Lombardi, and it's dated six months ago."

"Looks like you guys didn't waste no time gettin' a biscuit in the oven."

I stifled an embarrassed giggle. If Mother were in the

room, she'd be telling him not to be crude. "I still don't see how this is going to help. I mean, if I try to get a new passport under the name Nellie Lombardi, but my old one says Charlotte Anne Forast, won't they reject it? I mean, the first names don't even come close. Why didn't you change the first name?"

"The more changes you make, the more obvious the doctoring. Lucky that Nellie kept Willis's name and it was short. We left the big first letter, so you got a middle initial." He was pointing to the B. "Getting a first name changed is a piece of cake—and you have the best cake maker in the world right here in this room."

"I would never ask Bill—"

"To do anything illegal. I know, Nellie, neither would I. Charli fills out the application for a name change, and the judge signs it. He can hold a closed hearing and expedite the process because her life is being threatened. It's all perfectly legal."

"But the dates..."

"Let me worry about the dates. That's the easy part."

My head was whirling with all this. My respect for Guido grew. It may not all be strictly legal, but he had put together an amazing process in a remarkably short time. "Thank you seems pretty inadequate."

"When the biscuit comes out of the oven, just have him call me Uncle Guido. On second thought, you should call me Uncle Guido. He can call me Grandpa."

I still wasn't convinced it would work, but now I had hope. I hugged Guido and kissed his cheek. "Thanks, Uncle Guido."

He spoke quietly into my ear. "Tell your Auntie Stell that there's more than one way of joinin' the family." He stretched and gave a mighty yawn. "And now, ladies, I'm going to stretch out on this here sofa and take a little nap while the two of you go off and make yourselves beautiful, not that either one of you need much help in that department. We still have a wedding to attend tonight."

"Whose wedding?" I was almost afraid to ask.

"My nephew, Alberto, is marrying the lovely Nellie B. Forast. We'll miss the ceremony, but the reception makes a great excuse for a party." With that he gave me a wink and a gentle shove off the sofa, stretched out, and closed his eyes.

Another car came for us when it was time to go to the party. "Uncle" Guido opened the door next to the driver and motioned for me to enter. Then he and Aunt Nellie got in the back. The driver was young and very good looking. He grinned at me, and I smiled back.

"Didn't I tell you, Tony? Didn't I say we'd have the prettiest girls at the party?"

Tony looked embarrassed as he started the engine. "I'm happy to meet you."

"I'm Charli."

I didn't expect to enjoy the party. Between the funeral that morning and what was waiting for me in less than two weeks, how could I? Tony was about as different from Guido as possible. I couldn't believe it, but Tony and I got along well, and I was having fun. The fact that Auntie Stell and Jackie and her husband were there, too, helped.

About an hour into the party, Guido said something in Tony's ear. I pretended I didn't notice because I didn't want to hear another one of his comments about this being the best blind date Tony was ever likely to have. A few minutes later, Tony grabbed my hand and said we were going to have our picture taken. We went to the dining room and there was a wedding cake on the table, complete with a tiny bride and groom on the top.

"It's not up to Nellie's standards, but it's the best we could do." I was speechless. We had a couple of pictures taken. Then my relatives showed up, and there were more pictures. Guido poured some champagne and we had our own private party. The photographer said it wouldn't be a wedding without a shot of the bride and groom kissing. I'm pretty sure Tony enjoyed it as much as I did. When the photographer left, everyone else went back to the main party, but Tony took me out in the backyard.

"Some men can be real sons of bitches." His language startled me, but he looked sincere. "Uncle Guido told me your ex is a real horse's ass."

"Yes, he just won't let me go."

"You really think wedding pictures are going to change his mind?"

"I hope so." We found a bench and sat in silence. He put an arm around my shoulders. I felt comfortable and safe.

"I gotta tell you, Charli, I felt real funny in there. I mean cutting the cake and all. It was kind of scary, but part of me wished it was real." Then he kissed me again. I guess part of me wished the same thing. I got all teary eyed when I had to say goodbye at the end of the evening. "Thanks, Tony. You made tonight very special. I'll never forget what you did for me."

"Can I see you again? Maybe we could go to a movie or something?"

I shook my head and a tear escaped. "I'm leaving town."

Late that night I was still crying into my pillow. Why had I let him kiss me? Why had I wanted him to kiss me again? I didn't even know him. I'd never been attracted to boys like him. Well, maybe for a brief moment in high school when I'd pined for a James Dean bad boy. I guess the whole wedding thing made me wish for something else. I knew better. I knew that if the wedding had been real, our future would have been an apartment in a tenement, crowded with unruly kids. Our evenings would end in shouting matches more often than not. Not to mention that he was at least five years too young, and his grammar was iffy at best.

I turned the light back on and reached for the journal.

≫ ☉ ☉ ☉ ☉ ≪

JANUARY 7, 1951: - Daddy got leave for Christmas vacation and we went to visit his parents. His family is so different from Mother's family that I don't think Mother was comfortable. Granddaddy's very funny. He's a small man, and his hands shake so much that Grammy only pours him a half a cup of coffee at a time, but he and Daddy laugh together a lot. They have some really funny stories. Grammy is taller than he is. It's too bad we don't get to see them very often.

Christmas Eve was the best part of the whole visit. After dinner, we all went to sit in the parlor (that's what Grammy calls her living room). The Christmas tree had *real candles* and Grammy lit them and turned off the lights. It was so much fun! We sat near the tree and sang Christmas carols and Granddaddy told us funny Christmas stories from when Daddy was a little boy. Most of the stories were about presents they gave each other when they didn't have any money at all.

"Remember the year we almost got kicked out of church?" I could see by Mother's face that she was as shocked as I was. What had they done to get kicked out of church? "It was all her fault." Granddaddy was pointing at his wife. "She couldn't keep her mouth shut. She was yakking at me something fierce until Father Murphy stopped the mass." Grammy blushed and got up to get more eggnog.

Daddy was laughing again. "We were sitting in the front row, and she called Dad an s.o.b., and Father Murphy heard it. He told her to go wait in the confessional and he'd listen to her confession as soon as mass was over."

Grammy was back with her eggnog. "My great-grandmother's brooch was missing, and I was sure he'd sold it to buy another damned piece of equipment."

"Well, you never wore it. In all the years we'd been married you never wore it."

"It was the Great Depression. People were hungry. I couldn't go around wearing something like that when our neighbors were hungry."

"He sold the brooch?" Mother had very clear unbreakable rules about her jewelry. No one *ever* opened her jewelry box or her purse.

"No, the kids took it."

"Robert and I didn't even know it existed. It was Mary. She knew you never wore it, not even to church or weddings or anything. She thought you forgot about it."

"How could I forget the most precious thing I had?"

Daddy shrugged. He turned to Mother. "We didn't have any money. We ate beans three or four nights a week, if we were lucky. When we weren't lucky, we lined up at the church soup kitchen like everyone else. Mary got this bright idea that we could wrap up the wonderful brooch that Mother had forgotten about, and give it to her for Christmas. We were kids, what did we know?"

"I've never been so humiliated in my life. I had to walk over to the confessional in front of all our friends and neighbors. I could hear them snickering."

"When Ma got up and started walking, Mary got up and walked behind her. Then Robert got up. I didn't know why, but I knew I had to go too." I could just picture Daddy following his big sister and brother toward the confessional.

Granddaddy shrugged exactly like Daddy. "Hells' bells. I couldn't just sit there like a bump on the log and let my whole family take the walk. I got up and followed the rest of them." Even Grammy was laughing again.

"Remember the year we got that big contract from the city? That was the year I got you all the most expensive Christmas presents I could find." Granddaddy looked at Grammy. "Remember? I got you the pearl necklace and earrings?"

"Oh yes, I remember. The necklace was missing in the morning. Lucky for me I'd forgotten to take the earrings off when I went to sleep that night, and the burglar couldn't take them without waking me up." They all laughed, but it didn't sound funny.

"And you got Robert and me that fancy Lionel train set." Daddy was laughing so hard he could hardly get the sentence out. When they stopped laughing, Daddy explained that Granddaddy's big contract was cancelled on Christmas Eve, but the presents were already under the tree and he couldn't sneak them out of the house. He had run up huge bills to get the equipment for that contract, and he knew someone would be coming after him if he couldn't pay. He needed the money he'd spent, so he hid the presents on Christmas night after everyone else was asleep. He pawned them the next morning, but he didn't want the family to know that, so he told them the presents had been stolen.

Daddy laughed so hard he had to wipe the tears from his eyes. "It would've worked, too, except that I walked past the pawn shop a couple of days later and saw the train set in the window. I went running home to tell Dad there was a train set in McGivney's Pawn Shop that he could buy for us. He wasn't home from work yet, so I told Ma because I was worried they'd sell it to someone else."

"Damn, that woman was smart," said Granddaddy. "She made Frank stay home, and ran right down to talk to old McGivney. It didn't take her long to worm out of him that I'd hocked the train set and her pearl necklace, too." They all started laughing again. Granddaddy slapped his thigh and shook his head. "Those were the days, weren't they? Chicken one day and feathers the next."

"You ate feathers?" I asked, and it started them all laughing again. Mother said they should have saved some of the money when they had it.

"But then we might never have had any fun, because we never knew when we'd have money again. It all depended on the contracts. We had to enjoy it while we had it."

"And we sure had some fun, didn't we?" Grammy was still chuckling when she turned on the lights and started blowing out the candles.

Mother looked at her watch. "Oh, look at the time. It's way past your bedtime, young lady." She started pushing me toward the door.

"She can't go to bed now." Grammy stopped her. "It's time to get ready for church. We always go to midnight mass on Christmas."

Mother started to argue, but Daddy said it was a Christmas tradition, and Grammy would be upset if Mother broke it. So, I got to go to midnight mass! That was the first time I ever stayed up past the middle of the night. I might have nodded off during the sermon, but lots of people nod off when Father Donnelly says mass at home.

When we got home from church, Grammy said they always opened presents after church. She handed me a small box. It was a Mickey Mouse watch. I asked her if I could wear it to school and she said I could. It was a great Christmas.

When we got home I learned that Aunt Nellie and Jackie spent Christmas with Grandmother and Grandpa Sam. I haven't heard anything definite, but I'm sure Aunt Nellie's working on another divorce.

⏱ ⏰ 2013 ⏲ ⏱

"Dammit! I forgot to reserve a rental car. See what happens when you get old? You can't handle disruptions in the process. You said you bought the ticket, and I put the whole thing in the done column and took a nap."

"Not to worry. I took care of it."

"You're an angel."

"Did Kate say anything about losing her grandmother?"

"I'm not sure she knows."

"You didn't ask?"

"I didn't have a chance. I didn't even have time to give her my cell number." I related the conversations.

"What do you know about her husband?"

"Nothing much. I met him when I was there for Jackie's funeral." Even after four years I had trouble talking about it. "I wasn't impressed, but he seemed okay. I think he caught her on the rebound after her divorce. At the time I was glad she had someone. I spent my time with Aunt Nellie, who was a basket case. To be honest, I don't think any of us handed it well."

"You were there for almost a month. You must have more than just an impression."

"David, I'd just lost my twin—"

"Cousin."

"—and I wasn't inspecting my niece's new husband."

"Sorry."

"I do remember that he said they'd have to sell the house because Kate couldn't live there any more. It might have meant he didn't have much of a job."

David didn't say anything, and my thoughts went skittering back to Aunt Nellie. I'd taken care of all the nasty paperwork that lingered after an accidental death. Jackie didn't have a will, and I'd worked with Robert Aldeman to make things as painless as possible. It was more tedious than difficult since Kate was an only child. I could still hear Aunt Nellie's voice, pleading with me to stay, as much for Kate as for herself. I was tempted, but then Susan had written to say they'd found the perfect house for me. She was overwhelmed with things and could really use my help. Having Kate and her husband move in with Aunt

Nellie seemed like the perfect solution.

Every time I picked up a pen to write to Nellie or Kate, I'd remember Jackie and all I could get out would be a couple of meaningless sentences. I'd called a few times, but it made Aunt Nellie cry to talk to me. I shouldn't have let it happen, but I did. I told myself that they had bushels of relatives around them. I didn't even know when Kate moved out of Nellie's house.

My thoughts came back to the present as David took the turnoff to the parking lot. "You don't have to park. Just drop me at the terminal. I can manage the bag. It has wheels."

"I got two tickets. I'm going with you."

"David, I don't need a babysitter. I was negotiating international airports before you were born, and I can follow a GPS once I'm on the ground. Don't be silly. You have things to do here."

"Mom, it's not about you. I'm going for Kate."

Mother, God rest her little soul, often told me that if I didn't have anything to say, I should keep quiet. She didn't follow her own advice, but I tried to—when I remembered in time. We made small talk through the check in and it wasn't until we had reached cruising altitude and the captain had turned off the seat belt sign that David got serious.

"Mom, remember when I was little and we used to have 'grown-up' trips?"

"I remember." In spite of my anger, a smile tugged at my lips. It had started as a way to make him behave on those interminable flights, but turned into a lot more.

"You used to tell me that we were so high and going so fast, that the words would be lost in the clouds by the time we landed — no questions, no memories, no embarrassment."

"The precursor of 'what happens in Vegas.'"

"You know how you and Jackie always talked about being twins?" I nodded. "You also told me that you barely survived your premature birth, and your mother never managed to carry a child to term. Aunt Nellie never had any other children either."

"Where are you going with this?"

"Well, I've been thinking about all the pieces." His words slowed to a jerky crawl. "I just thought that maybe, if two sisters couldn't have children, that maybe one of them might befriend a girl in trouble, and if that girl happened to have twins..."

"David, I don't know what gave you that idea, but in a word, no." I had to laugh. This was so unlike David. "If you must know, we're only half cousins, if there is such a thing. Mother and Aunt Nellie had different fathers."

"But that's the only explanation."

"Explanation for what?"

"I'd rather not talk about it."

"Remember the rules, no evasions and only truth-telling."

"Some things a guy can't talk about with his mother."

"On a grown-up trip we're friends. You can't have rules that only work one way." He nodded and looked out the window. I could see he was struggling. "Written on the clouds, remember?"

"A long time ago Kate and I wanted to get married."

"*Married*? You couldn't get married — you're cousins."

"That's exactly what Aunt Jackie said. She said our children would be monsters, or stillborn, or something."

"I'd have said the same thing. Why're you so upset? You said it was a long time ago."

"You'd've said the same thing? Why would you lie to us? Was there another reason you didn't want us to get married?"

It took me a couple of minutes to catch up with his thinking. "David, we were brought up in a different world. It was a world without search engines or internet, and the highest authority we could access were teachers and nuns. We were taught that cousins shouldn't marry, and we never questioned it."

"God damn it!" David's face was pale, and I thought there were tears in his eyes before he turned toward the window.

"Can I get you anything?" The flight attendant probably headed our way because of his outburst, but our faces changed her mind.

"My son's lost a dear friend. I think he could use a glass of — "

"Scotch, if you have it," said David. I gave her my sweetest little-old-lady smile, held up two fingers and extended a credit card. The drinks came in record time. David downed his and reached for mine. I handed it to him. "As much as I want to lash out and blame you and Aunt Nellie, the hell of it is, we didn't question it either." He finished my drink and pressed the call button for another round.

This time I kept a firm grip on my drink. We didn't speak again until the meal had been cleared away, and we had coffee. "Did you know that twenty-six states allow first cousins to marry — and West Virginia isn't one of them? Or that an estimated one-fifth of the marriages in the world are between first cousins? Hell, we aren't even full second cousins, and second cousins can get married anywhere."

"No, I didn't know that." The coffee looked and smelled like Georgia swamp water. I wished I'd asked for tea. "What made you tell me?" It took so long I thought he wasn't going to answer.

"Yesterday I was feeling trapped by my life with Susan, and today I found out that Kate's life was a lot more miserable. The more I thought about it, the more I was filled with anger, sadness, and God knows what other emotions. It overwhelmed me. I couldn't handle the thought that things might have been different."

I reached over and put my hand on his. Are mothers allowed to do that? He didn't pull away. "You can't look back. You were so young, you don't know what might have happened."

After a minute he patted my hand and turned to me with a surprising smile. "Maybe I told you so you wouldn't be shocked if I kissed her with more fervor than you expect."

>> THIRTEEN <<

Two days after my "wedding," Guido called and invited himself to dinner. Aunt Nellie called him a rascal, but promised a good Italian meal. He showed up with a camera and a guest — Tony.

"I knew you'd have plenty of food." Guido seemed to fill the room with his boisterous presence and good humor. Tony hung back. Maybe he was embarrassed when he realized he hadn't been expected, or maybe he was just shy.

"Hi, Tony. I'm glad you came." As soon as I said it, I knew it was true.

"Here you go." Guido tossed two fat envelopes onto the coffee table. "I made two sets. Wanna look?" I sat on the floor opposite Guido, and Tony sank down beside me, leaving room on the sofa for Aunt Nellie. Guido opened the envelope with a flourish. "I figure Charli's a nice girl, right? So we can't have a weddin' without a courtship. Presto — a day at the beach." He pulled out some snapshots.

I looked at the pictures. One of the guys at the party was Tony, and he was never far from her. The girl's face was never clear. Sometimes she was looking the other way, sometimes wearing a floppy hat, once kissing Tony. "That's not me."

"It's a girl I used to know. I already had the pictures, so I loaned them to Uncle Guido."

"Pretty smart kid, ain't he?" There were a couple of

other pictures of the two of them in other settings—all with the girl's face in shadow or hidden. "After a decent courtship, we get the wedding." He opened the next packet of pictures and spread them out for us to view.

"That's a great shot." Aunt Nellie pointed to the picture of Tony and me feeding each other a bite of wedding cake and laughing too hard to swallow.

"I like that one." Tony's voice was meant for my ears only. His eyes went to the close-up of the wedding kiss. I felt my cheeks get hot. His hand brushed mine and the warmth spread. I moved away.

Guido pulled out a few newspaper clippings. One was a properly-dated wedding announcement, complete with a photo of the smiling couple. The other was an entry in the obituary section. "How did you do that?"

"Tricks of the trade, sweetheart, tricks of the trade." He pulled out a smaller packet of photos. They showed Guido holding my elbow to help me down the church steps, Aunt Nellie on one side and Guido on the other at the gravesite, and a few long shots of the large gathering of mourners.

"Who died?" Tony hadn't known about the funeral.

"I guess you did 'cause the obit says she's now a widow."

"Why? I understand she wants wedding pictures to warn off her ex, but a funeral would mean she's available again, wouldn't it?"

"She don't have to send the ex all the pictures. Some day she might want to marry a good Catholic boy. She'd have to show she wasn't divorced, wouldn't she?"

"I guess." The logic had a huge hole in it, but Guido shepherded us into the kitchen before Tony had time to think it through.

"Come on, we need some pictures of the happy couple fixing dinner for Uncle Guido and Aunt Nellie."

"I can't even pronounce some of these things, let alone cook them."

"Nothing wrong with living in make believe for a few hours, is there?" said Aunt Nellie. Her wind chime laugh harmonized with Guido's baritone and Tony's tenor.

Aunt Nellie outdid herself. I'd never had a meal with so many courses. We all laughed as I tried to memorize the names. First came the antipasti, which was some beets marinated in vinegar and a dish called caponata with eggplant, capers, and sweet tomatoes, and other good things. Next came a course called the primi. It was a small serving of pasta with a fresh tomato sauce, a hint of creamy ricotta, and thinly sliced fresh basil. The next course was what I would have called dinner. The meat was pork called porchetta with a rosemary crust, so tender I could cut with my fork. It melted in my mouth. It was served with fresh spinach, sautéed with red pepper and garlic. There were fried artichokes, and some kind of beans with olive oil and sage. They called those contorni. The dessert was homemade tiramisu made with thick mascarpone crème, infused with marsala wine. I will never stop marveling over Aunt Nellie's abilities. Nothing like this was ever on the menu at Al's restaurant.

Guido said he thought he'd died and gone to heaven. Tony agreed. We ate until we couldn't hold another bite, even though our mouths wanted more. Tony and I said we'd do the cleanup. Guido got some great shots of Tony with dish suds up to his elbows and me clowning around with the dishtowel. While we were cleaning up, the phone rang, and Nellie took it in the bedroom. She came out smiling.

"Good news?"

"Just a friend, Guido. I said I'd call him back."

"Sounds like our cue to leave, Tony."

As soon as I closed the door behind the two men, I felt like a bucket of cold water had been thrown over me. Aunt Nellie disappeared into the bedroom, and I put the kettle on for tea.

"Good news, Charli, Bill says he processed your request for a name change today. He's going to bring it over tomorrow night. Once it gets to Guido, he'll get the date fixed, and you'll be all set."

"Aunt Nellie, I'm so grateful for all the things you've done. I can't believe you put together a whole new identity for me. We actually have a plan for me to get away."

"Then why don't you sound excited? Something else bothering you?"

"I had more fun tonight than I ever had before."

"Don't tell me having fun bothers you."

"It's Tony. I really like him. Even scrubbing pots was fun. Every time he touched me, I felt it. I mean I really felt it."

"So? He's a nice boy."

"That's just it. He's a boy. He's at least five years younger than I am; he has no education; he probably hasn't read a book since high school, which wasn't that long ago. We have nothing in common, and shouldn't be attracted to each other at all, but we are."

"You have a lot in common, you're both young and healthy. I know this isn't something you ever heard at home, but love and sex are two different things. If you hit the jackpot, they come together. Your reaction is a good thing."

"How can it be good?"

"Did you think of Jamal this evening?" I shook my head. Other than thinking that my fake wedding looked a lot more real than the real one, I hadn't. "Sometimes removing the usual constraint of fear of pregnancy…"

"It can't end well if it goes any further."

"I don't know about that. It could end with you having the time of your life, if you let yourself go with your feelings."

"Oh, Aunt Nellie." Her cheerful laughter followed me to my room. I knew I had to get up for work in the morning, but I still reached for the journal.

≫≻ ⊕ ⊙ ⊙ ⊙ ≺≪

JANUARY 20, 1951: - It was Saturday, and the women were coming over. After hearing that Aunt Nellie was getting another divorce, I was surprised to see her laughing and happy when she swept into the house this morning with a new fur stole flung over one shoulder. I couldn't believe how well the stole matched her hair. It looked as though her own hair had been made into a stole. And then I saw the little heads and a tiny paw next to the head. Aunt Nellie was wearing dead foxes! Mother was already asking questions — like where did it come from, and how long had she been keeping *that* a secret.

"I'll tell you all about it when the others get here."

"Where's Jackie?"

"JJ's daughter took her to the zoo today."

Lucky Jackie went to the zoo. Who was JJ? I could tell by Mother's raised eyebrows that she didn't know either. I disappeared into my room to find a book to hide behind. I had to choose my seat carefully. It had to be out of the line of sight of the women, and it had to look casual. I decided to get my social studies book, and encyclopedia volumes covering Colonial America, the American Revolution, the growth of the United States. That was enough to justify the use of the dining room table. I would draw a series of maps of the United States from colonial times to the Gold Rush. That should take time, and get an extra credit mark for social studies (my least favorite subject). I love to kill more than one bird with one stone.

Speaking of killing...I thought about the dead foxes again. They looked rather sad as they dangled from the stole with their beady little glass eyes. Why did I think that was so terrible? I loved the feel of Aunt Nellie's mink, and I would stroke it any time I got close enough. If the minks had heads, would I still like the coat? I grabbed another volume of the encyclopedia and looked up "mink" to see if I could figure out how many of them it took to make a full-length coat.

I got my ruler and went into Mother's closet to see how big her winter coat was. By the time I came out of the closet, the women were already deep in conversation. Now how was I going to find out who JJ was? I sat hunched over the encyclopedia, but I couldn't read a word. I wished I could turn my ears like elephants do to get the sound to go in better.

"I still say it's wrong. You'd be deliberately going into sin." That was Mother's voice.

"Oh, grow up, Charlotte." Even if I hadn't recognized the voice, I'd have known it was Aunt Nellie. "You talk a good game of holier-than-thou, but I don't see you at the altar rail taking communion every Sunday." Now that Nellie mentioned it, Mother never does take communion. She takes me to confession on Saturdays, but I don't remember her ever going up for communion—or Daddy either.

"Just be careful," said Auntie Stell. "Remember what happened to Rita. I must say, I can't figure out the lure of the wine tasting. I don't even like wine. Champagne is good because the bubbles kind of mask the taste, but regular wine, especially expensive wine, is wasted on me."

"Oh, no," said Mother. "Good wine is mellow and easy on the tongue." That wasn't what she told Daddy when he came home with a bottle of expensive wine for their anniversary. He said he didn't think they should celebrate with a gallon of Dago red, and Mother said he'd just paid for a fancy label. Maybe she'd changed her mind when she drank Daddy's wine. When I grow up, I'm never going to drink wine or coffee. I've tasted them both and I think they're vile. Of course, it's possible that they taste better to adults and I'll change my mind when I become an adult. Maybe that's God's way of making children not drink things that are bad for them.

The doorbell rang and conversation stopped while Mother answered the door. I heard Rita's voice all the way from the hallway. "Why doesn't anyone tell me anything? My aunt is on track to be my stepmother-in-law and no one mentions it to me?" So JJ must be Prince Charming's father!

"I'm sorry, sweetie," said Nellie.

"Do you know how humiliating it was to hear it from Richard's little sister? When she came to the house she had Jackie with her. I was so surprised that she knew I was totally in the dark. It was awful. How could you do that to me?"

"Rita, I never dreamed you'd end up in an awkward situation. Whatever possessed that girl to go visit you today?"

"I had a doctor's appointment and the new rocking chair I was expecting hadn't been delivered yet. I called her to come and wait for the delivery."

"A doctor's appointment? Are you all right?"

"I'm pregnant, or hadn't you noticed? I have regular appointments. Now answer my questions."

"Rita, you weren't supposed to know. She said she'd take Jackie to the zoo."

"*Why* wasn't I supposed to know? I'm the one in the family most likely to be affected by it."

"That's exactly why, dear. This whole thing just happened — it wasn't planned or thought out by either one of us. Believe me, if I told you the whole story you'd see — it was just happpenstance."

"Then *tell* me the whole story. You owe me that much. You definitely owe me the complete story."

"I've only just finished telling everyone."

"We don't mind hearing it again," said Auntie Stell. "It's a great story." I felt like cheering. I was going to hear the story after all.

"There isn't much to tell really. I was just organizing the work for the day when JJ marched into the kitchen. To borrow a phrase from Mama, he was wearing his thunder face. I was grumpy already because I hadn't had my coffee yet. I had a lot to do and no time for nonsense. He stuck his nose in my face and demanded that I wear a hair net. I had my hair all tucked up under my chef's hat. What did he think the chef's hat was for? I'm a professional, and I know better than to let my hair get into the pastries."

"What did you say?"

"I told him I was an artist, not some frump serving prison food or a school cafeteria worker. I said that if he wanted donuts and pound cake, he could hire someone with a hairnet. Then I pulled off my chef's hat and gave him the full hair toss. 'You want me to put *this* in a hairnet?' Then I unbuttoned my white smock and took it off. 'Find someone with a hairnet. I wanted another hour's sleep anyway.' I was wearing that red dress with the plunging neckline and the matching heels." Her laugh floated over the clink of coffee cups. "His eyes nearly popped out of his head." Nellie gave a lower laugh. "That wasn't all that was popping out. He pulled his jacket closed to hide it, but you can always tell, can't you?" I am definitely growing up. I understood what Aunt Nellie meant when she said JJ's eyes weren't all that popped out.

"What did he say then? And why were you dressed up in your best dress in the kitchen so early in the morning?"

"If you must know, I was dressed for a noon appointment with my divorce lawyer. But when JJ cleared his throat and said, 'Perhaps we can discuss this further over lunch,' I changed the lawyer's appointment for dinner instead." Even though the women had heard the story earlier, they still laughed. "At lunch, I told him that as a true artist, I had to be myself in the kitchen. I had to look my best to feel my best to do my best work."

"You're an artist all right, a con artist. Did he buy it?"

"Sure did, but as soon as the words were out of my mouth, I thought I'd shot myself in the foot with that one, and I'd have to wear heels every day. But it turned out to be a really good move, because I started having lunch with

JJ more and more often. Now he calls me his foxy lady—and I have the stole to prove it."

"So my father-in-law's been dating you for ages? And I just hear about it today, and by accident? Is that right?"

"I don't think you should call it dating, but other than that I suppose that's right."

"I meant was that the right thing for you to do? How could you date my father-in-law without telling me?"

"I told you. We aren't dating. It's just a harmless flirtation. After all, he's a married man."

"And you're a married woman." Mother jumped in with the obvious. Aunt Nellie ignored her.

"You accepted his gift. Aunt Nellie, I'm shocked. You're the one who always told us never to accept a gift unless you're ready to pay the implied price. You're the one who always says never date the boss unless you're willing either to accept his terms or quit." Rita was still upset. "All of us girls came to you with our problems, and we listened to your advice. Now you're doing everything you told us never to do. Unless I've misjudged you and you *are* willing to accept what this implies?"

"Rita dear, good pastry chefs don't grow on trees. I think of the stole as a nontaxable benefit. He thinks my artistic temperament is cute. I'll be careful not to use it too often—just enough so he remembers he needs to keep me happy if he wants good work. Besides, I do follow my own advice. I *am* ready to quit if he expects more than good pastry and pleasant lunches. I enjoy the work, except for the early morning wake up part, but I don't really need to work. Pretty soon my divorce will come through, and I'll be just fine with Al's alimony check plus the child support I still get from Willis. I'm suing for a share of the profits from the restaurant, too." Does alimony last forever? If she keeps getting married and gets alimony from every husband, she could be rich.

"So if it's just a harmless flirtation, why the big meeting?"

"We don't have to have a reason. We enjoy getting together."

"That doesn't wash. I saw Mother's car out front. It takes more than a casual get-together for her to drive over the bridge." It took a second for me to remember that when Rita said "Mother," she meant Auntie Stell.

"All right, if you must know, I'm thinking about accepting an invitation for a weekend in wine country, and I just wanted to let the women know." What came next was too quiet for me to hear.

Then suddenly the women all started talking and the whole tone of the conversation shifted. I risked a peek and everyone was looking at Rita. Auntie Stell had her arms around Rita. Rita was crying!

Try as I might, there were too many voices for me to follow anything. I caught bits and snatches that I filed away to think about. Someone said she had to get home, and I realized I had nothing to show for all the time I'd been in the dining room. I knew Mother would look at my schoolwork when she had things cleared away, and I'd better have something to show her.

JANUARY 21, 1951: - I shouldn't have looked up mink and tried to picture them in a coat. I had a dream that I was wearing Mother's winter coat and wishing it was mink, and a whole swarm of minks came running. The first two climbed up the coat all the way to the top and settled on the collar. They wrapped their little tails around my neck and their fur was so soft I felt warm and cozy. Then other minks came and climbed up and arranged themselves all over the coat. I was happy that Mother got a mink coat and they didn't even have to die. I wanted to run and show her, but the minks had wrapped the coat so tight around my legs that I couldn't move. I woke up with my heart pounding and the blanket wrapped around my legs. Minks are carnivores. Good thing I woke up before they started biting. I don't think I ever want to stroke Aunt Nellie's coat again. It probably has little mink ghosts crawling all over it.

Mother says there's no such thing as ghosts, but when she said it Auntie Stell and Grandmother both started talking at once. Then Mother glared at them and they got quiet the same way they do when they start to talk about things I'm not supposed to know yet, like sex or childbirth. It makes me think that there really are ghosts, but I'm not supposed to know about them until I'm older. Could souls and ghosts be the same thing? They probably do exist because there are too many ghost stories not to have some truth. Anyway, they have a better chance of being real than Santa.

Mother says that only people have souls and go to heaven, but Betty's mother says there's a special heaven for dogs. She said the puppies that had to be put to sleep went to dog heaven. If there's a dog heaven, might there be a mink heaven? Thinking about the minks made me afraid to go back to sleep. I turned on the light and stuffed the crack under the door so the light wouldn't show. I read a few pages of my new library book about Edgar Allen Poe. That didn't make me feel any better. I got out my history book to read about early America until I felt sleepy, but I couldn't stop thinking about dog heaven.

Why would God keep dogs separate from people? Some people like their dogs more than they like other people, and I'm sure they'd rather be in dog heaven than have to live eternity with a lot of people. Mrs. Lafferty loves her cats a lot. She talks to them all the time. I think she'd like to go to cat heaven, or at least have her cats with her.

If there's a dog heaven, and then logically a cat heaven, where would it stop? I can't really imagine a mosquito heaven, but why would dogs have a heaven and not mosquitoes? Wouldn't it be funny if mosquito heaven was part of people hell?

We went to a late Mass and afterward Mother said that we were going to visit Auntie Stell so I could play with Sharon. I knew it was because she wanted to talk about what made Rita cry the day before. That was fine with me because Sharon might tell me more about what was happening.

As soon as we got in her room, Sharon started talking. "Rita's convinced that Dick (that's what she calls him now instead of Richard) stays late at the hotel for reasons other than work. She's in a terrible state because now she's about to have a baby, and the baby should have a father. We all feel really bad for her, but there's nothing we can do." Sharon was about to cry. "It was a fairy tale wedding, but they aren't living happily ever after. It's not fair." Sharon was right, it wasn't supposed to work this way.

"Come on. Let's get something to eat. Mother always says you feel better after you eat something." I took Sharon's hand and we went to the kitchen. I looked around for the plate of what she called her "factory rejects." There it was — the plate with cookies that were either broken or a little too brown on the edges. I brought the plate to the kitchen table and poured a glass of milk for each of us. Sharon didn't say anything, and I started listening to the talk from the living room.

"Why are we all accepting Rita's suspicions as true? We don't have any real proof. Did anyone ever stop to think that maybe things got away from him at work because he spent so much time with her before the wedding and during the honeymoon? Did anyone think that maybe, just maybe, he was trying to get a promotion now that he has a child on the way? Rita dear, this is your first pregnancy. A lot of women have serious mood swings, bouts of depression, strange changes of personality with pregnancy, especially the first. It's temporary." Aunt Nellie was trying to make Rita feel better.

"I am not crazy, temporary or not, and I resent what you're saying."

"I wasn't saying you were crazy; it's just hormones." I tried to remember the word to look it up later.

"You're not helping. Not one of you has said anything helpful. I don't know why I even came." Auntie Stell said something I didn't hear. "It's no use, Mom, I'm going home." It got very quiet. Sharon and I just looked at each other. The front door opened and closed. A shiver ran through my body. The curse had struck again.

"There's one way to settle this, isn't there?" Auntie Stell said. "We tail him a few evenings and see if he's working or dallying."

"We can't do that." Mother was shocked, as usual.

"Relax. I wasn't suggesting one of *us* tail him. I'll take care of it. I know a guy that owes me a favor. Now let's

216

have some coffee and hope Richard really is working hard for his family." I could hear Auntie Stell's footsteps coming toward the kitchen.

"Do you want help carrying the cookies?" I put on my wide-eyed innocent look.

"No. I want you two busybodies to get back in Sharon's room and amuse yourselves. I can see you already had your share of cookies."

"We only ate the rejects."

She shooed us out of the room like chickens.

The tap of high heels preceded Aunt Nellie's entrance. "I'll help, Stell. Are you really going to have Richard tailed?" Sharon and I froze in the hallway and listened.

"Yes. Guido will do it for me. With any luck, Rita will have to eat her words. If not, we'll have to cross that bridge then."

"I guess you're right. Guido's the man for the job. Let's just hope we're lucky because we all know how you feel about crossing bridges."

Sometimes living in our family is better than listening to the serials on the radio.

≫ FOURTEEN ≪

I went to sleep outraged by Aunt Nellie's suggestion about Tony, but I woke up thinking how much fun it would be to go to the movies with him. I knew it was a fantasy, but it cheered me up anyway. It was early afternoon when my supervisor poked her head out of her office and called me. "Your aunt is on the phone, and she sounds upset."

My mouth felt dry. This couldn't be good news. I croaked into the phone, "Aunt Nellie?"

"Charli, your mother called. She's frantic. She says there's a black car parked in front of the house, and it's been there for hours. I told her to ignore it, but she's really frightened. An hour later there was a car parked in front of our house, too. There's a man sitting inside. I don't know how long it's been here, but I'm worried. I don't think you should come home."

My knees felt weak. I grasped the edge of the desk and felt a chair being pushed against my knees. I sat. What was I doing dreaming of going to the movies like a giddy teenager? Jamal is a ruthless man, and now he's watching.

"What should I do?" I wrote down Jackie's phone number and hung up.

"What's wrong?"

"I got some bad news. Would it be all right if I use your phone for a local call?"

"Sure. Why don't I get you a drink of water?"

"That would be wonderful, Janice. Thanks." I dialed Jackie with unsteady hands. The phone rang and rang. Jamal had promised me two weeks. It hadn't been a week yet. One time years ago when I had a loose tooth, Daddy tied a string around it and told me he'd count to three and pull. He pulled after "one." I'd been angry and said he wasn't fair, but the tooth was out. Jamal was pulling the string after one week.

"Here's your water."

"Thanks, Janice. My cousin isn't home. May I come back a little later and try again?"

"Of course. Keep trying as long as it takes." I thanked her again and went back to my desk. At least I needed to look like I was working.

As the afternoon wore on, I got more and more worried. What if he'd had me followed? What if he knew where I worked? How would he kidnap me? Would it be violent? If I went to Jackie's house, could he follow me? Might someone else get hurt, like Jackie or Kate? If he wanted a baby so badly, he might even take Kate, too. What if the men didn't know exactly what I look like, and took both Jackie and me? My thoughts were spiraling out of control.

It was time to go home when I called Aunt Nellie. I didn't know where else to turn. The only other number I knew by heart would connect me with Mother. Then it came to me—how had they known to watch Aunt Nellie's house? Mother must have told them to make them leave her alone. When Nellie didn't answer, I burst into tears.

"What's wrong, Charli?" Janice handed me a tissue and sat on her heels in front of me. "Everyone else has gone home. We're the only ones in the office. You can talk to me. Is there anything I can do?"

My mind shifted into overtime. I barely had enough money for a meal, let alone a hotel room. Maybe she could lend me money for a cab to Oakland. Grandmother would shelter me. This might be a good time to reveal that I was pregnant and needed the job. I might get help for today and a few more months on the job when I grew too big to disguise it with loose clothing or blame it on overeating.

Sticking to the truth as far as I could, I began the tale of leaving an abusive husband who was determined not to let me leave. I'd been staying with my aunt, but now he was watching her house, and I couldn't go back there. I hinted that he might be involved in organized crime. "Charli Forast isn't even my real name. A friend of his felt sorry for me and got me the papers." Uh-oh, what if she thought I'd gotten the job with a false resume? Too late to worry about that now. I plunged on with the story. "I never thought he'd find me. I was going to go to my cousin's house, but she isn't answering her phone. I don't have money for a hotel, and I don't know what else I can do."

Her face flickered through emotions too fast for me to interpret them. Then she reached over and hugged me. "You can stay with me tonight. We'll have all weekend to get things sorted."

What a relief. "I couldn't impose." Of course I could. What choice did I have?

"It'll be fun to have the company. I have a studio apartment a couple of blocks away. It's small, but you don't take up much room."

"What if he knows where I work?"

Janice thought for a minute. "No problem. We'll go the

other way, duck into that five and dime on the corner. I'll buy you a big red shoulder bag and floppy hat to match. Stuff your raincoat in the bag. We come out the other door, and walk to my apartment as two other people." She hugged me again. "I read a lot of mysteries."

"You're wonderful to offer to take me in for the night, but I can't let you spend money on a bag and hat, too."

"I've had my eye on them for a month. I wanted to buy them for the beach, but I go so seldom, I was having trouble justifying it. So, you could say you're doing me a favor." That got a weak smile from me.

I'd intended to call Jackie until I got an answer, but Janice didn't have a phone in her apartment. "I'm at the office most of the time, and it's one more expense I don't need." Between worrying about Jamal's men, worrying about Aunt Nellie not knowing where I was, and the lumpy sofa, I got little sleep that night. I woke up feeling as though I'd been run over by a truck, and had dark circles under my eyes.

Janice suggested I stay in the apartment and rest. "You're welcome to stay here as long as you like. I'll tell the office that you called in with the flu. That'll buy you some time to decide what to do." I wasn't convinced, but I was too distraught to argue. "I can't wait to get back tonight and have a nice long talk. Why, I don't even know your real name." She laughed. "This is so exciting. I feel like I'm in the middle of a novel."

"I just hope it's one with a happy ending." She left me a key in case I needed to go out for anything. As soon as she left, I poked around in her closet and found a scarf to put over my hair, and a big jacket. It was too warm for a jacket, but it changed my appearance. As silly as I thought

Janice was with her ideas of disguise, I practiced a shuffling walk with my shoulders hunched and my head down. I grabbed a few dimes and went to find a pay phone.

"Aunt Nellie, thank God you're home. I've been worried sick."

"*You've* been worried! We had visions of you huddled in some doorway all night. Where are you?"

I gave her the address and told her about Janice. "I was worried she'd fire me, but she's giving me sick days and telling everyone I have the flu. She thinks it's exciting."

"I'm so relieved you're safe. After I talked to you yesterday, I called Guido. He said he'd be right over and to have your stuff packed. He was going to take it to Jackie's. I threw things in the suitcase, so I apologize for the state it's in."

"So my things are at Jackie's?"

"No, your suitcase is riding around in the back of Guido's car. Turns out Jackie's away for a few days visiting her in-laws. By the time Guido told me she wasn't home and I tried to call you, the office was closed. The name change paper's in there, too, along with a letter from Bill saying he approved it due to extreme endangerment, or something like that."

"Are the cars still in front of the house? What should I do?"

"Just sit tight. I don't think the car will be here long. The one in front of your mother's is gone."

"It probably left as soon as she gave them your address."

"Anyway, Guido walked over to the car and talked to them, blocking the view of the front door while Tony took the suitcase to the car. He told them his girlfriend was getting nervous about them being there, and he had some friends that would make sure they parked somewhere else."

"Why is Guido doing all this for me? I mean, I'm grateful because I think he's saving my life, but I can't help wondering what he's getting out of it."

"I think he enjoys being part of the family again."

"Again?" Of course, Aunt Nellie was married to his cousin Al.

"How would you like to be a red head?"

"Huh?" It took me a second to switch gears.

"I think you'd look great with red hair, and get your friend to cut it for you."

"Are you serious?"

"Dead serious. Guido says the guys in the car were armed. He's coming to spend the night on my sofa. Listen, call me tomorrow, okay?"

I went back to the apartment and lay down on Janice's bed. I didn't think I'd be able to sleep, but when the doorbell rang, I woke up with my heart racing. I tiptoed to the door, thankful for the peephole. "Tony, what a relief to see you."

"I brought your suitcase." He stood there, waiting to be invited inside. I stood aside. "Charli, I've been thinking." He caught my elbow and guided me to the sofa. "Do you want to live with me?" I relived visions of us together, washing dishes and laughing. It was wrong, but warmth came with the vision. "I live in an old house with a couple of other guys. We'd have our own room." The vision changed. I saw myself, barefoot and pregnant, living in a frat house. Suddenly, Tony looked a lot younger.

"Tony, you've been swell through all this, but by now you must realize that it's much more serious than a boyfriend I can't shake." He nodded. "Uncle Guido's been calling in a lot of favors for me, and I appreciate it. Doesn't that tell you something?"

"Yeah, he told me to make sure I wasn't followed when I came here."

"Remember the first night when I told you I was leaving town? It's time for me to go. I'd never forgive myself if anything happened to you, Tony. I'd like to know that whatever happens to me, wherever I go, I have a real friend here." I took his hand, and it was warm and comfortable—no electricity, no butterflies.

Janice was thrilled to spend the evening cutting and dying my hair. "This is the most exciting thing that's ever happened to me. I hope I get to know how the story ends. Golly, it would be like reading a book where someone tore out the last chapter if I never hear from you again." It was fiction come alive for her.

Hours later I was wrapped in a blanket on the sofa worrying about Aunt Nellie. I dug the journal out of my suitcase and tiptoed to the bathroom where I could read without disturbing Janice.

$$\gg \; \odot \; \odot \; \odot \; \odot \; \ll$$

JANUARY 30, 1951: - "Who else is coming?" There were too many cups for just the three sisters and Grandmother.

"Jean and Edna."

I knew it was important if Jean got a babysitter. "Edna moved back to San Francisco?" Edna was younger than Jean, but her boy was a lot older. He was her husband's son by his previous wife. I barely remember Edna because her husband keeps changing jobs and they move more often than we do.

"She's visiting Jean. That deadbeat husband of hers has a new job and she's staying with Jean until he gets them an apartment." Deadbeat husband? I thought deadbeats were people without jobs. Every time I hear about Edna, her husband has a job; it's just a different job in another place. Maybe I'll ask more about that when Mother isn't so busy. Another family puzzle. "Why isn't Rita coming?"

"Why not stop asking questions? You said you were dusting. I haven't seen you go near the bookcases." Ugh. The bookcases. I figured out why we don't have bookcases that go all the way to the ceiling like the ones in movies. It's so Mother can use child labor to dust them. It's not like anyone reads any of them. The only ones that get used are my encyclopedia volumes. While I was dusting, I grabbed the encyclopedia volumes I was going to use for this week's extra credit report. I needed "C" for Curie and chemistry, "R" for radioactivity, and the "XYZ" for x-rays.

I had everything I needed and was sitting down making notes about Marie Curie long before the doorbell rang. It surprised me that she was married. I didn't think married women worked in those days.

Aunt Nellie's the only woman I know who likes her job. The cousins work because they're single and they can't live with their parents forever, and all they talk about is meeting the right man and getting married. Of course there are lots of women teachers, but that's kind of like being a mother except with more kids. For the nuns it's different. We're the only kids they'll ever have, and they do it to serve God—at least that's what Sister Mary Agnes said. It doesn't make much sense to me. If God wants us to learn things, He could make us know it at the right time—like he makes us learn to walk and talk. We could just know a little more each morning when we wake up until we know all we're supposed to know. It would be easier than homework.

The steady buzz of conversation in the living room got quiet. The clink of a coffee cup being placed on a saucer sounded very loud.

"Well, ladies," said Auntie Stell, "I have bad news. Guido says that wolf in sheep's clothing that married Rita *is* fooling around. I couldn't sleep a wink last night worrying about her. I kept changing my mind about what would be best. I'm hoping you can help me decide. Do we tell Rita she was right, and he's cheating? It's so close to her due date, I can't bear to think about it. Can we keep it to ourselves until the baby's born? It would be horrible for her to face the birth of her first child knowing that the father was a louse."

"You knew your first husband was a louse before Albert was born, so you should know what it's like," said Mother.

"Charlotte, not now." Grandmother scolded Mother.

"Sorry, Mama."

"You should be apologizing to your sister, not to me."

"Never mind." I could picture Auntie Stell waving off any apologies. "I've been thinking about this ever since I talked to Guido. Maybe Dickhead's just having a little fling. I think we should let him know he's not getting away with anything. That might be all it takes to make it go away. Maybe he's just doing it for a thrill. I mean it's not as if the wedding was an impulse. They planned it for almost a year, he must have been in love with her, and people don't fall out of love that fast. He just needs a wake-up call."

"That's a great idea." The unknown voice had to be Edna. "Maybe he's trying to impress his buddies. If we let him know it might have consequences, he'll stop."

"I disagree." Nellie sounded emphatic (I love it when I get to use a new word). "A man who cheats once will cheat again. If he's cheating now, when he can feel his baby moving inside his wife's womb, he's not doing it to impress his buddies. Rita needs to know right away, before she has the baby. That way she'll be so busy loving her new baby and being a mother, she'll get over it sooner."

"But she won't be able to work. How will she live?" Auntie Stell was worried.

"Any good lawyer can get her a decent settlement with child support payments. If she stays with him until the baby's born, she'll be overwhelmed with all the responsibilities of motherhood and will hesitate to leave him. It's comforting to have a husband around when you're a new mother for the first time. If he's there and gets to hold the baby before she leaves, he won't want her to go. He'll promise anything to keep that baby safe. Rita needs to assert her independence while she can."

"If he'll do anything to keep the baby safe, that means he'll stop cheating when the baby's born."

"I didn't say he'll *do* anything; I said he'll *promise* anything. He's a cheating husband. The promise will be forgotten, and he'll cheat again. Making a clean break now will be better for Rita and the baby."

"I think we should give him a warning. Even if he starts cheating again after the baby's born, how can that matter? The baby'll be too young to understand. Besides, that doesn't seem to stop *you*, and Jackie's old enough to understand what's happening."

"Charlotte."

"It's all right, Mama. She's right. Jackie does understand, and she knows how hard it is to live in a house where there's cheating and lying. If Richard continues cheating, and I'm sure he will, the house won't be a happy place for the baby. Even very young babies can feel when their parents are unhappy. Unhappy parents have colicky babies, or worse."

"I think you're wrong, Nellie." Auntie Stell always thinks the best of people. "You can't judge Richard by what Willis did. You should know that. Maybe his promises will mean something. After all, they were engaged for almost a year and he never strayed."

"That we know of."

"Don't be so cynical, Nellie. Maybe Stell's right. Maybe he's just afraid of Rita."

"Afraid of Rita? What're you talking about, Charlotte?"

"Don't pretend you don't understand what I mean. Afraid if they...you know...that maybe he'll hurt her or the baby."

"If they what? Oh, you mean if they have sex. For goodness sake, everyone knows that's an old wives' tale. As long as the pregnancy is developing normally, there's nothing harmful about having sex. In fact, it's actually beneficial for many reasons. A lot of women enjoy it more during pregnancy, and it keeps the couples close in more ways than one."

Sex during pregnancy. A three-word phrase with two words I'm not supposed to use at my age. It seems Mother doesn't like to use those words at her age either. I wonder about sex during pregnancy—Mother says it's bad; Aunt Nellie says that's an old wives tale. Does that mean Nellie's wrong? Or does it mean that Mother's an old wife? She's not *that* much older than Aunt Nellie.

"I'm certain you're wrong, Nellie. How could it be all right? Women lose babies all the time, and most of the time the doctors don't know why it happens. It could very well be because they let their husbands...you know."

"It's called having sex, Charlotte. I don't know how you ever got pregnant if you can't even say the word. It's just a word; saying it doesn't hurt."

"All right, girls." Grandmother always called them girls. "Stop teasing Charlotte for keeping her language genteel. Animals have sex. People make love. It's called making love for a reason, because if there's no love, they shouldn't be doing it. It's not necessary to use common language. Besides, Charlotte has more reason than the rest of us to be careful about anything that could cause a woman to lose a baby. She's had the sorrow of losing a baby, and can't afford to take these things lightly."

Mother lost a baby? She loses her car keys sometimes, but I wouldn't have thought she could lose a baby.

"Please, can we get back to Rita?" said Auntie Stell. "What are we going to do about her husband? Do you think he loves her or not? Isn't that the real question? If he loves her, we should do something to discourage his bad behavior. If he doesn't love her, maybe Nellie's right that the sooner she leaves him the better. Getting the father entangled with the children if there has to be a divorce makes things even worse."

"Amen. Willis dotes on Jackie. It makes it really hard because he keeps taking her places and buying her things all the time."

"What's wrong with that?"

"For one thing he's spoiling her. More important, she can get anything she wants if she waits until her weekend with her father. I can't teach her things like saving up for what you want, or earning the privilege of going somewhere. Any time I say she can have something when her report card shows that she's applying herself in school, she comes home with whatever it was she wanted after a weekend with her father. He's buying her love."

"Why're you complaining? The more he buys, the less you have to spend."

"It's not about the money. It's about life. All she has to do is say she loves him and he buys her whatever she wants. That's how girls can go wrong. It becomes a pattern of trading love for what they want—and love takes many forms as a girl gets older." Now I understand why Jackie has such a fancy dollhouse and all the furniture.

"What does this have to do with Rita and Richard?"

"Sorry, Stell. I just get exasperated with Willis. I thought once the divorce was through, I'd be through with him and his problems, but I guess I never will be." I heard the clunk and rattle of a cup and saucer being put down on a table with a little more force than usual. "All right. So to follow up with Stell's thoughts of it hinging on whether or not he loves her, I guess we need to determine that part first. How can we tell if he loves her?"

I got out a fresh sheet of paper and held my pencil at

the ready. I heard a giggle that built up into a roomful of laughter. How could they think that was funny?

"Oh, Aunt Nellie, that's what we've been asking *you* ever since we noticed that boys and girls are different."

"I guess it's one of life's Unanswerable Questions," said Aunt Nellie. "And do you want to know why?" I nodded, even though she couldn't see me. "Because, ladies, in spite of all the sappy love songs, love is *not* eternal." Aunt Nellie gave one of her dramatic pauses, making everyone wait for her next words. "Love is not eternal, but our great hope is that the *commitment* to love is eternal. Admit it. Aren't there times when you want your husband to just go away and leave you alone? At that moment, you aren't really in love with him. Then he turns around and you see something in his eyes, or he does something silly, or maybe he says something and his tone of voice hits you just right, and ready or not—you fall in love with him all over again. That's what marriage is all about—making an effort to be alert for those little things so you can keep falling in love again every time you hit a bump in the road."

"Aunt Nellie, you're the smartest woman in the world. Sometimes Johnny wakes up with breath that could peel the paint off the walls and I look down at his sorry ass and want to tell him to get lost, but then he reaches over and runs a finger down my cheek, or buries his face in my neck and mumbles something I can't even hear. Yeah, Auntie, you're coming through loud and clear."

"Okay. So let's assume that Richard is committed but he's just in one of those moments when he forgets. Now we have to ask how to get him to look at Rita again and see what he saw when he asked her to marry him." Auntie

231

Stell was trying to get a plan of action.

"The problem is that there's a big difference between just turning away, like Edna does when Johnny smells like an old ashtray sitting in stale beer, and turning to someone else. Turning to someone else could be poor judgment, or it could be his leopard spots that will never change."

"I refuse to believe that," said Auntie Stell. "I think he's just showing off."

I hope she's right, but I think Aunt Nellie knows best. She was right about Willis. I think Aunt Nellie understands more about the curse than anyone else in the family. In fact, we might be the only two who know there *is* a curse.

The words in the other room became a blur of sound, and the words on the page in front of me became a blur of print. The curse isn't getting any weaker. It's just spreading to more women as the family grows, and I'm no nearer a solution than I was when I started. I just hope my list of dos and don'ts work.

I jumped when Auntie Stell clapped her hands and said, "All right, ladies, I've decided. Nellie is too quick to believe the worst. I think that Richard is basically a good person who has made a mistake. I'm going to talk to Guido about letting him know that he wasn't nearly discreet enough, and Rita knows about his playing around. Guido can let Richard think that he's willing to persuade Rita to forgive him quietly and not mention it for the sake of the baby, if Richard promises never to stray again."

"*Gracias a Dios.*" Grandmother liked Auntie Stell's solution. "Now let's have some more coffee. Come on, Charlotte, I'll help you in the kitchen." I turned back to my work in case Mother or Grandmother glanced into the dining room from the kitchen. Once the two of them started chattering in Spanish, I turned my attention back to the living room.

Then Aunt Nellie started asking Edna about her husband's new job. I listened closely to see if I could find out why Mother called him a deadbeat, but I didn't hear anything new. They were talking about his new boss when Mother and Grandmother came back with the coffee and dessert.

"Speaking of new bosses," said Mother, "what does Al think of you eating lunch with your new boss? Has he seen the fox stole?"

"What fox stole?" Jean hadn't seen it yet. I worked on my report while the story of the fox stole was retold, but I kept my ears open for anything new.

"What happened to the weekend in the country?"

"I never planned on accepting that. It was just a tease of an idea that I enjoyed thinking about when Al was being a jerk, not that Al has stopped being a jerk. He still gives me a hard time every morning when I crawl out of bed to get to work. Every day I hear the same thing. 'If you'd quit that damn job you could sleep later in the mornings.' Yesterday I told him if I heard that one more time, I'd stuff his bed with ice cubes."

"I bet that shut him up." Jean was laughing.

"Not really. He said he thought I already had. The only difference would be that the little ice cubes would thaw quicker."

I wasn't sure what that meant, but Grandmother was worried. "Nellie, are you making *any* effort to make things work? You know you can enchant him all over again if you put your mind to it. You're the one who just gave the speech about falling in love being a continuous process."

"Maybe so, Mama, but I'm not sure it's what I should do. He's not making any effort to win me over. All he does is nag and remind me that I wouldn't be so tired if I didn't try to do two jobs. It sounds to me as though all he really wants from me is my work in his restaurant. It's depressing. His cook follows my directions about cooking, and Al prints my menus and implements my decorating suggestions, but neither one of them have learned anything. They're still greasy diner people in disguise. The hotel gives me a chance to do spectacular things every week — sometimes more than once a week. I have a staff of eager young helpers, an appreciative boss, and I'm having the time of my life. I'm going to enjoy it while it lasts."

"You think it won't last? Yet you're willing to sacrifice your marriage for it?" Grandmother sounded as confused as I was.

"Mama, you should know better than any of us that nothing lasts forever. I *am* willing to sacrifice a marriage that is no longer a marriage. I won't stay with a man whose main interest in me is my ability to cook."

"Willis kept coming back to you because you were a good cook." That was Mother again, pulling the conversation the wrong way. I wanted to know why Aunt Nellie sounded so sure the hotel job was temporary.

"Willis kept coming back to me because I was good looking, a good wife in and out of the bedroom, *and* I was a good cook. That was the last item on the list, not the first, and certainly not the only item."

"I still don't understand why you're pushing Al to the breaking point for a job you don't think will last. You know if you quit, he'd be happy as a clam. He thinks you're good looking, too."

"I'm good looking enough to add class to the restaurant. The regulars don't argue about the higher prices if I flirt a little. No, Mama, I think it's over unless he makes an effort to revive the marriage. And as for why the other one is temporary, doesn't anyone remember my advice about dating the boss?" I didn't think anyone could've forgotten. "If his son thinks he can hurt my niece and get away with it, he'll find out that his foxy lady is more of a fox than he thinks. He seems to have forgotten that the fox is a carnivore."

The women laughed at that, but I felt a chill go down my spine. I hoped I wouldn't dream of fox stoles with real foxes tonight.

Maybe I'll be a scientist and never get married. Marriage sounds like a lot of work. Not only do you have to cook and clean for more people, but you always have to worry about what your husband's up to when he stays out late.

➤➤ FIFTEEN ◄◄

"How do rental cars keep that new car smell? I'm sure they aren't all returned smelling that great."

"It comes in a spray can." David punched the address into the GPS. "You ready for this?" I nodded. Maybe not, but I wasn't going to be any more ready in the morning. "What's your plan?"

"I don't really have a plan. I thought I'd knock on the door and see what happens. If things look normal, I'll apologize for dropping in without notice. Maybe claim I dropped my cell phone or something. Since you're here, we might say you're in town on business and we came tonight because you have a meeting in the morning."

"Claim you were so excited to see her again that you forgot to call. I'll be shocked and say something about your memory slipping."

"I guess. The gray hair has to be good for something." I tried to calm my nerves by looking out the window and trying to pick out things that let me know I was in Texas and not some city on the east coast. Space? Newer buildings? It sure wasn't Boston or New York, but I soon tired of the game. All I could think about was how desperate Kate had sounded on the phone.

The GPS guided us through the city and into a neighborhood of old rundown houses that must have been lovely a few decades earlier. Many of the yards were neglected, and rusted cars cluttered a few driveways. The machine announced our arrival at our destination. I spotted the number at the same moment the front door flew open, and a woman I recognized only by the masses of red hair flying in all directions emerged, looking back over her shoulder. Her worn blue jeans and tee shirt suited the area. David saw her and pulled to the curb. We were halfway out of the car when the door flew open again so hard I heard it bang against the wall, and a man came out. He was waving his fist and shouting, although I couldn't distinguish the words.

I began to move forward, and in my peripheral vision I saw David run past me. Kate turned toward the door, and I caught a glimpse of her face. Blood was running from her nose and mouth, but what I'll always remember was her look of sheer terror. I may have screamed. David shouted, and the man's head turned toward us. Almost negligently, his arm moved forward, and his open hand struck Kate at the top of the sternum, propelling her backward off the porch and down the half dozen steps to the overgrown cement walkway. Kate was the only thing not moving as I grabbed my cell phone. David was running toward the house, and I tore my eyes away from the scene for the two seconds it took to dial 911 with shaking hands. I watched as the man came down the stairs, stepping around Kate at the bottom.

The line opened and I blurted out the address. I sounded hysterical, but that didn't matter. "We need an ambulance and police. The woman's unconscious or worse. Maybe a head injury. the man's coming after my son! Hurry!" I was screaming into the phone and running. "Yes, yes, I'll keep the line open."

"Oh my God, he's killed her this time." A woman ran past me. I stopped to catch my breath. More people appeared.

The man, who'd been approaching David, stopped and looked around at the gathering crowd. Thank God we decided to come in the evening when most people were home. "Damned lush couldn't even stand up straight. I tried to grab her," he said to no one in particular. Then he looked straight at me. "You saw that didn't you? I tried to grab her shirt, but it slipped out of my fingers." Only then did he look down at Kate. David was kneeling next to her. His fingers were on her neck, feeling for a pulse.

My heart beat fast enough for both of us. "Is she…"

"She's alive. Did anyone call an ambulance?"

"I did." I remembered the phone in my hand. "Are you still there?" She was. "She's alive." I relayed the question. "Is her breathing normal?"

"I guess so. The blood is bubbling out of her nose, but she seems to be breathing all right."

I extended the phone to David, but he didn't take it. I acted as go-between for a few more questions.

The man, who I assumed was her husband, squatted on the other side of Kate. "Let's get her inside until the paramedics arrive." He reached forward.

"NO!" I even startled myself with the shout. "Don't move her. She could have other injuries." The man stared at me. "The 911 operator says not to move her." She did say it after she heard my shout.

It seemed like an eternity before we heard sirens approaching. Kate's hair was turning a dark sickly red as blood pooled around her head.

The ambulance arrived with a black and white right

behind it. Many of the neighbors melted back into doorways. David hovered over the paramedics while I told my story to the police. Kate's husband told them the same story he'd told earlier.

"So you say he pushed her, and he says he was trying to save her." The cop looked bored. I had to convince him that it wasn't only my word against the husband's.

"Officer, just look at her. How could she have fallen on her face *and* on her back. "Ask that woman." I pointed to the neighbor, the only one who seemed to care enough to stay around. The cop turned to the neighbor, and I watched the paramedics. "David, you have to tell the police what you saw. He needs another witness."

The police decided to take the husband with them, and I promised to give a formal statement later. David walked over to the ambulance and asked if he could ride with Kate. "Who're you?"

"Her brother. We just flew in from Virginia. Please. I don't want her waking up all alone."

"Okay, but stay out of the way."

"Promise." He tossed me the keys and climbed in the back of the ambulance.

"Wait! Which hospital?" The doors slammed and the driver took off, sirens blaring. Now what? I could never catch up to them, let alone follow through red lights and stop signs. "Never mind," I said to the back of the ambulance, "I can call all the hospitals in Houston until I find you." I turned toward the house. Maybe I could make a cup of tea while I searched for hospitals.

"Memorial Hermann Southwest." It was the neighbor who'd spoken to the police.

"Was it on the ambulance?" Guess I'd been too

239

distracted to look.

"We're in Sharpstown, *the* place to live in Houston—forty years ago. Memorial Hermann Southwest is the closest hospital. It's a good hospital, even if it is around here."

"Thanks. Are you a friend of Kate's?"

"Maybe not a friend, but I've called the police a couple of times, and I've tried to get her to press charges or go to a battered women's shelter or something." She gave me directions to the hospital. "Can I give you my name and number? I'd like to know how she's doing." I entered her information in my phone and promised to stay in touch.

The door of the house was still wide open. I went in and found Kate's purse. Luckily, her keys were in it. I took the purse, locked the door, and started for the hospital. The neighbor's guess was right. David was pacing in the lobby of the emergency room, pale and worried.

At last a doctor came out. David jumped. "Is she all right?"

"We can't really tell yet. She's had a rough time. The CT scan shows some bleeding around the brain. We're calling in a neurosurgeon to decide whether or not it warrants inserting an intracranial pressure gauge in her brain. If it doesn't get worse, it should heal by itself. If it gets worse, we'll have to drain the blood."

"But she will get better?"

"It's too soon to tell."

"What about—"

"I really have to get back to her. It's a borderline case. The neurosurgeon will probably want another CT scan when he gets here to see if there's been any change. Either way, it'll be hours before you can see her. Why don't you two go get something to eat? I'll call if they want to do the procedure. Come back in the morning around ten. She'll be in the ICU. I promise to call if there's any change."

We found a chain restaurant near the hospital and picked at our meal. "I forgot to tell you, I changed our hotel reservations. The paramedic told me about a motel less than a mile from the hospital."

"Good idea, I wouldn't have thought of it."

"I'll get us settled in and go back to the hospital. I really want to be there when Kate wakes up."

"Of course." After David left, I checked my watch and calculated the time difference. It was almost too late to call. David and Susan might be having their problems, but it was only right to let her know that we had arrived safely.

"Hello." My tongue froze. Why was a man answering the phone? It wasn't a wrong number, I'd used speed dial.

"I'm calling for Susan Lombardi?"

"Just a minute." I heard a muffled shout. "Susan, telephone." His hand came off the receiver. "She'll be with you in a minute." He set the phone down with a clunk. The television was on in the background.

"Hello." Susan was annoyed.

"I wanted to let you know we arrived safely."

"Oh, it's you. That's good. The mayor and I are just going over a speech he's giving tomorrow. The immigration issue needs to be handled delicately."

"I'll leave you to it, then." The mayor? Was that what she called laying the groundwork? David certainly had turned the curse upside down. I was surprised at how calm I felt. It took less than a second to decide to say nothing about this conversation. At least I had a clear conscience about my plans.

I opened my suitcase. Bypassing the novel I'd packed, I reached under a few layers of clothes for the old journal. I needed the comfort of the women around me tonight. They all had their problems, but they all survived them. I liked to think they came out the other side stronger and wiser for the experience. I prayed that Kate and David would not be exceptions.

>> ⏰ ⏲ ⏱ 🕐 <<

FEBRUARY 3, 1951: - I got a plate of cookies and a book and found a nice out-of-the way place in the hall to sit. I brought a small piece of paper that fit into my book so I could take notes. I had a feeling this was going to be interesting.

As I settled into my spot, I had to use all my will power not to eat the cookies all at once, but they were my excuse not to be in my room. "Sorry. I was trying not to get in the way, but Mother doesn't let me eat cookies in the bedroom." It sounded good to me.

Conversation was really quiet, even though they must have been getting impatient. Auntie Stell was very late. Even Aunt Nellie seemed unusually quiet.

I don't know why time moves so slowly when you're waiting for something, but it took so long that I got bored with the conversation and stopped paying attention while I read. After what seemed like hours, I heard the doorbell, followed by absolute silence. Mother hurried to the door. "Stell, oh my God, Stell—what's wrong?"

I could almost feel the walls of the house bow inward as every woman in the room gasped. Confident that no one was paying attention to me, I leaned over and peeked through the doorway. Auntie Stell was pale and leaning on Grandmother.

"Richard's in the hospital." The reactions came so fast I didn't even try to sort out who said what. It all amounted to the same thing—why and how bad.

It was Grandmother who answered. "He has a couple of broken ribs, two black eyes, a broken nose, but what's keeping him in the hospital is a broken leg that needs traction. Rita's fine. She's all weepy and seems to have forgiven him for everything she thought he was doing. I was about to tell her he wasn't worth her tears when Stell started wailing like a banshee and I had to drag her out of there. She hasn't stopped crying, but at least she stopped sounding like a professional mourner."

"Mom, what's the matter?" Jean was leaning over Auntie Stell.

"Get her some tea, Charlotte." Mother scurried off to put the water on for tea. She was back before I could say Jack Robinson, afraid she'd miss something.

Auntie Stell talked through her tears. "It's all my fault."

"The doctor said he was mugged. How could that be your fault?"

"I told Guido to make sure that snake didn't hurt my little girl any more. I told him that he should make sure Richard knew that he couldn't cheat on Rita with imp...impun... without someone knowing. I should have known better. Guido went too far. He couldn't just threaten him, he nearly killed him."

"Stell, calm down." Aunt Nellie never got flustered.

"How can I?" Auntie Stell's voice was almost a squeak. "A man nearly died because of me."

"Guido may not speak perfect English, but he's not

243

stupid. You told him to let Richard know that his little games had not gone unnoticed, and his wife would hear about it if he didn't stop. Guido knew you wanted to make Rita happy by stopping Richard from playing around. What would make him think you wanted her to be a widow? That's not Guido's style."

"What do you know about his style?" Auntie Stell's voice made me think of the word ominous. (Another new word.)

"I know enough to know that in his line of work he wouldn't be walking around today if he were stupid." I couldn't hear Auntie Stell's muffled answer. I wonder why Guido wouldn't be walking around if he were stupid. Lots of stupid people walk around every day. A lot of them drive cars, too. Daddy is always calling other drivers stupid idiots.

"Well, this changes everything," said Aunt Nellie. "With Richard in the hospital for weeks, and Rita doting on his every moan, there's no way to get them apart now. So it sounds like time for a fresh pot of coffee. How about it, Charlotte?" I hoped Mother wouldn't notice me on her way to the kitchen. She didn't.

"Jean, go help her so she doesn't heat up the sludge in the bottom of the pot."

"Nellie, don't make fun of your sister. She had a rough time as a child, and it made her extra thrifty."

"Mama, we all had a rough time. Charlotte isn't thrifty; she's miserly. She adds old stale coffee to a new pot because she hates to waste anything — even old coffee."

I slipped back into the kitchen for more cookies. By the time I got back with more cookies and milk, Auntie Stell and Grandmother had left to visit Richard, and the women were talking about Aunt Nellie and Richard's father.

"No, I decided not to go on the wine tour. I just enjoy flirting. But in the end, I'm still married, even if I'm working on that divorce, and I've decided that even a bad marriage is as good an excuse as any to turn him down. After the divorce, we'll see what happens. In the meantime, I'll enjoy his charming company."

FEBRUARY 4, 1951: - Daddy came home late last night, and I didn't know it until this morning! He says he has a few days off because the ship is in dry dock having its bottom cleaned. That's funny because ships don't poop, and they live in the biggest bathtub in the world.

At breakfast, Mother said we were going to visit Richard at the hospital later in the afternoon. She said it was important to show Rita that she has our support. I could tell Daddy didn't want to go, but Mother had already decided. "We won't stay long, and afterward we can go to that burger place you like so much." Daddy and I were both happy about that.

When we got to the hospital, we learned that children under twelve aren't allowed into the hospital rooms. I had a book with me, so I didn't mind waiting in the lobby. I settled down to read.

One man kept walking by me as he paced up and down. Every time he walked past, I pulled my feet in and tucked them under the chair until he passed. After I'd done that a few times, I looked up as he passed. It was Guido! "Mr. Lombardi?"

"Yeah. Do I know you?"

"My Aunt Nellie is married to your cousin Al. I think you know my Auntie Stell, too."

"Is Stella here?" He looked around the lobby.

"I don't know. My parents are visiting…" I suddenly realized I shouldn't talk to him. He nearly killed Richard, and there's the whole thing about Auntie Stell's first husband. Even if Aunt Nellie says he didn't do it, I was scared.

"Someone in your family sick?"

"No, just someone we know." Was that a lie? Richard isn't a blood relative.

"That's good. That it's not your family, I mean." I nodded. "Me neither. I'm waitin' for a neighbor. His wife just had an operation." I nodded again. "Well, say hello to your aunts for me." I nodded once more and he walked away. I pretended to read, but I kept watching Guido. If his neighbor came out and they left, I'd know his story was true, but what if he wasn't?

Then I looked over the top of my book and my eyes met Guido's! I jerked the book up over my face. Why would he watch me? Could he want to know when my parents come out, just like I want to see when his neighbor comes out? I really wished they'd hurry. What if Guido *did* nearly kill Richard? The more I thought about it, the more frightened I felt.

Finally, my parents stepped out of the elevator. I wanted to shout, but I didn't. I just walked as fast as I could and grabbed them. I'd never been so happy to see my mother in my life. "Guido's here!"

"Guido Lombardi?"

"Yes. He says he's waiting for a neighbor, but what if he isn't?"

Daddy was looking at me like I was crazy. "What are you talking about?"

246

"What if Auntie Stell was right, and he's the one who attacked Dickhead?" Mother gasped and Daddy took hold of my arm and marched me outside so fast my feet barely touched the ground. I'm sure I'll have bruises in the morning. Mother and Daddy were speaking at the same time, and neither one of them was listening to me.

"Where did you hear that dreadful word?"

"If I ever hear you say something like that again, I'll give you a spanking you'll never forget."

"What word? What did I say?" My arm really hurt, and I hadn't been spanked in ages. Maybe screeching an octave above normal worked because they both stopped talking and looked at me, then at each other.

Mother looked at her toes and said nothing. Finally, Daddy said it. "Dickhead."

"That's Rita's husband's new nickname in the family. Auntie Stell called him that the other day." Mother's mouth opened and closed, but no sound came out. Laughter exploded out of Daddy, then Mother started laughing, too. I was furious. Not only did they drag me out of the hospital like a two-year-old throwing a tantrum, but they followed it by laughing like they'd invented the first knock-knock joke.

"Never say that again. It's not his nickname."

"If it's not a name, what does it mean?

Mother pursed her lips. "It's just a bad way of calling someone stupid."

"It means his brains are in his — "

"Frank!" Mother cut him off, but I understood. By that time, we were at the car and Daddy opened the door for Mother.

"I think Auntie Stell was right about Guido." I'd gotten

sidetracked by the whole Dickhead thing.

"What about Guido?" Daddy shut my door and walked around the car.

"I think he feels guilty. He's all nervous and jumpy and he was pacing up and down the lobby. I had to pull my feet in every time he passed, and that's how I noticed."

"How do you know it was Guido? It was probably someone else."

"I know it was Guido because I called him Mr. Lombardi, and he answered. He said to say hello to my aunts." I had Mother's attention. "I think he's nervous about Richard. After we talked, he sat far away from me, but he kept watching me. That made *me* nervous. I'm sure Auntie Stell is right."

"Right about what?" After Mother explained, Daddy laughed again and started the car. "What an imagination. People waiting in hospitals are always nervous in case they get bad news. It's a coincidence that we were all there at the same time."

Mother put her hand on his arm. "Turn off the engine, Frank. It may be a coincidence, but could you live with yourself if something worse happened? What if Guido really did try to kill Richard? Maybe he's in there right now, finishing the job?"

Wow! Even I hadn't gone that far. I thought he wanted to apologize, or maybe make sure Richard was all right. Finish the job? Could it be possible?

"Please, Frank. Go back in and see if everything's all right."

"And do what? Walk in and say 'Excuse me, Richard, has anyone come in to kill you since we left five minutes ago?'"

"Have your keys in your hand and pretend you're looking for them. If everything's all right, you can hold them out and say you found them." Mother's terribly clever sometimes. Daddy made a face, but he walked back to the hospital. We didn't say a word the whole time he was gone. I could barely breathe. I should've been worried about Daddy going after a murderer, but I wasn't. He couldn't get hurt in the middle of a hospital, could he?

Daddy was gone a long time before I started to worry. What if he was in trouble? Maybe we should go in and see what was happening. Or maybe we should go in and call the police. I was afraid to say anything because I didn't want Mother to worry, too. I started holding my breath while I counted to thirty and let it out slowly for the rest of the minute. This is always a good way to not think about something, but I couldn't keep doing it because I started to get dizzy.

"I'm going to see what's taking him so long." Mother opened the car door.

"No!" I shouted. "You can't leave me alone out here with a murderer on the loose. I'll go with you."

"You'll be safe in the car. Keep the doors locked. I'll be right back."

"No, I won't be safe. He knows me, and he knows I know who he is. I could swear that he was here. He could be looking for me right now to shut me up for good." My fear grew with every word. "You can't leave me." Mother hesitated. "If you go, and something awful happens to me, just remember..." I had intended to say that I told her so, but I thought of a better ending. "...just remember that I love you."

"All right, you can come." I breathed a sigh of relief.

249

Just as Mother was opening my door so I could get out, I saw a man running toward us.

"Get in!" I grabbed Mother's skirt and pulled. "He's coming!" It had to be Guido coming to get me. "Hurry!" Mother must have heard the terror in my voice because she slid into the back seat and slammed the door. By the time she had the door closed, I'd pushed down all the other door locks. She reached over and locked the last door. I sat down and grabbed her. Her arms went around me, and I don't think she'd ever hugged me so tight. My heart was pounding so hard I could hear it. No, that wasn't my heart; someone was pounding on the car window. He'd found us! I buried my face in Mother's dress, muffling my scream, and listened for the sound of shattering glass.

"For God's sake, open the door." Mother's arms relaxed and I sat up and looked. Daddy was peering through the window. I was limp with relief. "Get your keys and start the car." He was shouting so we could hear him through the closed windows. Mother and I looked at each other. If Daddy knew how scared we were, he'd never stop laughing. I nodded, and I knew we had a pact of silence. I didn't want Daddy laughing at me again tonight.

Mother stepped out of the car. "What happened to your keys? And what took you so long?" Daddy laughed. I love it when Daddy laughs, as long as he isn't laughing at me.

"I'll explain later. Turn on the headlights so I can find my keys. I was waving to show you that everything was all right, and my keys flew out of my hand. I tried to find them, but..." It didn't take long to find the keys.

"Let's go get some burgers," said Daddy. He laughed again as he started the car.

"What's so funny?" Mother was as anxious to hear the story as I was.

"Damn, I haven't had so much fun since Mom and Dad came home and found my sister Mary on the couch necking with the captain of the football team." He laughed some more. "Come to think of it, Mary might not have had so much fun since then either." That made him start laughing again.

"Are you going to tell us what's so funny, or not?"

"As soon as I catch my breath." Daddy was making us wait just to tease us. "I decided to look for Guido in the lobby before going back to Richard's room. I didn't see him at first, and then I saw him with another man, so I called out to him."

"Did he recognize you?"

"Yep. He shook my hand like I was his best friend. We were still shaking hands when a nurse came over pushing a wheel chair with the biggest woman I ever saw."

"I don't see anything funny."

"I'm getting to it. Guido said the man he was with was his neighbor, and they'd come to pick up his wife after an operation. Guido asked me if I'd walk to the car with them. It turned out Guido wanted me to help get that woman into the car. The operation was on her knee, and she couldn't put any weight on one leg." Daddy was laughing again.

"It was funny?"

"Oh, it was funny all right. Guido has a two-door sedan, and I could tell right away that she'd never get in the back seat. Even with the hospital attendant, it was all we could do to steady her while she moved from the wheel chair to the car. The whole car listed to starboard so bad I thought the tires would bust."

"That's not funny at all. It's terrible to make fun of people because of a physical handicap. You're not setting a good example."

I know Mother's right, but it was hard not to laugh. Hanging over the back of the seat, I could see Daddy's good humor evaporate, but when we got to the burger place and started eating it came back.

"Daddy, tell us about the time your parents caught Aunt Mary with the football player. Did they get mad at him? Was he her boyfriend?"

"Getting caught wasn't the funny part, even though I thought it was funny. It didn't take us long to figure out why plain Mary was being sparked by the most popular guy in school. That was the funny part—while he was spooning with Mary, the rest of the team was passing bottles of my dad's bathtub gin out the basement window. Mary should have known she didn't have a shot at the captain of the football team."

≫ ⊙ ⊕ 1965 ⊕ ⊙ ≪

I looked in the mirror and didn't recognize the person looking back at me. Yesterday I had medium long mousy brown hair; this morning I have a new-penny pixie cut. It didn't just brighten my hair—it brightened my attitude. Janice did a great job. I told her I was going to stay a redhead forever and ever. She gave me a hug as she went off to work. I said I'd push the key under the door when I left, and I promised to keep in touch. I packed and put some dimes in my pocket for the pay phone.

"Aunt Nellie, I love the new haircut."

"We had some excitement in our quiet little neighborhood. Someone tried to break into the house last night." My heart thumped. "I told you Guido was sleeping on the sofa. By the time I woke up, he'd already called the police. They were here in record time." It sounded like she was stifling a laugh.

"What happened?"

"One of the wheels fell off the car as the intruders were driving away." I laughed with her. "Guido said they'd been careless with their maintenance when he dumped the lug nuts on the coffee table. He also says the cops can't hold them long, and I should be careful because they might not be so obvious next time. I say let them watch me all they want, as long as that's all they do."

"Be careful, Aunt Nellie."

"Don't worry about me. I'll be fine. You just pack and be on the sidewalk at exactly ten. Guido will pick you up. Your grandmother asked if you might be willing to stay with her. She says she's lonely without Sam, and it's perfect for both of you."

"Are you sure? I mean, what if Mother comes to visit and sees me? She can't keep a secret if it's locked in a trunk."

"I know, but you'll be staying in Donald's old place. It's an addition in the back with its own bathroom, and the connecting door's always closed. You'll be fine." I remembered that closed door, and the one time I was allowed through it to see Uncle Donald's drums. It was messy and smelled funny.

"What if *they* find me? I can't put Grandmother in danger. She'd probably have a heart attack if someone tried to break in."

"Don't worry. They're looking for a frightened brown-haired girl named Charli or Charlotte in San Francisco, but that girl no longer exists. Instead, an elderly widow in Oakland takes in a sassy redhead named Nellie."

"Call me Nellie B. It'll keep us from getting confused."

"As much as I loved Charli, I can't wait to meet Nellie B."

Grandmother met me at the door with a big hug and a whiff of rose talcum powder that made me feel safe even before the door closed behind me. By the time I got settled Grandmother had a bowl of homemade soup on the table.

"Are you sure this is all right? If Jamal locates me somehow, it could cause trouble."

"Nonsense. I'd have asked you right away, but I didn't think you'd like living with an old lady. The house is much too big for me, and I know I should sell it, but I can't leave the garden. It makes me feel close to Sam." She spooned soup into her mouth. "Did you have any trouble getting here?"

"Guido brought me." I laughed. "He's such a teddy bear. You know, when I was little I used to be afraid of him?" To lighten her mood from thoughts of Sam, I told her the amusing story of Guido and the hospital. She didn't laugh.

"Guido's always been willing to walk through fire for Stell." Grandmother's eyes seemed to be looking backward through time. "It's a case of what might have been. She was convinced he was responsible for Leonard's death because he told her not to come home that night."

"The other day at Aunt Nellie's, he explained it to her." Oops. I just revealed my eavesdropping.

"After Nellie married Al, and we got to know Guido,

254

Nellie and I both tried to tell her. Do you think she listened this time?"

"Maybe. She stopped glaring at him, and she did come to the 'wedding' party."

"Good. Guido's been doing little things for her ever since Walter passed away — like keeping her lawn mowed, although she doesn't know he was the one. She thinks it was her son. I'll set her straight. Guido couldn't kill anyone, even though the guys he sent to warn Rita's husband nearly killed him. He meant well."

"You mean to tell me he really *was* behind the mugging? And Mother never said anything? She hates to feel foolish, and it would've justified her fear that night."

"Which is exactly why your Mother was never told. If your mother knows something, it eventually becomes common knowledge. What would Rita have thought of her mother if she knew she'd engineered the attack on her husband?"

I nodded. "Just this morning, I told Aunt Nellie that Mother couldn't keep a secret."

"She's only kept one secret in her life, and that was because she believed I'd kill her if she ever breathed a word of it."

"What was it?"

"I threatened your mother with death. I don't want to kill off the whole family." Grandmother was smiling, but I knew I'd never learn that secret.

We ate in silence. I suppose we were both thinking about secrets. It's funny how the brain connects things sometimes. "Grandmother, do you think Mother's religious?"

"I suppose so. Of course, no one knows what's in

another person's heart."

"Why doesn't she ever go to communion?"

"I guess because of the divorce."

A mouthful of soup went down the wrong way and I coughed and coughed. Even when I could speak again, my voice came out a raspy whisper instead of the shout I was thinking. "Mother's been divorced? All those terrible things she says about Aunt Nellie—and *she's* been divorced?"

"I guess I misjudged your mother. Apparently she kept two secrets."

≫ SIXTEEN ≪

The bed next to me had that hotel pristine look to it. David had spent the night in the hospital. I checked my phone for messages. "She's still out. I'll call if anything changes." I guess no call meant no change.

I asked the desk clerk if she could give me directions to walk to the hospital. While she was drawing a map, I smelled coffee. "My son's been at the hospital all night and their machine coffee is terrible. Is there somewhere I can get some food?"

"Sure, room service makes box breakfasts all the time. I'll make it for two." Within minutes I had a bag with hot bagels wrapped in foil, cream cheese, coffee, and all the fixings. They even remembered napkins and stirrers. "If you take a cab, you'll be there in two minutes. If you walk, you'll get there with cold coffee." I took the cab.

At the hospital I was directed to the ICU. I paused in the doorway. David was sprawled in a chair with his eyes closed, innocent and vulnerable as a child. Kate's head was bandaged, and she was connected to tubes and machines. Her face was pale and almost translucent. I wondered if they'd shaved her beautiful red hair.

David's eyes opened as I tiptoed into the room. "I didn't mean to wake you, but I come bearing gifts."

"You don't have to whisper. In fact, we'd all love it if she wakes up."

"No news from the doctors?"

"They haven't rushed her to the operating room, so the pressure must be stable. That's a good sign." I nodded. "Ahhh, coffee and bagels. You're an angel, Mom." We ate in silence.

A small sound came from the bed. I'd never seen David move so fast. He stood over Kate, holding the hand without the needle and tubes. Her eyes fluttered a few times, and then opened, and focused.

"David, you're here."

"Yes, Kate, I'm here."

"David, did you see her? She's beautiful. The most beautiful thing I ever saw. She's perfect. Her tiny hands with their long fingers and tiny little nails, her toes look like beads from a pearl necklace. She has your eyes." Kate's voice was low, but clear. I looked at David, and watched the tears flow down his cheeks and disappear into the day old stubble before reappearing as silver drops falling to their clasped hands.

I walked quietly to the door and left them alone. I struggled to keep back my own tears. It wasn't hard to figure out what was happening. In a few minutes I'd tell the nurse Kate was awake. She might be living twenty-five years in the past, but that would probably pass, based on my store of TV medical knowledge. Even if she didn't, would that be so terrible? She'd have no memory of that bastard who nearly killed her.

>> ⊕ ⊕ ⊙ ⊙ <<

FEBRUARY 22, 1951: - Rita had her baby! We went to visit them today. His hands are so cute with their tiny, tiny fingernails. I didn't get to hold him. Maybe Rita remembered what happened to her wedding book. They named him Richard, Jr. Auntie Stell's staying with them for a few days to help Rita because Richard's still on crutches. Everyone's happy. Well—almost everyone.

When Rita went to the bathroom, and I was leaning over the crib, Auntie Stell told Mother that Guido found out that she thought he put Richard in the hospital. It makes her angry because she doesn't know who told him. She said if Rita found out about any of this, she'd kill the person who told her. Mother didn't say anything. Maybe she had the same thought I had—it could have been Daddy. Maybe Daddy was laughing so hard at the hospital because we were so afraid of a man who was only helping his neighbor, but he couldn't let Mother know he was laughing at her for going along with my fears.

Some of the laughter might still have been about the poor fat lady. I wonder how Guido got her out of the car when they got home without Daddy or the hospital attendant.

$$\ggg \oplus \oplus 1965 \oplus \oplus \lll$$

Even the journal couldn't distract me from the thought that today was the day Jamal was to call Mother's house to make final arrangements, and I wouldn't be there when he called. I patted my rounding tummy. "It's all right, baby. I'll take care of you," I whispered. "I won't let him take you into those radioactive mines or marry you off to the most expedient husband." I wanted to bury my head in the pillow and wake up tomorrow, when it was over. I swung my legs over the edge of the bed. Big girls don't hide in the closet.

The day ticked by in a succession of infinite seconds. When the phone rang, every nerve in my body knew it was Aunt Nellie. Grandmother was outside repotting something. I had to answer it. "Hello?"

"I just got off the phone with your mother. That man is diabolical. When she said you weren't there, he said he wanted to talk to her anyway. Charli, he played her like a cheap violin. He talked about how much he wanted her to live with the two of you, and when she was startled by the idea, he said he'd extended the invitation long ago. He sympathized with her having to raise such a headstrong child with almost no help from the father. He listened when she said how hard it had been, and told her what a wonderful job she'd done. In fact, he'd heard so many wonderful things about her, he wanted her to come and visit so he could get to know her better, she could even stay if she liked. She'd have her own driver and maid always at her beck and call. What's a beck anyway?"

"He didn't say anything about me not being there?"

"He said that pregnant women were notorious for erratic behavior. He knew your love was strong, and you'd come back when you were ready. It might even make it easier for you if your mother was there, ready to help you through the pregnancy and childbirth. It would help you feel more at home in an unfamiliar culture."

"What did Mother say?" My hands began to shake. I was glad I was sitting down. "If she goes, I'll have to choose."

"She said she'd think about it. He asked her full name and birthdate to start working on the visas. When she said September, he said, 'Perfect. I'll have Cartier's in Paris make the jewelry with diamonds and sapphires.' Then he pretended to be upset because he'd spoiled the birthday surprise."

I groaned. "How could Mother resist?"

"She wants to talk to you."

"Aunt Nellie, what can I say that can compete with diamonds and sapphires?"

"Tell her the truth, Charli. Your mother may have her faults, but she's not stupid."

"Can I have a day or two to think about it?"

"You're being a coward, but call her tomorrow. I'll tell her you're visiting an old university friend today."

I went out to walk in Grandmother's garden. I think I understand why Grandmother works so hard in it. It's a world of its own, secluded from view from the street or the neighbors. It's so peaceful I could almost forget that Jamal's out there looking for me – almost.

By nightfall I knew how to convince Mother. I listed my arguments on a piece of paper so I wouldn't get sidetracked or forget something in my anger or frustration. I had no doubt that there would be plenty of both. I went over the points again as I tried to sleep. Was there anything else?

Isolation had to be the main point. She'd never see her family. If we'd spent years in San Francisco with Daddy stationed in San Diego, she wouldn't leave her family easily, would she?

What good were jewels if you only wore them around the house? She could visit the neighbors in them, but what would she say when she visited? Women weren't educated, most could barely read or write, and none of them spoke English.

It wasn't safe to go out alone. There were beggars everywhere, and we lived behind a thick stone fence and the iron gate had armed guards. If she did go out on the streets, she could be kidnapped and held for ransom, or worse. Think of it—a white woman was probably worth a lot, even an elderly white woman. Of course, I invented that part, but I'd be careful to say "probably."

In the morning I thought of one more thing. If she said that a short visit wouldn't hurt, I'd remind her that it takes time to custom make jewelry, especially from Cartier's. It was going to be months before her birthday came around, so any visit would have to be pretty long if she wanted the diamonds and sapphires.

At breakfast I asked Grandmother if I could practice on her. She added the idea that she and Auntie Stell would visit Mother for coffee. She would say how much she missed the visits with just the three of them. She'd switch to Spanish halfway through to emphasize the special bond the three of them had. Brilliant. I'd try to time my call to be around the hugs-and-kisses-we-love-you time.

When Grandmother left to pick up Auntie Stell, I made a big pot of tea. I paced and talked to myself until the appointed time for the call. Pouring what must have been my fourth cup of tea, I realized I couldn't talk very long unless I got rid of the earlier cups of tea first. Then I looked for some crackers to settle my stomach. I couldn't put it off any longer. I dialed.

"Mother?"

"Charlotte Anne, it's so good of you to call, but you picked a bad time." I should have thought of that—how did I miss it? Of course, she had company. I heard coughing in the background. "Just a minute, dear." She covered the receiver, and I heard muffled sounds. "Mama and Stell are over for coffee, but they've just gone to the drugstore to get some cough medicine for Stell." Grandmother was a quick thinker.

I let her tell me about Jamal's invitation, and the jewelry. I agreed that he was the soul of generosity, but… I told her that I couldn't live there. It was too strange and foreign. She tried to persuade me, but I went through my arguments. Surprisingly, Mother listened. By the time Grandmother and Stell got back from their errand, Mother was convinced to make Jamal wait for her answer. I knew the jewels would keep tugging at her, but at least I'd made her think about the other things, and the women would keep her close.

>> ⏲ ⏱ ⏰ ⏰ <<

MARCH 3, 1951: - "They can't transfer you to another ship." I stood outside the kitchen door, frozen in my tracks. Transferred? Where?

"Charlotte, it's a big promotion for me. This is my dream come true. I'll have my own command. It's just a little minesweeper, but it'll be *my* little minesweeper. The U.S.S. Grackle, AMS 13. Doesn't that have a nice ring to it?" Mother sniffed and mumbled something. "Look at the bright side—South Carolina's warm. You always complain about the cold damp San Francisco winters. Little minesweepers aren't out of port for long periods of time. In fact, I'll be home most holidays and weekends."

"But our families are here."

"It could be worse; we could be going back to Maine or Rhode Island. Charleston has a huge Naval base. There'll be other Navy wives and you'll find friends soon enough."

"Friends aren't family." Mother's voice broke. That's when it hit me, and I ran to my room to cry in private. I finally have a real best friend. Betty and I never have the kind of fights where we say we'll never talk to each other again. And how can I leave Jackie? Charleston, South Carolina is all the way across the country, which means we won't even come back for holidays.

Now that I'm writing this, I realize I won't have anything else to write about once we move. I'll be in sixth grade next year, and lots of sixth grade girls have boyfriends. Of course they don't get married, but even so, I'm leaving just when I'm on the brink of needing this information. Any friends Mother makes in Charleston will never discuss husbands or sex or anything else I need to learn — only family talks about those things.

JUNE 15, 1952: - I can't believe we've been in Charleston a whole year! It's crazy that I'm in junior high now. I'll have a locker and everything. To top it all, it's going to be a fantastic summer! Jackie's spending a whole month with us! Mother said that Aunt Nellie left her husband, and I absolutely choked on my cereal when she told me.

"When did she get married?" My voice was almost a squeak.

"Just after we moved east. She married that hotel owner."

It took me a few seconds, but it all came back in a rush. "So Aunt Nellie is Rita's new mom? What a hoot!"

"No, she's *not* Rita's new mom. And where do you pick up those dreadful hillbilly expressions?"

"There's another hotel owner?"

"If you must know, Miss Nosy Parker, it's the same hotel owner, but Rita's no longer married to his cheating son." So Aunt Nellie had been right—again.

That brought back all my angst (how's that for a new word?) about a curse. We've been in Charleston a whole year, and I'd totally forgotten about the journal until I started thinking about Jackie. I don't believe in curses, but really, what else could explain the transient (another new word) nature of the husbands? Even if I don't know what happened to all of Auntie Stell's husbands, I know for a fact that Grandmother didn't have anything to do with the deaths of her husbands.

I wonder what Mother thinks of Aunt Nellie now. Mother sees things differently all the time—even the same things. It's almost like her world is a kaleidoscope and every now and then someone twists the end and she wakes up with a different view. Sometimes she likes a person, and other times she surprises me by talking about that person in a way that sounds as though she doesn't like her. I wonder if her view of sin is flexible. I don't think so.

I have to hide this again and get ready to go pick Jackie up at the airport. I can't wait to hear all about what the women are doing. I guess it's back to late night writing when Jackie's asleep.

JUNE 16, 1952: - It's seven in the morning and Jackie's sleeping like a baby. Between the late night talk in the dark and the time change, I'm betting she's going to sleep a lot later than usual. I learned a lot of new stuff about what's been happening in the family. There are more divorces that I hadn't heard about. Edna got divorced, Patsy got married and then divorced, not to mention Rita that Mother already told me about. Too many for it to be coincidence. OK—so it's not a curse, but what is it? Any man who marries into this family has a very high likelihood of either being killed or cheating over and over, even if he promises not to do it again and means what he says. It makes me shudder to think about it. I pray every night that the curse really has missed Mother.

I may not have much time to write, so I need to record at least a synopsis of what I learned last night:

Rita and her baby came to live with Nellie and Jackie. That worked out pretty well for Aunt Nellie, because Rita stayed with Jackie while her mother (Jackie's, not Rita's) went "wine-tasting" with the hotel owner.

Jackie didn't know how it happened, but Mr. Hotel-Owner's wife found out about it, and there was a big ruckus ending in divorce. I don't know how I remembered, but it was as though Aunt Nellie was sitting on the end of my bed saying, "He'll learn that a fox is a carnivore." I was so distracted that I nearly missed the next sentence.

"Mommy wouldn't go to bed with him again until his son agreed to pay alimony and child support to Rita."

"So you were Rita's step-sister until the divorce?"

"No. This was before the marriage." I was shocked into silence. Thankfully, Jackie couldn't see my expression in the dark. How could she be so casual about her mother going to bed with a man she wasn't married to? I blurted out the first thing that came to my mind. "This didn't bother you?"

"What? That she was using him to force Richard to do the right thing?"

"That your mother..." I was trying to be delicate.

"Ha!" Jackie's outburst made us both freeze, listening for footsteps in the hall. We both breathed a sigh of relief that no one seemed to have heard. Jackie picked up her pillow and tiptoed over to my bed. "Move over." Once our heads were six inches apart she whispered, "You do know about sex, don't you?"

"Of course."

"Can you keep a secret?" I nodded and our heads bumped. It took a few minutes for us to quiet our giggles. "Even from your mother?"

"Especially from Mother." We giggled again.

"Mommy says that sex, and love, and marriage are all different and have different reasons. She says sex can be very powerful, and a woman must learn to use it properly. Men, especially men with lots of money, can do almost anything they want to do. Women can't follow the same rules."

"You mean the rules of the church? Like the commandment about adultery?"

"Mommy would never commit adultery."

"But she — "

"Adultery is when you're married. She never did it when she was married. *He* was married, but she wasn't. So *he* was the one committing adultery."

I was pretty sure adultery and sex were the same thing, but Jackie was positive that they weren't. I didn't want to waste time arguing over it, so I said I understood. I'll look it up when I get a chance. "But once Rita got the money she needed to bring up her baby, then they got married?"

"Not right away. His divorce took a long time, because his wife wanted him to give her so much money. Then Mommy said she wasn't sure he loved her." Jackie giggled quietly. "It took a long time for him to prove how much he loved her — a long time and a lot of really nice jewelry."

"Money doesn't prove love."

"It helps. He spent money on us, and he didn't go away. Mommy said he could have had any woman he wanted, but he didn't go out with any other woman, and he kept asking her. She wanted him to earn her, so he wouldn't think she was cheap. Once he proved he loved her, they got married, and we lived in this wonderful big house with everything you could even dream of having, with servants and riding lessons and everything."

"That sounds wonderful." I was *so* envious. I'd give *anything* for riding lessons. Mother said we couldn't afford it, and she signed me up for tap dancing.

"It *was* wonderful, for a while." I could barely hear her, even though her mouth was only inches from my ear. She sounded frightened. I reached out and took her hand. It was cold and trembling. She threw her arms around me and started crying. I felt her body shake, and her tears were hot as they soaked through my pajamas. It made me feel so sad that tears came to my eyes, too. After a few minutes, she calmed down a little.

"What went wrong, honey?" I'd never called anyone honey, but I wanted to let her know I cared about her and felt bad that she was crying.

"I'm not supposed to tell anyone. Mommy says if Aunt Charlotte knows, then everyone knows, and no one will ever like me, or want to play with me again."

"Oh, Jackie, that can't be true. I'll never stop liking you, no matter what. You know that."

"Really? Are you sure?"

"Yes, I'm sure." I hugged her tight.

"You promise not to tell anyone — ever?"

"I promise."

"It was my birthday, and we'd spent the whole day at the amusement park. When we got home, my favorite dinner was waiting for us with a giant birthday cake. It was the best birthday I'd ever had." She started crying again. I didn't say anything. What could I say? Who cried about a perfect birthday? There had to be more. I patted her back, and held her. "After I went to bed, he came to my room and said he forgot to give me my special present."

She was quiet for so long, I wondered if she'd decided not to tell me the rest of the story. "Did he give you the present?" I felt her head nod.

"He said that he was my daddy now, and he wanted a birthday kiss. He sat me in his lap and he kissed me on the mouth. I didn't like it much, but I'd seen a few other fathers kiss their daughters on the mouth."

"I've seen fathers do that, too."

"He said he'd bought me a new nightgown just like Mommy's. And then he said he wanted to see how lovely I looked in it, because I was as pretty as my mother, and I was getting to be a real grown up. He kissed me again, and he closed his eyes and made a funny little growl in the back of his throat. Then he gave me the package and started moving around like he was as excited as I was while I was unwrapping the present." She had to pause again while she cried.

This story wasn't going to have a happy ending. "If you don't want to tell me, it's okay." I really wanted to know what happened, but I didn't want to make Jackie cry anymore.

She sniffled. "There isn't much more. He wanted to

help me put it on. I didn't want him to, but he said that was part of the present. He kept saying he was my daddy, and he loved me very much. I didn't know what to do. He pulled up my nightie, and started putting his hands on me. I pushed his hands away, but he wouldn't let me pull my clothes down. His hands kept touching me. I was really uncomfortable, and frightened. I was afraid that it would make trouble for Mommy if I made a scene."

"And then?"

"And then Mommy stuck her head in and asked what was keeping him so long."

"And she saw?"

"Uh-huh. Then everything got crazy. Mommy snatched me off his lap and the next thing I knew, I had my coat on over my old nightie, and we were in Mommy's little convertible driving away so fast that I had to hang on to the door every time we turned a corner. Rita was already asleep when we got to the house, but Mommy rang and rang the bell and pounded on the door until Rita woke up."

"You were lucky your mother caught him before it got any worse and he..." That wasn't the right thing to say, so I stopped talking. I gave her another hug and got up to get her a tissue. "You didn't do anything wrong, so what makes your mother think no one would want to play with you anymore?"

"She doesn't think anyone will believe that she got there before he did any more than touch me—or that it only happened that one time. She says people might think that she knew about it and let it happen so we could get the presents and the money."

I thought about Mother's kaleidoscopic view of things. She had said bad things about Aunt Nellie before, when she was divorcing Willis. Maybe Aunt Nellie was right. I hugged Jackie again. "I believe you, and I promise I'll never tell anyone."

I don't think I want to write any more in the journal. It's too hard. The writing's not hard, but thinking and writing about all the unhappy things that happen is hard. I don't understand why things don't work the way they should any more now than I did when I started. I'm going to put the journal back behind the drawers. Who knows? Maybe if I read it when I get older it will help me understand things better.

➤➤ 🕐 🕑 2013 🕐 🕑 ◄◄

David stood next to me in the corridor, his face a study in anxiety. Kate's room overflowed with doctors, nurses, and equipment. I wanted to put my arms around him, but I contented myself with slipping my hand through his arm. "David, I'm sorry. It must have been dreadful, and you had to suffer alone."

He gave me a crooked little non-smile. "I suppose we all have secrets, don't we?"

"I suppose so." He had no idea. I was now the keeper of four generations' secrets, but I would do what my mother couldn't do—let them be buried with me. Mother had revealed Grandmother's secrets to me as I sat by her deathbed, but she never told me she'd been divorced—and I never let on that I knew. Viewed from the twenty-first century, most of the secrets are pretty humdrum, but the people they belonged to didn't have that perspective. Even Jackie's secret no longer held the importance it once had. My own secret, like Kate and David's, only held the power to harm the children involved. Aunt Nellie had been the last living person to share my secret—and now only I knew.

Kate's door opened, interrupting my thoughts; medical staff and equipment began to trickle out of the room. It was another five minutes before a nurse said we could go in. The doctor was talking to Kate and smiling. Smiling was a good sign.

He turned to us. "I was just telling Kate that we're moving her out of the ICU to a monitored bed on another floor. If all goes well, she can go home in forty-eight hours. We'll give you instructions and a list of things to watch for."

"Can she travel?"

"That depends. She'll need a lot of rest, and a rough ride could be injurious."

"We'd planned to leave the stage coach in Texas and take a plane to Virginia."

The doctor smiled at the weak joke. "We'll see." He told Kate he'd see her the next morning and left. David followed him out the door.

"Kate." I wanted to smooth her hair, but her head was swathed in bandages, so I took her hand. "I want you to know that we love you, and we'll take care of you. David loves you so much."

"You know?"

I tried to blink back my tears. "I do now."

"She mustn't ever know. I mean, she's all grown up and has children of her own. It could be devastating if she found out now. I don't know how she'd react. She might hate me forever for it."

"Yes, dear, some secrets can never be told."

"You *do* understand." She smiled.

"Yes, Kate, I do, and I'm so sorry you had to make that decision and live with it. I can't imagine how painful it must have been for both of you — and to keep the secret all these years, hurting alone." I lost my battle with the tears.

David spent another night in the hospital, after a visit to the hotel for a shower and a short nap. The next day the doctor was even more optimistic. He said one more day in the hospital with no complications and he'd let her fly. That night David came back to the hotel with me.

"David, are you awake?"

"Yes. Thinking about the role chance plays in our lives." I let a few minutes pass.

"Aunt Nellie used to say that love, sex, and marriage are three different things. Once in a great while the stars and planets align and a couple get all three, but it doesn't happen very often. That's one of the problems with our society — we expect it to come as a package."

"Sometimes respect and friendship can substitute for love."

"What are you planning to do now?"

"I don't know, Susan will never give me a divorce. Not when her political career is just beginning."

"Everyone makes compromises sometimes."

"I know. Susan said that if I wasn't going to live in the new house full time, I shouldn't have my name on it. I guess you could say I bought my half-freedom."

"So it's all worked out for you to spend half your time with me?"

"Yes, but now that…Kate…"

Even in the dark I could see the penny drop. I rolled over and pulled the covers up to my chin. "Uh-huh." I was already in that never-never land between sleep and wake when he had another thought.

"Would Kate even want me around? I mean, still married to Susan?"

"David, her face glows when she looks at you. Besides, didn't she just walk away from her own husband? My eyelids started to close again.

"But what if it causes a scandal? That would be a disaster, not just for Susan, but think of the children. If she's running for office, things never stay hidden. There's nothing the modern politician likes better than to sling a good sex scandal into the newspapers. Our kids would be mortified. They'd never forgive me."

"Scandalous behavior? Under my roof? Remember what Susan called me when your son and his girlfriend spent a week at the beach? She said I was the last surviving Victorian." If she ever suggested there might be a breath of impropriety in your actions, I'd gather my righteous indignation and say, "Good God, Susan, get your mind out of the gutter. She's his *cousin* for Christ sake. They grew up together."

"We did have a lot of golden summers together. And there was the year of the epidemic wherever it was you were teaching, and you sent me to Aunt Jackie."

"Not to mention the troubles in the Middle East when I waited it out in Greece for two months, but I sent you back."

"Good times."

The doctor was there when we arrived the next morning. He agreed to release Kate the following morning if nothing unexpected happened during the night. David got out his phone. "Before I make reservations, Kate, how much time do you need at home to get whatever you can't live without?"

"I don't want a single thing from that house."

"Papers, credit cards, passport?" I hesitated, but it had to be said. "Will you tell your husband where you're going?"

Kate sounded defeated when she answered. "You brought my purse. It has the useless credit cards. They're all maxed out. I never had a passport, and," she didn't meet my eyes, "he's not actually my husband."

My reaction was instantaneous, but David's painfully strong grip on my shoulder kept me from blurting it out. Why hadn't she walked out before this?

"Kate," he moved me aside and put his arms around her, "that's the best news I've heard since… That's the best news in forever."

I resolved not to ask why she hadn't left earlier. No, I'd probably ask eventually, but I'd wait until she was stronger. The good news was that without a legal connection, the man who put her in the hospital had no reason to try to follow her, I hoped.

I left David at the hospital to spend the day with Kate. I got directions from the desk and went shopping. I picked out a new wheelie and amused myself filling it with clothes for Kate, including a couple of cute cloche hats to hide the bandages.

≫ SEVENTEEN ≪

As much as I loved living with Grandmother, I worried about putting her in danger. I hoped I could get all the papers in place soon so I could stop showing my face around. I worried about being recognized, despite the beautiful red hair that I decided I'd never change. The next few weeks I had plenty of time to worry as I stood in lines and sat in waiting rooms. The woman at the social security office was an older Janice. She read the letter from Judge Aldeman about my life being in danger and was thrilled to help. The passport people actually called the judge to confirm his signature on the letter. After that, I had no trouble getting my passport the same day, so I could leave the country immediately. After I had my passport, I took the test for a brand new driver's license, opened a new bank account, and even applied for credit at Sears.

Jackie brought over her old maternity clothes, and my transformation was complete. I missed Aunt Nellie terribly, but we'd agreed there should be no contact. Jackie and Kate spent a lot of time with me while the older women continued their coffee meetings, usually at Mother's to cement the idea that she'd be unhappy elsewhere.

One day Grandmother came home from one of the coffee visits with a postcard from Janice. She'd used the information in the personnel files, so it went to Aunt Nellie's house. "Great news. Call me when you get this." I dialed the number, hoping something other than idle curiosity had prompted the postcard.

"Charli, I've got something for you. Do you have a paper and pencil?"

"Hang on." I grabbed Grandmother's grocery list. "What's this all about?"

"You know how we charity types stick together? Well, I talked to this guy who runs a cultural exchange thing. He sends teachers all over the world. When I told him about your linguistics degree and the MA in English, he was practically slobbering over the phone. I told him you'd have a baby, and he said it was no problem. All of the assignments provide housing, and household help is available and affordable. Charli, this is perfect for you. By the time school starts, your baby'll be old enough to travel, and once you sign up for this, you can be in a different country every year."

"Did you tell your friend I was running from someone?"

"Give me a break, Charli. I don't like stories with sad endings. I told him you got in trouble and the guy took off." She laughed. "I flipped it around and said the guy was running because your father's looking for him."

"Thanks, Janice. I owe you one."

"Okay, as down payment, tell me you're in a safe place."

"Yes, I'm safe, for now."

"That pays for my friend's name and contact info." She dictated and I took down the information. "I didn't give him your name, just tell him Janice sent you." She was still enjoying living in a mystery novel.

➤➤ ⊕ ⊕ 2013 ⊕ ⊕ ◄◄

Susan was away, signing the papers for her new property. David and Kate were out for a drive, and the house had a mild smell of garlic from the leg of lamb roasting in the oven. I poured a small glass of wine and stared out at the deepening twilight, content that a new normal was settling into place. I smiled at the thought. Conventional wisdom says that young people adapt well, and old people are upset by change. Nonsense.

I no longer have the tunnel vision of the child who'd obsessed over the failures and ignored the successes. I'd grown up in a world of women. Even though men played a huge role in the conversations, they played a minor role in my young life. It never occurred to me that there might be a flaw in my mother's view of marry-once-and-done. I just knew it didn't match reality, and I used the idea of a curse to put a name to something I couldn't yet conceptualize.

I had ignored the many terrific relationships in the family. A marriage doesn't have to last forever to be successful. David and Susan had a good marriage—until it wasn't. Grandmother had more than one successful marriage. In spite of all my fears and their constant arguing, my parents stayed together until "death do us part"—their own brand of success. Even Aunt Nellie triumphed. She and Bill were together until the end, although they never married. They had the same constraints that face David now, and they made accommodations.

But the gold medal of love and romance went to Guido, who'd pursued Auntie Stell from the classroom